THE ADVENTURES OF ANGIE MERK

A Romance

BETTY MANDELL

DEDICATION

For Isa, Vicky and Mary, whose spirits buoy me daily.

CHAPTER ONE

2018, Columbia, SC

I think I'm in love with my divorce lawyer. I fell in love when he took my bony old hand in his bony old hand at our first meeting. Dan's hand fit around mine. Warm. Strong. For an instant, his hand was my world, like that moment in the shower when the water is the perfect temperature, or the first bite of a hot pastrami sandwich when you're starving. Or the spoonful where shortbread, strawberries, and whipped cream align. I thought: I'd like to cuddle with this guy.

While I wait for Dan in his conference room, the seriousness of my infatuation is clear. I want to hold his nice hand and straighten his tie and cook him a pork loin with rosemary, garlic mashed potatoes, and brussels sprouts with onion and bacon. Upon further reflection, the proposed menu would be too heavy if our first assignation occurs in the summer. Better would be cold poached salmon. I want him to feel full, but not stuffed. I want him to savor every bite. The idea of biting leads to the idea of licking. Now I'm lightheaded.

So, what do I like about this ancient guy? He's traveled.

He's smart. He's widowed. He wears a professionally pressed shirt. His masculine smell has my eyes drifting shut to savor the memory.

Angie, consider! Is every divorcée so desperate for affection? Could a robotic alien with flashing red eyes, a swiveling head, and webbed feet, reciting "I'm so sorry" in an electronic squeak, also elicit romantic feelings?

In the three weeks between our first meeting and now, I have imagined Dan and me as the main characters in the romance novels I read every week. Sometimes we sit down to a medieval feast, where he is a knight, and I am the undiscovered princess. His appetite is strong for meat and fruit. Sometimes we have a meal on a train leaving Paris to check out his newly inherited estate in Bordeaux. In this story, I am the victim of a life-changing scam. His rags-to-riches story interweaves with my riches-to-rags story. Other times, I'm a nurse in the war, feeding the beautiful and wounded soldier restorative soup after having foraged for ingredients under enemy fire. He is grateful and in love with me. In my fantasies, we are always eating a meal I have supervised or prepared, and then we have sex. The sex scenes are not as well-developed as the eating scenes since I have trouble imagining perfect young bodies. I wonder why there are no novels with old folks.

My smartphone ring insists I return to the present. I swipe right to get Rachel.

"Hi, sweetie."

I imagine Rachel, slim and tall, sitting in her home office, the control center for her family. Even at home she would be fashionably dressed. I'm lucky to have her as my daughter. Even more fortunate to have her living in the house directly across the street. More accurately, I live in the house across the street from hers. When her cancer was diagnosed, the house was available, and I snapped it up. I had just separated from Steve.

"Are you there?" she asks.

"Yes, I'm here in Dan's conference room, awaiting his entrance."

"Mom, don't minimize what's happening. Your life is on the line."

"Was my 'hi' too chirpy? Don't worry."

"I am a little worried about you. Sometimes I think you are not taking this process with the seriousness it deserves. Don't let his attractiveness lead you astray."

"You will be pleased to know I have enough sense not to bring him cookies."

"Mother!"

"Don't panic. I'll tell him everything." I take a deep breath. "Thanks for checking. You're doing a great job of mothering me. I believe I can focus on what he needs to know."

"Just let me know what happens." I can hear the exasperation in her voice.

"Okay, I'll settle down. I am anxious about how this will work out," I tell her, then my mind goes to scolding myself.

How can you even think of flirting and cooking when your daughter is so ill? It isn't right for you to even feel male-companionship starvation. Angie, your job is to get the money. You need money, you deserve money, you earned every blasted penny this lawyer can get for you. Your life, and Rachel's life, will be easier if you have enough money.

My soon-to-be ex-husband should be punished. I took a lot of nastiness. He should be run out of town. Some people think I should slash his tires. I only wanted to be treated like a person with a brain and interests of my own. If he had treated me like my friends treat me, I'd still be doing his laundry, cooking his food, and trying to be nice. The worst thing happened when he retired: he became a picky eater.

Heavy drapes frame the windows of the conference room, squeezed small by heavy furniture. The circular arms of the leather chairs say make yourself at home, the massive table says, sit up straight.

The object of my fantasies, Dan McCloud, and I had our first meeting in the hallway of this fancy office building, where prints of Columbia's historic buildings line the walls. Rachel had Dan's name and telephone number from a friend of hers who highly recommended him. The first appointment was set up for him to meet me and let Rachel have her say. She did. She told Dan her dad was mean to her and to me. Dan made sympathetic noises. Remembering the handshake of the first meeting, I struggle to concentrate. Today's meeting is for him to get the details. I hope my personal interest in him doesn't send me to la-la land.

I glance out the window. I am inexplicably comfortable in this room. The view of the noble church across the street is sharp in the late-afternoon sun. The slanting light enhances its ocher color, the color of a Mexican church. The local Episcopalians wouldn't have used that color if they had ever traveled south of the border. Now that I think of it, a pumpkin flan is that color too. Steve wouldn't eat the last one I made. He didn't like the color. His rejection felt personal.

To calm myself, I look around the room. The window is clean, and I love clean windows. They bring the outside in so the serenity of nature spreads through you. Even as they symbolize goodness, they also suggest the world is in order. I'm grateful for the sense of peace washing over me.

Ancient oaks arch the road to Dan's office, making the August day look cooler than my car's temperature gauge indicates. The light sweat I worked up in the thirty steps between my car and the front door is evaporating. I'm relaxed. I'm sitting on the side of the table so Dan can sit at the head. How typical of me to automatically give him the male power position. I'd move to the head of the table, but it wouldn't feel right.

Luckily, I have recovered my senses between these meetings. Being in his presence made it difficult to focus on what went wrong in my marriage. What I want in the divorce kept slipping from my mind. My plan today is to focus on getting the money.

I become aware of Dan's footfalls down the hall toward the door. My recovery and relaxation are shot to hell. I am alert from skull to toes. When the door opens, he comes in to stand at the head of the table.

"Nice to see you again." He nods without an instant of eye contact. "You go by Angie, right?"

My lips tighten as I internally scold him. You could be friendlier, Dan. I want us to be friends. I want to be able to invite you to my house and cook for you.

"Yes, that's right." I smile, rising from my seat. I make him take my hand. I don't get the same buzz as before, but his hand is warm and strong.

"Sit over here on this side." He waves his hand to a seat facing away from the window and sits down.

It feels like an order when I am old enough to believe nobody orders me around anymore, dammit. Still, the old habit of niceness kicks in.

"I'm comfortable here," I say and even wiggle a bit for emphasis.

"I want you to sit on this side." His tone firm, he motions again with his arm.

I'm puzzled and appalled. I slam my papers on the other side of the table. I get up, my resistance evident as I move to my new seat.

He smiles at me. "Thank you." His voice softens. "Lydia

always sat in that seat. I have difficulty focusing on the business at hand when a female client sits there. I can almost see her, so it helps to be able to look to the other side of the table."

This time, I don't smile back. I am shocked by his willingness to share such a private quirk. The business at hand jolts me to what is.

A summary of my situation flits through my mind. Separated, no retirement investments in my name, no golden parachute out there, very little cash on hand. Dan being of the male gender is irrelevant. Money is what's important. I don't care how much he makes or how much he charges. I don't care what side of the table he wants me to sit on. I do care what he thinks I will have when this divorce nonsense is over. I'm going to need a lot of money over the next few years. Rachel doesn't deserve to have medical debt. And I don't deserve to live poor any longer.

When he smiles, my heart softens even as I wonder why he opened up. Luckily, I have a question prepared so I don't appear demented or upset. Time to get down to the nuts and bolts of why I'm here.

"Is Steve's pension a marital asset?" I blurt out.

"Yes, it is. It was earned during the forty-year marriage. Anything obtained during the marriage is marital property. Inheritances, if kept separately, are not."

I want to focus on what is important, but the length of his eyelashes is getting in the way. I maintain eye contact and smile a bit. Recent research indicates long eye contact is useful for falling in love. Dan, the southern gentleman, looks at me with his bright blue eyes, not yet watery or red-rimmed. Then he focuses on the yellow legal pad he takes from his folder.

Dan looks like an older Tom Cruise but not as rugged as an elderly Bogart. His brown plaid jacket is probably a mixture of silk and cashmere. The light blue shirt and dark blue tie are a nice match to the coat. If he likes nice clothes, he probably likes good food.

I return to the task at hand. "I'm the one who moved out. Will that count against me in recovering the money?"

"Not if you can persuade me, as your daughter did, you had good reason to leave."

Is food rejection a valid reason for divorce?

The conference room has become a sauna—or maybe it's my blood stirring. The table is hot to the touch where the sun hits it.

He's older than me, but his hands resting on the tired leather folder don't look any older than mine. How does he keep up like that? He told me at our first meeting he eats blueberries to stay healthy. That couldn't do it. His starched shirt looks like a one-a-day laundry bill. He'd have no trouble with that. He's an attorney, for Pete's sake. The question is, will I get more income and a big check when this is over?

"Did he ever cause you to have a bruise or a cut?" Dan's question brings me back.

"No, nothing like that. Really just fussing at me all the time. I didn't know how to turn it off."

What would he do if I reached out and put my hand on his? Probably jump up and run out of the room. Or his eyes would register horror, and he would look at me sadly as if to say, you poor thing. Maybe he would twist my hand and hurt me. Maybe I can bring him a cake. Angie! Stick to business. He may be just another mean man. You don't know him at all.

He looks at me over his glasses with what appears to be intimate eye contact. There is an instant tingling. Unintentionally, I smile at him. Is batting my eyes too forward? His mind seems sharp, but his skin is a little gray. I'm lucky that like all females, at four in the afternoon, I can add color to my face. I don't care what he thinks of my face. Dan may be a rat in sheep's clothing. You just never know.

"Angie, your husband is a selfish man, but since he only abused you emotionally, it is hard to get more than fifty percent of the assets. Most judges believe no marriage is perfect. They don't reward complaining." Sympathy shows on Dan's face. I think he wants me to have more money.

"What about his pension?" he asks.

"He chose the pension arrangement, and I signed on with the option that gave it all to him."

"You're telling me Steve chose the pension option that excluded you?" His mouth drops open.

"Of course, he did. Then he would have more money for his lifetime."

Steve has a narcissistic personality disorder. He was raised by parents who made bathtub gin in the Great Depression. He never joined the American "see what I got" scene. When I met him, he had decorated his meager apartment with different-sized clear glass jugs filled with dyed water. They were lined up on the windowsill so the sun shone through them. I thought they were a clever decorative item rather than a cheap way to fill space. What did I know? I was twenty-two.

"He never bought you a new car?"

I shake my head, and my earrings swing back and forth. A kaleidoscope of car scenes slows my response—pushing a car all the way to the movie house in Boulder, changing a flat tire on the side of a freeway while driving cross-country with four children asleep in the back of the station wagon. Even now, I can feel the heat of those post-midnight truck stops in Oklahoma, bugs circling the lights, the dark void beyond scaring me. One scene is vivid: Steve driving fast on an icy road. We skid, and after a long time, we come to rest against a snowbank. Why the hell was he driving so fast with children in the car?

"What kind of a car are you driving now?" Dan breaks the silence.

"Rachel helped me buy a lightly used Subaru. It's red. I call it 'Candy.'" I smile, thinking about the pleasure of not worrying whether or not the car is going to start, or stop, for that matter.

Thinking about cars, another scene stands out. We were living in Chapel Hill. Steve had an exchange professorship. I started the car in our driveway when I was taking the children to school. A terrible rattle ensued; my hand shot out to stop the engine. The rattle quit, but panic came over me since I do not like the children to be late to school. I opened the front door and yelled, "The car is dying." Steve followed me back to the car and stood where I pointed. Then, in his lecturing uniform of khakis, ancient English tweed coat, light blue shirt, and loafers, he bent down in front of the car. He rocked up and down rather quickly, then rose up, triumphantly holding the bumper overhead. I backed out of the driveway with the rattle killed. I was amused. I felt in sync with his ability to solve the problem. Crazily, I also felt taken care of.

A trace of that warm feeling transfers to the here and now. I face Dan as directly as I can and tilt my head a bit. I open my eyes as wide as possible without feeling as though I'm named Dolly. I want him to like me.

I'm pleased I can remember the original question about a new car.

"The idea dismisses itself. We always drove junkers since he was pretty good at finding tight engines. The cars usually drove forever but looked atrocious. Steve loved to tell the story of driving our rust-covered blue Chevy in L.A. A couple of blondes in a white convertible pulled up beside him at a light. One of them sneered and said, 'Hey, mister, does it itch?' Then they zoomed off laughing. He thought that was a funny story."

"Maybe it is." Dan smiles but doesn't laugh.

I smile back. Is he flirting with me? Does he like chocolate? Maybe a warm spice cake with a buttercream frosting to go with his jacket. Is cream cheese a required ingredient for the frosting of a hummingbird cake?

Back to cars. "One of the reasons I left was I was driving a car with unreliable brakes. Steve insisted they were fine. One thing I hate is when the brake pedal hits the floorboard before the car is fully stopped."

I don't want to seem paranoid, so I don't mention I thought he was trying to kill me.

"Hard to imagine! So, Mr. Merk didn't like to spend money."

I shake my head so my newly cut hair falls over one eye. I pull it back and tuck it behind my ear.

"Steve spends money as easily as a rock flies; he can't do it. He does spend money if it's on something where he can make money. I spent my money making our lives decent, so I'm scrambling, and he has lots of money in his account. Also, I'm still working to make sure I can take vacations with my daughters. He refuses to help with the doctors and hospital bills from Rachel's mastectomy."

I shake my head to release the pain and start in a new direction. "He told me once he had hidden money in the house, but he wouldn't tell me where it was. He just said I'd find it if I looked."

I never looked. Now I'd probably tear the house down to find it. I just never thought I would divorce him.

Dan's eyes widen. "Hidden money?"

"Who knows? All I have is the recent Merrill Lynch account statement, but I believe there is more. The money isn't properly accounted for after this many years of two salaries and no spending."

"Is that the Merrill Lynch account statement?" Dan's thin, knobby, but strangely strong hand points to the folder I have taken out of my well-worn canvas book bag.

"Last week I went back to the house when I knew he was away. I wanted to get the key to the safe-deposit box. I was looking to see if he still had ten thousand in cash in there. I had seen it a couple of months ago. I would have taken half, but the key wasn't in its usual place. I don't want to go more in debt to fix my house."

"He'd hidden the key? Your name is on the box too?"

He doesn't draw back in dismay, but a sweet outrage comes into his voice. Maybe he'd like a key lime pie for being so nice. I make it slightly tart, not at all gummy. It's not to be confused with what's in the freezer section at our local grocery store.

"I guess so. Anyway, when I went into the house to find the key, I looked at the top file folder on a pile of papers in the bookcase. There was his Merrill Lynch account statement, one-point-one million. I just took it." I felt like a sneaky thief, but I knew it would be useful.

"That's a lot of money." One of Dan's eyebrows raises.

"Steve has no debt. Only his name is on the house, and there's no mortgage."

"Ah, the house is in his name also?"

"Everything's in Steve's name. Two badly running cars, the roach-infested house, the ill-gotten money, the grave plots, the pension, the art collections, everything. The only thing in my name is a substantial Visa card debt."

What had I been thinking? If I'd made him pay for stuff, we wouldn't be in this pickle. I didn't want him fussing at me. He fussed about how much toilet paper I used, for crumb's sake.

Dan looks up when I push the papers across the table. "You say 'ill-gotten money'?"

"He always cheats on taxes. I recently received a letter from the IRS saying he was asking for innocent spouse relief for last year's taxes because we still owe several thousand dollars. Since I always did the taxes, he thinks he's not responsible. I wrote them back, and I hope I gave them a laugh."

I give Dan my warmest smile. "I told them he had never paid his share of taxes. The note included the information we were in the process of a contentious divorce. I wrote, 'I have trouble believing he has the gall to ask for such a thing.'"

Dan gives me a full-out smile, just short of a laugh. It's a twinkling smile, the mouth and the eyes. "Sounds like you took care of the issue." He gives a satisfied nod. "What other papers are here?"

"I have the last two jointly filed tax returns. As I said, we still owe on last years' taxes, but I believe he should pay it."

"Why is that?" he asks.

"We both put money on the taxes equally each quarter, but his accounts being much larger produce higher income. I was putting in proportionally more money than he was to pay taxes. Besides, now I would have to put it on my already loaded credit card."

My credit card is so loaded it staggers when I pull it out of my wallet. Why had I thought it was cute or wifely or unselfish rather than stupid to pay more than my share? I knew I was enabling the skinflint.

"I'll look into the taxes. Has he given you any money since you left the marital home?" His voice is somber again.

"Not a penny. Why would he? I make enough to support myself like I always have. I did, however, have to cash my mother's bonds to buy my house."

I sold those bonds at a loss. It makes me angry to think

about it. Now, I'd really like more money. I need to secure my future and help Rachel. The law says in a marriage dissolution the distribution will be half and half, so I always believed I would get half of the value of everything. It's too bad I have to spend all this money just to get my due. I don't have a pension, just Social Security. I ran my psychology practice as a small self-owned entity, so the investment money is important.

"Your mother's bonds? Are they inherited?"

"Yes, my mother died five years ago."

"Have you kept them separately?"

"I've never used the money before having to buy my house. It's in a Morgan Stanley account."

A timid knock at the door puts a temporary halt to the interview.

"Come in," Dan shouts at the door, then turns to me. "I think you've met Pam."

I nod.

"Do either of you want water or coffee?" she asks.

"Water would be nice," I say. She's not even offering a cookie, much less a pastry. I could use a brownie at this time in the afternoon. The best brownies are made with orange-infused olive oil. My mouth waters.

Pam presents a bottle of water wrapped with a linen napkin. I smile and say a thank-you, but she doesn't smile back. Then she smiles at Dan. "Anything for you, sir."

The instant judgment of male-identified woman darts through my mind. Don't expect much cooperation from her. My better nature kicks in. *Don't be so judgy*.

As I rise up from my seat to take the water, I catch my reflection in the pretty wall mirror surrounded by expensive silk flowers. My new haircut helps me look younger. Short hair elongates my neck and softens the overall image without taking away from my high cheekbones and narrow nose. The fifteen pounds of weight loss since leaving the marital home six months ago has trimmed my shoulders and hips, and my blouse hangs nicely on my frame. I'm dressed for work in black draped pants, a blue-print blouse, and a crisp white overshirt. Since I regularly meet with clients, I dress upscale-casual, and with a little effort, I look well turned out.

After getting the nothing-for-me nod from Dan, Pam turns and leaves.

Dan cuts short my enjoyment of the cool water. "How much did you put down on your house?"

If he didn't seem so interested, I would be annoyed at this intrusion. I am still trying to convince myself the house is an investment, not an indulgence. The fact that it takes money rather than gives money doesn't make any difference. It will appreciate, right?

"I put down one hundred twenty thousand by cashing in inherited bonds and took an equity line of one hundred thousand. I thought I only needed eighty thousand for the loan, but I've used most of the extra twenty thousand for repairs."

The incompetent inspector didn't find half the stuff needing repair. One whole corner of the exterior siding was rotten. The laundry room floor had to be replaced. I don't know how that presumed professional missed the six-inch hole in the wall that allowed the resident to judge the weather, and the squirrels and mosquitoes to enter. The house was so full of crap he couldn't see the damage. Furniture lined every inch of the walls; couches and tables loaded with papers blocked every pathway; the kitchen sink was piled with dirty dishes. Cheetos and pork rinds in the pantry filled out the picture.

I want to believe that with three animals and a toddler they didn't plan to be deceptive. They seemed like nice people. When the previous owner showed me around, the dirty dishes were the only thing she was embarrassed about.

The supposedly dry basement floods in heavy rains. I'm going to see about gutters to move the water away from the house. The electrical outlets hidden by the wall-to-wall furniture get hot when you plug in a lamp or the vacuum. The inspector missed those fire hazards. I worry about plugging in the coffee maker and the blender at the same time.

"Do you like the house?"

His question surprises me, but I want to look like I'm savvy, so I hide the problems from him.

"It's perfect for me. I've spent a lot of money fixing it up, and I still have things to do."

"Are the appliances in good working order?"

The refrigerator they left was filthy and moldy. My sister visited and bought me a new one. I didn't have enough cash on hand, so we pretended the purchase was for my birthday. The washing machine shakes violently when it spins, so I have to lean on it or it will walk away. I believe it wants to take the stairs into the basement. The stove is gas, and it has turned out to be great. It obeys every order I make with just the perfect heat.

"They're just fine." I'll show him I'm not a complainer. "As an example of how Steve saved money, he took the ancient furnace out of the house on Corley shortly after we moved in. For the decade we lived there, we never had central heat or air conditioning. He liked to be competitive with people about how little could be spent on the energy bill." My air-conditioned cottage is like living at the Plaza.

Fighting the energy war kept us sleeping in the same bed. Snuggling was the only way to stay warm when the temperature dropped to freezing in the bedroom. No sex, just another warm body. When he traveled and I was alone in the cold, I used to clench my muscles to stay warm. Now they're saying you can lose weight sleeping in the cold. It's a wonder I'm not skin and bones.

"How did the two of you stay married for so long?"

"He was away a lot. I'm very adaptable. Mostly one thing is as good as another for me, except for food. When I cook, only the best ingredients will do."

Dan ignores my food reference. "He couldn't have been away all the time. You have four children."

Heat warms my cheeks. "We got along pretty well in the early days." I shrug. "I went along with whatever he wanted."

I knew how to do it all. Like my mother, who was widowed early with three small children, I believed it was what you did. I managed the house, the children, the job. I raked at night so the yard was decent. The idea of going to a movie never entered my mind. Since I was healthy, I delivered babies easily. I convinced myself activity was better than rest. To this day, I have trouble just hanging out. Was I the grand martyr? Stupid? Competent? Or just a patsy?

I try to move my head like my friend Caroline does while keeping my eyes turned to him. When Caroline and I are out together, she attracts men like a newly opened box of chocolates attracts children while I stand by like three-month-old Halloween candy. Waltz Wednesday was delightful last week. The tall, thin guy and I had a good time dancing together. I imagined strawberry-and-rhubarb pie. When I watched Caroline dance with him, my heart sank. I lost my appetite.

My stomach turned out to be right. At the end of the evening, he gave her his card and asked her to call him. Is that how it's done? He asks you to call him?

What the hell is the matter with me? My daughter says the haircut is cute. Two other friends have gone to my hairdresser because of me. I asked Jodi if she thought going blond with my hair would be good. She replied, *"I won't do it,"* and curled her lip. I guess silver is all the rage in the over-sixty crowd. The clothes my daughter insists I wear are widely admired.

Without warning, the image of my beautiful daughter prepped for surgery, the horrible black marks on her chest, a track for the knife to slice her flesh, and the white cap hiding her thick, dark hair surges into my mind. My eyes close. I shake my head in an unsuccessful attempt to stay present and sink into nothingness.

"Are you okay?" Dan's soft voice breaks in.

"Not quite."

"You're not planning on going back to him, are you?"

"I wouldn't consider it."

He frowns. "I have seen some strange things. So, what's the trouble?"

"Dan, my daughter is sick, and I can't think of it without feeling ill. I need money to help her with her treatment."

"Her dad won't help, will he?" He speaks in a whisper.

"He's somehow gotten it into his mind her breast cancer isn't happening. He may think she's making it up. A friend of mine, Caroline, thinks he has early-stage Alzheimer's disease, but I keep telling her he's always been like this."

Dan sighs deeply. "My wife died of breast cancer. It was quite real."

We sit quietly, enveloped in a cocoon of suffering.

When he breaks the silence, his speech is halting. "I'm sorry. No need to be frightened."

He reaches over and places his hand on mine. I see it, but I don't feel it. I've been waiting for this moment. Now it's happened, but I've gone to the place in my brain that is a black hole.

"Many cancer patients do just fine." He hesitates. "Let's go back to Steve," he says in a firmer voice. "Does he not know the illness is serious?"

Time has slowed. Dan's question is hard to process. Several internal repetitions are required before it sinks in.

He removes his hand from mine. I pull it from the table to rest in my lap.

"I haven't directly experienced Steve's reaction to Rachel's cancer. He has a knack for drama, so he tends to steal any emotional scene. When he watched our son's birth from behind a one-way training mirror for nurses, he hopped around like he was stomping the life out of gargantuan tarantulas. The nurses never asked how I was doing. They always asked me how he was."

We were living in Toronto then. I was working on my doctorate in psychology. Steve had his first academic job. We moved several times around the city with two small children that first year. The situation was so stressful, I had back spasms.

Later, I was pregnant and hid my condition as long as I could from the Psychology Department. The University of Toronto was conservative. They didn't believe in a home life for graduate students. My son was an easy third birth. Since then, I've always said I'd rather give birth than go to the dentist since I had such quick deliveries.

"So, it's hard for him to empathize or even sympathize with anybody else?"

"Right, plus there's a 'they hate me and want to do me in' element in his dealings with other people. When he retired from the university, the venom he had directed toward others became directed toward me." My lips tighten.

"So he'll believe you are trying to take him down rather than just getting on with your life."

"Exactly! He believes the money and art belong to him. Once he made a comment to a colleague of his suggesting I was a stay-at-home mom."

"With thought distortions like that, we may have a difficult time arranging a proper settlement. Have you thought of what you'd like?"

I have thought of what I'd like. The thoughts are indecent and involve you, sweet Dan. I mentally shake my head to return to the task at hand. I hope my thoughts don't show in my eyes. Then again, maybe I hope they do. Either way, he looks impervious.

"I thought I would ask for three hundred fifty thousand. I believe I can manage on the income from that and any social security when I quit working."

"With the size of that Merrill Lynch statement, I couldn't in all conscience ask for that little. We'll start with five hundred fifty thousand plus half the sale of the house." Dan slaps his hand on the Merrill Lynch paper.

"Whatever you think is best. He won't agree to anything." I shrug my shoulders.

"At least we will have a reasonable request on record. Who is his lawyer?"

"Herman Castro," I tell him.

"I've dealt with him many times. He's experienced, so he'll understand the situation," he says.

My mind goes to a psychotherapy client of mine who had Herman as her lawyer. He wanted to hire experts. She believed he was running up expenses for his own purposes. In the end, she felt he had caved to her husband's willfulness. I don't care if he's a good lawyer for Steve, but I do hope she has gone on to a good life. I liked her despite her anxieties.

"I have been to court with Mr. Castro as an expert witness for the opposing side in a case or two, many years ago," I relay potentially relevant information. "I would have to think long and hard to recall anything about these cases. He will, at least, know who I am."

Dan looks up from his notes. "I'm surprised we haven't run into each other earlier since you are a psychologist who will go to court."

"I 've done very little court work over the years, but I find the courtroom fascinating." I try the overly long eye contact to no avail. The book entitled, *How to Make Him Fall For You,* has been of no use, so it will go into the Salvation Army bag.

Dan looks down to make a note on his legal pad. Then he raises his head to look at me, his face serious. "I love to go to court and help people get what they should have. I want the dissolution of a marriage to turn out right and to have a fair settlement. That reminds me, you mentioned art. What is it? How can it be divided?"

"There are several art collections. I'd say there are forty to fifty bronze statues. At one time, he had collected about seventy of them. He used to brag they were worth a half a million, but he did sell some at Sotheby's in New York. He has also given or sold a bunch to museums."

"What are these statues?" he asks.

"They're late nineteenth-century bronze statues, with a variety of themes. Some show a romanticizing of work, some have more classical themes. They're French or German mainly, a few from Belgium or Sweden. They're mostly signed by the artist and have foundry marks."

They sat all over our house. When she was a teen, Rachel loved a four-foot statue of a nearly nude warrior with his sword raised to shoulder height. The unliftable hunk of metal sat near the window in her room. She draped her lacy bras and panties over the sword. What could one say? Turn swords into clothes hooks? Peace, not war? The lacy bra will deflect the might of this sword? Seems symbolic, but I can't get a political rallying cry from the visible contradiction. Are swords phallic? Maybe I missed my teen's sexual blooming.

"Some of the best examples are in the city museum. Probably the easiest thing is to go see them. I called the museum and tried to get the records of whether he had sold or given the bronzes to the museum. They wouldn't give me anything. They said he was the only one who had signed the forms."

"We can get that information. Is there any way to place a value on the statues?"

"He will undervalue them, but even so, I would like to get half the value of them rather than have a bunch of them sitting in my living room."

"Sometimes when it's difficult to agree on a value, the practical way is to divide the number of items in half. You used the plural when you spoke of the art. What else is there?"

"He has Guatemalan textiles, Guatemalan masks, and jade from Guatemala in every form: raw, carved, and polished. It's as if he was determined to bring Guatemala back in little pieces and put it in our backyard."

"If I'm hearing you right, he's been a big collector. Are there other assets?"

"I believe there's an account with the earnings from his real estate dealings. For a decade, when housing prices were going up, he made money buying and selling small apartment complexes. I'm not clear on the details as that was twenty years ago."

I justify my ignorance with an internal review. I was busy teaching at the university, tending to the children, the house, the yard. I went into private practice later. I didn't know what he was doing. He spent his summers researching and buying art in Europe. He always had money to buy stuff. He also always sold stuff and made a profit.

There was a lot of cooking to be done. We're talking about a family of six. I perfected great pots of nicely seasoned lentil soup, cheap and filling then, chic and healthy now. I do regret seasoning them with hot dogs or sausages. I hope earlier versions of ground-up meat were cleaner and healthier than what the research indicates now.

"I don't know where the money went. We lived as paupers. I never had anything new, and the children had used crummy bikes. Thinking back on it, however, he always rode a top-of-the-line bike." My voice changes pitch. How did I live so long with such a penny-pincher?

"Calm down, Angie, we'll try to rectify the situation as soon as we can. I'll issue the necessary subpoenas, and we'll hire someone to read the bank statements. We'll need someone who can find the money."

I sit up tall. "No! I mean, I can read the bank statements. I don't think we need to hire anyone to do that. If we can get the records in here, I'll go over them. I'll know what to look for."

I have never hired experts to do anything I could do, nor maids or landscapers. Steve did repairs, badly. He installed cabinets in the kitchen. The handles were catawampus by two inches. The toilets he fixed ran less but didn't stop running.

Dan shakes his head. "Trust me on this, please. Keep a consultant in mind. Pam, my assistant, knows who to call. It has been a while since these transactions occurred and records are sometimes hard to find after this long. I'll consult with my wife, Lydia, and see if she thinks we can find the money."

Lydia? What's that all about? I thought she was dead. Rachel's internet review told her he was widowed. He told me she died of breast cancer. How can he consult her?

CHAPTER TWO

Oaks dominate the landscape in the blocks near my house, their massive roots forcing the sidewalk to rise unevenly in spots. Since it's early fall, the oaks' brown leaves are raked into piles at the curbs. The changing of the seasons reminds me the divorce is taking a long time. Dan says he's swamped.

My friend, Caroline, and I are walking through the residential neighborhood not far from the University of South Carolina. She's up for anything, has done everything, and mostly, she leads the way. When I have a problem, I go to Caroline. She helps me change overhead light bulbs. We are on our way to work out at the senior citizens center. Someone is cooking bacon, so I'm distracted again. Bacon falls in he same category as butter and cheese. Not particularly healthy, but essential for the good life.

The walk is pleasant with older brick houses, tidy yards. A few leftover asters color flower beds. Camellia bushes show small buds indicating they will bloom in about a month. The morning smells fresh, without a hint of the mid-afternoon heat still to come. We are in the habit of not needing a sweater. I'm pleased I got a good night's sleep so my legs are peppy.

Twice a week, we walk a mile and a half to the center, work out some, and then we go back to my house. The seasons change but the pattern remains the same. I fix us each a bowl of mixed nuts and fruit, dried and fresh. The first time I presented Caroline with dried apricot, she picked it up tentatively with two fingers and brought it to her face for close inspection.

"What is this?"

"It's a dried apricot. It's good for you."

"It looks like a dried something, perhaps something you wouldn't want to talk about. I'll take it home to taste it so if I have to spit it out or upchuck it, I'll do so on my own time and in the privacy of my own bathroom." The next time we were eating our snack at my house, she said simply, "I like dried apricots."

I vary the fresh-fruit combinations. I might have melon and blueberries or pears and mangoes. Caroline had never had mango, thus eliciting the same routine. She took a slice home in a plastic bag so she could investigate it. Same response. The nuts and dried fruit from Sunny Land Farms are expensive and delicious. Since I left Steve, I have persuaded myself I eat so little I can spend what I want on food. It's not like I live on lobster, although I did indulge in a pricy lobster roll last week. Delicious!

Does Dan like lobster? He would have to like shrimp since he is a South Carolina native. I bet he likes lobster too. Maybe he doesn't. I asked Rachel to investigate, but she told me definitely no. His food preferences were not for her to search. Besides, it is unlikely there is a place on the internet where any indication of Dan's food likes and dislikes are revealed. What if he is a picky eater? My spirits fall.

Caroline looks at me. "You seem to have something on your mind. You're awfully quiet."

She reads me like the instructions on a microwave dinner. Do I have large type on my forehead? I have several problems on my mind this morning. I have a problem with a man at the senior center. He bothers me because he looks seriously depressed. My divorce is moving slowly—although it keeps me seeing Dan, so I don't mind much. Gene, the man at the center, is the easiest issue to put on the table.

"Sad Gene won't smile at me. I worry about him."

"Don't be concerned. I'll take care of him. What else is on your mind? I have the feeling the Gene issue is the tip of the iceberg."

I hesitate and consider insisting on the Gene issue, but since this is Caroline, I don't. "Sex. Sex is on my mind. I haven't had sex with another person in so long, I think I won't be able to do it if the opportunity comes up." I think for a minute. "Maybe it's like everything else: if you want it done right, you have to do it yourself." My fantasies about Dan are starting to annoy me. I seem to be doing all the work, even though imagined, in this relationship.

Caroline laughs. As we walk along, we pass a persimmon-colored maple tree. Winter has come but the tree has retained its colorThe tree is picturesque with its round shape against the blue sky, its branches hinting at its internal strength. Caroline doesn't see what I automatically see, but she's grateful when I remind her to look. I point, and she nods. We're in a spot where the trees drip over the sidewalk so we can't walk side by side. When the sidewalk widens, she turns to me as I catch up. She has a half smile on her face, and excitement lengthens her stride.

"I know what would be helpful because you need some confidence. I have a friend who is a stud. He likes to have sex with anybody, so he would love to have it with you. He has some numerical goal in mind, but I haven't paid much attention to that. We screwed several times a couple of years ago. He's sympathetic and wants his partner to have a good time too."

"How would that work? I would eat steak tartare, even though it nauseates me, so I could have an evening of anticipation and end up actually having a romantic sexual experience?"

"Romantic sexual experience is a little highfalutin, but George is up for helping women 'get it off,' as the saying goes. Let's take it from the top. First, I give you his name and number. You simply call and invite him to your house."

We are moving too fast for me. As long as this "stud" was abstract, I could go along. Now Caroline has him coming to my house. "My house?"

"Yes, your house." She points a finger at me. "You wouldn't be having sex in my guest bedroom, that I guarantee."

"What's so special about your guest bedroom?"

"Let's not get distracted here." Her voice is emphatic as she has intuited my avoidance strategy.

"Okay. What do I say to him?"

"'Hi, George. This is Angie Merk. My friend, Caroline, gave me your number.' I'll get to him first, let him know your situation. That you're going to call."

"Why don't you give him my number and have him call me?"

Caroline's recently lightened hair flies out as she shakes her head.

"No way! You're the one who wants him in your bed."

Do I really want him in my bed? Since I sleep in a twin, we'd have to use my guest room with its queen-size bed. More sheets flopping on my line. More neighbors disturbed by a clothesline barely visible unless it has clothes on it. I live where people like to be la-di-da. They don't want undies flapping in the wind.

"That's true enough. After I introduce myself, what comes next?" I ask.

"Do you want to feed him one of your fabulous meals or just supply a nice bottle of wine and some cheese and crackers? The two of you could even converse, at least a little bit."

I shake my head. "I could never cook right away for a complete stranger." I pout, my lips drooping. I like Dan so much I'd ask him what he'd like if I'm ever in a position to offer dinner. "Usually, I have to know what someone likes and dislikes. I could serve leg of lamb to a vegetarian, maybe oysters to a gagger, nuts to someone who's allergic. You don't cook for a stranger. That's a recipe for disaster." What I like to do is cook for people I love. The thought saddens me.

"Yet you plan to get in bed with him?" She gives me her raised-eyebrows look of astonishment. "Never mind. Let's move on. You say, 'I'd love to share a nice bottle of wine with you. Can you come over Friday night?'"

"Oh, shit. I already have something on Friday night," I say, feigning disappointment.

Her lips purse. "Ninny, you pick the night." She slowly enunciates the words. "And when you talk to him about sharing the bottle of wine, you need a low, half-laughing voice, particularly on the word 'share.'"

"You are so smart. I never would have thought of that."

"Say it." Her eyes narrow.

"What?"

"Say the sentence. I want to hear you ask the question."

I feel more than a little uncomfortable. I'm supposed to imply we'll have sex after the wine. I give it a try. Caroline hoots and makes me try it over and over. I look for an out, but the sidewalk here is too regular to fake a fall.

"Okay," she says finally. "Now what will you say to him

when he appears at your door on the night you have free for him?"

"Don't be snippy," I tell her.

"Look, you need practice. We haven't even gotten the wine open. By the way, you let him do it."

"So, he rings the doorbell. When I open the door, I see he's standing there. I say, 'Hi, come on in.'"

"No! You look him up and down, and you say, '*Wow*, Caroline didn't exaggerate one little bit,' and you smile a big smile. Put everything in the smile—admiration, welcome, hello, pleasure, and whatever else you've got, then you put out your hand."

"Hand?" I ask.

"Your hand, we're not ready for the boobs yet." She sighs dramatically. "This is going a little slowly for me. Pull him inside and sit him where you can sit next to him. Have the wine at a distance, requiring you to bend over and show cleavage."

"I have to wear something to show cleavage?"

"Yes, and it has to be tight around the ass and easy to get out of. Chat and have wine. At some point, you put your wineglass down and hold your hand on it for longer than necessary. Then you turn toward him, you take his hand, and pull him into the bedroom, laughing a low laugh. I expect he'll take over from there, just follow his lead."

"What's going to happen?" I can barely walk straight. My head is going to explode.

"Three things will happen. The exact order is up to him. He'll kiss you like he means it, he'll take off his shirt, and he'll take off your dress. Whenever he takes off his shirt, you run your hands slowly over his chest and make cooing sounds."

"I remember how to do that. So, he kisses me and takes off my clothes. How big is this guy?"

"I told you. He's a stud. He's muscled, not yet fifty, over six feet tall. He's big and blond, nice looking too."

Two full minutes of silence, then I confess: "I can't do it. I'm too scared. The idea of putting my hands on a big strange guy's chest like that is too intimidating. I've changed my mind. I don't want sex. Rather, I want to romp with someone my age I can cook for. Someone who has wide-ranging food tastes. Someone who likes to dance."

"I can imagine that's what you want." Caroline nods sagely and walks on.

My mind fills again with the memory of the last Waltz Wednesday. Caroline and I go to a community center in Charlotte for these dances several times a year. The long drive is worth it. Last time, I danced with several good dancers. The taped music is not good waltz music, and the hall is only a cut above a barn, but, for me, the overall effect is of being Fred Astaire's dance partner. We are twirling and graceful. I smile, thinking about the beauty of our dancing. I have difficulty concentrating on the stairs up to the center. I'd rather be in the arms of a good dancer.

Caroline and I sign in at the counter in the small social room and go to the gym. The gym consists of two rooms. The first room is filled with leftover Curve's equipment, some of which is held together with black duct tape. The usual group inhabits the circuit room while Lenore wipes down the equipment. She has skinny arms and legs and an outsize belly. Each Wednesday, while she wipes and wipes, she tells us how her horse is. She tells us how bad she felt when she gave up the horse, but how relieved she was when the original owner took him back. We shared in her pleasure when she described the horse's move back to Texas. We were delighted to follow her retelling of it eating and sleeping well. We were frightened with her when tornadoes were in the area where the horse lives. I secretly wish the horse would kick the bucket because I'm tired of the stories. The group of us remain polite and sympathetic. Maybe the others don't want the horse to die.

When the horse whisperer goes silent, Michelle talks about her house. The workers—plumbers, painters, roofers, electricians—don't do what they said they would. They send outrageous bills. Turns out, she lives in a teeny house. I drove by once to see it for myself. I had pictured a mansion.

Shelly, the last of the denizens of the circuit room besides Caroline and me, is perky and dark-haired and distinguished by her matching outfits. Today, she is in blue. Even her workout sneakers coordinate. With the permanently worried expression on her face, she tells us how her son and his wife and child are doing in their small apartment in New York. These women are all sweet and good-natured. I'm fond of them.

Inevitably, there is talk of the temperature in the gym and on the street. It is either too hot or too cold or too humid. These days it is too cold. Everyone has a holiday story often involving a relative who isn't behaving well. Often, someone has a sick, money-draining dog, another entrancing topic. When anybody is missing, we talk about them, reviewing their current concerns. I suppose they talk about us when we aren't there. Are we the unfriendly exercise freaks? Both Caroline and I increase our resistance loads. Sometimes we work hard enough to sweat.

When we leave the circuit room, we go down the hall to a larger room with treadmills and weights. Caroline goes over to where Gene adjusts a treadmill. She walks right over beside him, catches his eye.

"You look so grumpy," she says to him.

He reaches over the handlebars to give her a weak hug and peck on the cheek.

"That won't do." Caroline straightens herself and tosses her hair. She points to the ground where he is to stand. He goes to where she points. This time, he greets her with gusto. She laughs, then turns to the universal machine to practice her lat pulldowns. This requires pushing a bench under the bar hooked to the weights. I realize I'm staring, as are the three men in the room. We all return our focus to our muscles.

———

THE NEXT NIGHT, Caroline and I go to a dance bar. The music is so loud, I am tempted to plug my ears with bits of paper napkin. A golf pro stands in front of me and offers his hand as a way of asking me to dance. Since it is a slow dance, I allow myself to relax and feel his body against mine, my hair against his cheek. The pleasure of relaxing in a man's arms is profound. This tiny moment reminded me of what I had been missing from my marriage after it turned sour. When we sit down together, he tells me he has a girlfriend who understands. He asks if I would like to come back to his house, I suppose to meet his girlfriend? I politely decline. He didn't even offer wine or dinner.

———

CAROLINE and I are at the gym again. It's Friday, and today, we're starting in the weight room.

"Gene, where've you been? I missed you dancing last night. You never come." Caroline pouts, involving her whole face. "You hardly deserve your kiss today."

Gene moves as fast as he can to get his kiss and hug. Then he greets me cheerfully.

I watch Caroline work her magic: eyes, body, hair, and

smile. I try to imitate the posture and motions, but it's hopeless. Her green eyes seem to light up under her long, straight bangs. I don't think hair is my problem. My hair is okay since it's a shiny mix of silver and black and widely admired. I danced once with a guy who referred to my eyes as the "big blues," so I don't think my eyes are the problem either. Caroline is naturally friendly, while I tend to focus so much on what I'm doing I probably appear uninterested.

Gene follows us to the circuit room. He only uses the leg press and crunch machine. Caroline migrates over to him, and they catch up further on relatives and mutual friends. I feel left out. I also experience a flashback to a time with my sisters when they laughed and played. They pointed at me, making fun of me. In my memory, I'm standing by the side, left behind, or like I'm not there. Just like here in the gym.

I start my rounds on the machines, as does Caroline. She keeps chatting. I watch the clock so I can remind her of when to move to the next machine. Gene leaves, and she turns to me.

"What's the matter?" she asks.

"I had a funny sense of being left out when you and Gene were talking."

"When I glanced at you, you looked standoffish."

"What?"

"Now that I think about it, you looked a little scared or something."

"Maybe I was afraid to join in. Something bad might have happened." I frown.

"Gene wouldn't bite you."

"No, I wasn't scared of Gene. It's more like I wouldn't be graceful or fit in well."

"Sounds like an old insecurity to me." She shakes her hair.

"Sure does. I wonder where it comes from. I think of myself as reasonably friendly."

"You're on the reserved side of friendly," she says.

We have this soul-searching (for me) talk while moving from machine to machine. I slowly move my arms up and down with heavy weights. I do leg presses to no good purpose I can see unless I can solve my fear of joining in.

When we complete the circuit, we head back to the room with the paltry cardio opportunities. The room has three treadmills, two bicycles, and not a single elliptical machine. Caroline stretches her hamstrings while I practice full-depth squats. After two years of pain in my knees, I can finally sit on my haunches. Why I am bothering to become more flexible, I don't know.

The hero in a romance novel I read was delighted the heroine practiced yoga. My imagination went wild. I prepared him a gourmet meal before we got down to the business of sex. I can't remember the book title or the author, but I can remember how, in my fantasy, he was pleased with my flexibility. Surely, I have more motivation than that for two years of wondering if my knees would hold me going up the steps to my house.

Caroline startles me with an abrupt interruption of my thoughts. "So, you feel like you don't fit in?"

"I'm going to have to think about when and why I get that crazy anxious feeling." Psychologists like me are supposed to have figured out what in our past plays out in the present.

We head out past the white-haired front desk volunteer and through the automatic door. The weather has chilled over the past several months and Caroline takes a few minutes to zip up her puff-coat. The city is trying to improve the small park we walk through. Now a creek runs through the park, which was once a lake and a marsh. Technically, the area is a flood plain. The city horticulturists have sensibly planted water grasses to fill some of the low areas, but the new cement walks still sometimes sport puddles.

"What do you think my chances are of having a fling with my lawyer?" I ask as we head up the hill into my neighborhood.

"I can't be positive. At your Christmas party, he flirted with everyone. He did eat like he hadn't had anything tasty for months. Maybe you can get to him that way. I wonder if it's true. I remember him having three helpings of shrimp salad."

I remember the party too. I was surprised he came. His telephone message in response to the invitation tucked inside a Christmas card was curt—*"I will attend your Christmas party."* As the hostess, I was busy despite my best efforts to have all the food ready. I even had my grandchildren primed to get people drinks. The image reverberating in my brain is of Dan speaking and gesturing a bit wildly to some friends of mine. I don't remember who. Now that I think about it, we did have a moment in the kitchen together.

"Now we have a great idea. What do you feed men so they think about sex?" I ask.

"You have me there. You're a great cook. I tell them if they want to eat with me, they have to ask politely and take me someplace fancy. I do keep cereal in the cupboard so they can make their own breakfast. When I want coffee, I make enough for them too. The only one I keep overnight these days is Tim."

"I don't know anything about modern sex. What's a Brazilian?" I want to make my fantasies more realistic.

When she recovers from her choking-and-coughing spell, she looks me in the eyes. "You're serious, aren't you?"

"Yes."

"A Brazilian is a full-wax job—no hair left from stem to stern."

"I assume they use a general anesthetic."

She ignores my shudder. "You can imagine Tim, since he's an air-traffic controller, likes me to have a pubic haircut he calls a runway. Really, Angie, sex has always been the same. It's what the two of you agree would be interesting and exciting."

"I want to know about diseases. I read about warts and herpes. I don't think gonorrhea is a problem, but I'm not sure. Steve brought crabs back from Guatemala two times. He told me he got them from toilet seats. They weren't too difficult to get rid of."

"He had sex in Guatemala, probably with whores. You were lucky crabs were the only thing he came back with. He really shit on you in a number of ways, didn't he? You deserve better. You know, you have many attractions. You're good-looking, you are wonderful company, a sympathetic friend, you can cook, you'll have plenty of money."

We stand in companionable silence. We view the too-short dresses in the window of a fancy clothes shop near my house. Then, I can't help myself, I want to know how intimate partners manage. I rarely get into this stuff with clients, and the romance novels aren't true life.

"Do you and Tim have dinner and watch a little TV and then shower together?"

"Different things, different nights," she says.

"So, I suppose you're not going to tell me if oral sex is expected by all men these days?"

"Well, I don't do it even if they want it. I tell them it's missionary or nothing."

"Is there usually a lot of smooching on the couch beforehand?" I ask.

"With Tim, not much. When he's in the mood, we'll dance a bit. Of course, I love that. Once I told him, 'You dance with me for twenty minutes or you sleep in the guest bedroom.' He didn't even laugh. He said, 'Put the music on.'"

"You're very helpful to let me know how it is with people. What would Zoey and Alice have to say about sex? They're both married."

"Zoey's marriage is strained at this point because she is spending so much time taking care of her mother. They're probably not having sex."

"I wasn't aware of that. She seems to mention she and Frank go out for this or that event or tailgate together with a bunch of people for every game."

"The marriage will probably come through all right in the end. Since they don't have children, they don't have that strain to manage."

"You should have been the psychologist. You catch the undercurrents that pass me by," I say.

"I know you have two modes, one for inside your office and one for outside."

"That's true. What about Alice?"

"She's either an incurable romantic or crazy. This is her fourth marriage, you know."

"I know there was an early one she doesn't talk about. Maybe it was annulled. She has a son," I tell her.

"Yes, but he's old enough not to put a strain on this marriage."

"You're right. Besides, he's in law school and reasonably independent. I think he has a girlfriend, so he and Alice didn't become semi-married to each other between Alice's marriages."

"What do you mean?" she asks.

"Sometimes when a mother divorces a father and the boy child is a teenager, he becomes the love of her life, not sexually, but emotionally. He starts to accompany her to concerts, for example, or they eat out together as if they are a couple.

The pleasantness of the relationship makes it hard for another potential spouse to 'break in.' When the teenager is more independent, it doesn't happen."

"Interesting. I can see what you mean." She smiles at me.

"What's your prediction for that marriage?"

"Humm. I suspect she'll get bored. She likes to have her way. John's a great guy, but my guess is she gets tired of accommodating someone else. It all feels so great in the early stages."

"If I could find someone who likes my cooking, I would never get bored."

Back at my house, I focus on the grapefruit and kiwi. I love to cut fruit. The rounds of sliced kiwi are geometrically, artistically perfect. They are a luscious color and look sweet. I am efficient in peeling and sectioning aromatic grapefruit. The tart half-moons are a gift to the recipient. Kiwi adds sweetness to the tart citrus, green to the pale pink. I recommend the mixture frequently to my friends and relatives.

Caroline drinks water with ice; I drink it without. She eats prunes; I eat dried apricots. We have been doing these walks and workouts for several years. I fell once and twisted my shoulder. She fell once and hurt her knee. While we sit and eat in my dining room, we talk about whatever is on our minds.

"Money is another thing I want to talk to you about," I start. "There is a mystery about the money. Dan doesn't want to talk about this part of it. I believe Steve has one or even two bank accounts where we have no paperwork. I don't know how he has kept it secret, but the money doesn't add up."

"I'm with the lawyer on this one. If you don't have the paper trail for money, it doesn't exist."

"It's just he made so much money buying and selling real estate for about a decade, he didn't have any place to put it.

He got rent regularly, and he always sold the buildings for considerably more than what he paid. At one time, he had quadruplexes and the large apartment building where we lived in the basement. I seem to remember him telling me he was worth a million dollars. That was before he retired and started the Merrill Lynch account. It's a dim memory."

"You'll have plenty of money when you split the Merrill Lynch account. You're not like me. Every month, I get my annuity check supplementing my state pension. The extra money is slowly seeping away. With the price of gas going up, I'm going to have to decide whether or not I can afford to go kayaking with the group."

"I like the kayaking and hiking group. I'm actively grateful you included me." I pat her hand across the table.

"I knew it would suit you." She nods.

"I know you're in a tough place about the money. If my daughter didn't need every penny I can scrounge up, I'd offer to pay your portion of the cabin rental when the group goes away. Although I must note, you did buy a fancy computer last week." I cock my head.

"That's for the layout work I do. The computer is a business expense, but I could never let you support my expenses."

She pushes her bowl away, licks her lips, and raises her eyebrows to indicate she liked the medley. She smiles. "The computer is a treat, no doubt. You know I like the technical stuff."

"If the shoe was on the other foot, you'd be helpful to me," I tell her.

"You've got a point there, but this coming weekend will be inexpensive. The group does such a good job of keeping expenses down. When we all crowd into a state park cabin, the expenses go to nothing. I'm looking forward to the trip. It's also great we share the responsibility for arranging our outings." We nod approval of each other, then her face saddens. "By the way, how is your daughter doing?"

"She goes in regularly now for follow-up blood work. So far, so good! Did I tell you she found a clinical trial on the web? No? She found out about it from the Young Survivor's Coalition. She made her doctor sign her up for it. She'll go to Wake Forest for some kind of vaccine."

"That sounds promising. Will she be in a placebo group?"

"Evidently, they're not having a 'no treatment' group but rather groups with different amounts and schedules."

"Is the research group going to pay her for being a guinea pig?" She gets her jacket on, but we keep talking.

"No, and she has to make the drive up there regularly. She believes it's worth it. She's making a lot of effort to keep up with the Survivor's members from all over the country. Some of them are professionals and they have a personal interest, so they all keep up with the latest research. She keeps up better than her doctor as nearly as I can tell."

"She has the bigger stake in it."

"True. I feel a little worthless since I don't have enough information to have an opinion on whether the trial is worth it or not."

"She'll do the best she can. Is she feeling well enough to be back at work?"

"She is, but she's still falling a bit behind with doctor's payments. She was so good at finding affordable insurance. It has a high deductible, but the insurance is paying for most everything after that first five thousand dollars. When, and if, I get some serious money, I'll help her with her increasing debt. I consider it all to be family money."

"I consider it my duty to keep telling you to look out for yourself first. Will the family need to vote on whether or not you pay my cabin expenses?" She grins at me.

I grin back. "Nobody tells me what to do with my money.

If I want to give my money away, I will. The children can't complain because I help them a lot."

"Indeed, you do. I'll see you Wednesday. How about eight o'clock to load the kayaks?"

"I'll be there."

When Caroline leaves, I feel deserted. Now I know I don't have the courage to have sex. I don't have a way to find out about any other bank account. I still don't know how Caroline reels them in like she does. Dan is out of reach, except in my nighttime thoughts. The day is young, and I have energy. I am restless.

When I don't want to clean the house, I go to my office. Even when no clients are scheduled, I drive the seven minutes, listening to NPR, and relax.

My daughter, myself, and Connie, a close friend for twenty-five years, own a small office building. Since the parking lot is spacious, clients are not frustrated or annoyed as they meander the short walk between reasonably kept flower beds. A ramp beside the stairs invites children to romp. The exterior looks like a house and the inside is very friendly. People like to sit in the waiting room. I like to sit in front of my computer. I also like for people to sit on my couch and tell me their stories.

My office is not meant to impress. The modern couch where people sit is plain with two small pillows for hugging. The pillows have a bright geometric print. My chair has a caned back to encourage me to sit up straight. The desk is not between me and my client; rather, it is pushed up against the wall, and the computer and printer rest on it. I was once in a therapist's office with an antique French desk between the therapist and the client. What nonsense!

My phone sits on the desk to my right. Any incoming calls go to an answering machine. New health research indicates convenience can be deadly. You are supposed to get up

THE ADVENTURES OF ANGIE MERK

and go get whatever you want. I am trying to get up and down more.

I open the metal door with the double panes, close down the rickety security system. As I turn the key to my office door, I'm safe in a world separate from all my worries. My office is my second home, but without the requirements to clean or cook or think about Rachel. In contrast to my house, the natural light here is dim and relaxing so table and floor lamps are required.

Invoices beckon, they always do. The to-do stack is on the floor within easy reach. Invoices are mindless work, and I am always behind, so they get filled out, copied, and sent in an endless stream, but I am not tense about them.

On the days when clients come through my door, I welcome them. I dress like a small-business owner—pants with a sweater in the winter or a dressed-up T-shirt in the summer. Never a jacket. I don't look like an expert, but since I'm degreed, people usually listen to me. They're in pain, so they want help.

Sometimes they strangely bring my issues with them. When I worried about being old, a new client came in. She was sixty, and her hips hurt. She was scared of becoming immobile to the point of obsession. In helping her refocus, I soothed the edges of my own fear.

Several divorced women have shown me how important it is to minimize disappointment and treasure freedom.

Sometimes my secret issues walk in. I didn't know I was overindulging my adult children until I saw a client suffer the consequences of having weak boundaries, of being afraid to say no. I never did have to rescue a child from prison or drugs. I'm recurrently grateful for that.

People bring their six-year-olds to me. The children's parents tolerate bad behavior when they are preschool age, but the teachers won't put up with it. The parents bring the child when the teachers complain the children are disrupting their classes. Usually, the parents know their children are behaving badly, but they don't want to blame themselves. I don't blame them either; instead, I talk about other strategies they might consider. The blame issue disappears as does the defensiveness, so they're open to change.

Lots of times, children have stuff on their minds interfering with their ability to learn. They worry about monsters under the bed, tornadoes, a parent's demise on their deployment. If a child is afraid of a parent or sibling, they can have difficulty learning math or learning how to read.

Another group of children who come to my attention are older and addicted to electronics. They are sullen and uncooperative. They are disrespectful and don't listen.

I encourage parents not to shout at their children. Respect is a two-way street. I recommend they take control of their children's environment—i.e., the electronics. When the child has done what you want them to do, then they have earned what they want—time with their games. The principle is the frequency of a behavior is increased when you reward the behavior. Parents have to learn to reward the behavior they want. Too much talk and what the child learns is to tune them out.

Sometimes my prescription works like magic. One teenage client was a perfect example. She was behaving like a wild child. Her parents had taken away her cell phone, her lifeline. They kept increasing the time she couldn't have it, so she was not going to see it for eighteen months. I finally persuaded her parents to give her time on her cell phone after she had done the basics, attended class, and finished her homework. They were amazed at the speed of her transformation. She had instantaneously returned to her sweet self.

I want to change Dan's behavior. I want him to flirt with me, to pay me some fun attention. What could I reward him with? The only thing I have control over is the money I send him. How would he react if I told him, I'd send him the money after he flirts with me three times for fifteen minutes each time?

He'd just charge me his usual fee for the time, and I'd be sad and angry.

CHAPTER THREE

The weather has started to turn to spring again. A sense of adventure, as well as the early morning bird calls of a forested neighborhood, surround me when I leave my car to help Caroline with our kayaks.

"No need to drag it. Let me help you carry it," I shout to her.

Caroline flashes me a smile. "It's so easy when we do it together."

She has pulled her kayak trailer from her backyard to the side of her house. The trailer is a converted motorcycle trailer. Some soldering of the upright aluminum pieces to the bottom beams to eliminate swaying successfully modified the rickety reject. Since other members of the group have trailers too, I rationalize not having to mess with one. Even with her experience of pulling it on the highway, Caroline is careful not to get herself into a place where backing up is required.

None of us are strong enough to carry our kayaks alone. Caroline's trailer holds four. We grab the handles at each end of my boat, lift it down from my car, slide it into the trailer, then place hers on top of mine. Lifting the kayaks, I appreciate my bicep strength. Last night, my daughter helped me load my kayak onto my car so I could bring it here.

I love to drive around town with my orange boat on top of my red Subaru. I get looks of interest from guys in trucks and Jeeps at stoplights. They're always too young, but I smile at them anyway. When my kayak is on my car, I try to find time to go to the grocery store. It empowers me to come out of the store and see it. I can think people say to themselves, "There goes a competent woman."

Caroline's SUV pulls the trailer easily, with plenty of room inside for four people, four personal flotation devices, four paddles, and four suitcases. Zoey's big cooler can even sit in the trunk. Our food for the weekend and our gear will pile high enough to restrict Caroline's ability to see out the back window. I believe we look upscale outdoorsy, hauling four kayaks. Nobody knows we're not going white-water kayaking.

The air is mild for March, with only a hint of coolness. Since we could hit some cold weather farther north, we dressed in pants and long-sleeved T-shirts.

"I'm looking forward to seeing Zoey and Alice. It's been a while since the hiking trip in Tennessee," Caroline comments.

After we're settled, she moves the trailer out of the driveway, missing the curb as she turns into the street. "I worry about the kayaking," she continues. "I'm not as experienced as some of the others, and you know I'm not a good swimmer."

Caroline is strong at dog paddling, but because she doesn't know the classic strokes, she believes she can't swim well.

As she talks, I work to comfort myself. Kayaking is not a big fear for me as long as I make sure I am following someone who knows how to read a river. I am a good swimmer, so it's no big deal if I turn over. Still, I have never lost my balance, and I don't want to land in the river since the water is cold. I imagine the kayak over me, making it impossible to breathe.

To lose the image, I turn to reassure Caroline. "There's a range of experience and skill levels in the group. With eight of us, it will be pretty slow going."

"I hope so," she responds instantly. "This stretch of the French Broad is supposed to be a mix of Level one and Level two." She smooths out the worry muscles that have made a deep vee in her forehead.

"Don't be so concerned. You'll do just fine. You always do." I pat her shoulder.

She slows to turn the corner to Zoey's street. "There's the cooler on the sidewalk." Caroline nods her head and points as she turns the steering wheel with one hand, and the SUV glides into position next to the large receptacle.

Zoey's house is a step up from Caroline's and mine. She has a heated pool with tropical plants in her backyard. A maintenance man keeps the yard tidy. As Zoey closes the heavy oak front door, the sun hits the red highlights in her hair. She's light on her feet and moves quickly down the front stairs.

"I hope I have everything," she calls to us.

Caroline smiles. "You're always super ready."

Caroline and I move our stuff around in the back. We transfer the food that needs to be kept cool into the large cooler and load it into the trunk.

"You guys are dependably on time." Zoey's shoulders relax.

"We're both anxious to get out of town, for different reasons, mind you." We all chuckle and exchange eye contact.

Caroline wants to get away from her sister Susie. Susie had a knee replacement, and she exaggerates her pain. Caroline is fed up with her dependency. I had a full week of difficult clients. We know our reasons will be fodder for sympathetic discussion later when the wine has been sampled.

"We'll have to move stuff around to accommodate Alice." Zoey surveys the back of the SUV.

We all know Alice brings more stuff than the rest of us. She's the fashionista of the group. She keeps up to date with the latest outdoor fashions. Neither Caroline nor I pay any attention to current modes. We tend to replace clothes when they have holes in them, so the tops and bottoms may not match perfectly. In contrast, Alice always has a color-coordinated bandana tied around her neck.

I'd keep current if I could, but I always have too much else on my mind and not enough cash in my wallet. I wonder if her sense of style has anything to do with her four marriages. Do men go out of style and get replaced like the shape and length of jeans? I go for comfort, so I pride myself on packing light for a weekend under the assumption that if something happens to one pair of pants—like spilling chili on myself as I have done—I can wear my travel outfit.

Alice lives around the corner from Zoey in the same development. Her two-storied brick house has white columns supporting a small porch. Her friendly but stinky dogs come leaping up to greet us. I force myself to pet them, but it's a chore because they slobber and throw their heads around. These are big dogs. Petting dogs is supposed to be relaxing, but these dogs leave my hands smelling bad. The smells I'm attracted to are cooking smells, like yeast breads, spaghetti sauces, and roasts. Too soon for lunch, best to focus on the dogs, after all.

Maybe I should get a dog, considering the research says you'll live longer. On second thought, no, I want to feed my family and friends, not a dog.

Alice's current husband comes to the door. "Here, Jack, here, Jill!" As one would expect, he's tall and good-looking. He sends Alice an air kiss, which she acknowledges with a wink.

The golden labs hold back, their tails wagging their bodies, then reluctantly obey his follow-up whistle.

Alice and I retrieve her kayak from the backyard. Water spills out when we turn it to load it.

"Did you go on Wednesday's outing?" I wonder if she has time to join a subgroup that goes on regular floats on the Saluda River after work. I often have late afternoon or early evening clients, but I'd like to go. They take beer. Maybe I'd be more casual and relaxed about kayaking if I practiced wielding my paddle while under the influence.

"The weather was perfect for the evening float, not too cold even at seven. The river otters are out in the early evening." Alice smiles, then takes a big plastic baggie from a larger paper bag. "Will this salad stuff fit in the big box?"

"Let's try it. Usually, everything fits in Zoey's cooler." I move around to help.

Alice and I push and prod, something squishes a bit, but it all goes in.

"That does it." I slam the lid, luckily missing her fingers as her jump back shows off her good reflexes.

We take our usual places in the car. I ride shotgun with Caroline while Zoey and Alice sit in the back.

"I wonder if we'll have enough to eat," Alice says.

We aren't two blocks away from the house. Everyone smiles since it's a common joke for the group. We always have way too much food. I tend to gain two pounds on every monthly weekend trip. The following week of near starvation usually returns me to my pre-vacation weight.

Foods I rarely eat—spaghetti, cheese, brownies, bread—all get devoured on these trips.

The four-hour ride is interrupted by a plea from the shopping cabal. Alice and Zoey know every outlet store along every major highway within a six-state radius of Columbia. We stop at a house-wares outlet. I can't help myself, and I buy three berry boxes, rationalizing that they will make nice gifts for the birthdays the group celebrates.

Caroline doesn't mind, so we stop at a Land's End outlet where Alice and Zoey buy wicking, easy-care hiking shirts. I push the merchandise around, but I'm not much of a clothes shopper unless I know I want something particular. Then I find it and buy it. Successful shopping puts everyone in a good mood.

The rules are when we stop for gas, everyone contributes, and when we stop for food, everyone pays their own. The rules are clear. Stepping outside the rules is punished by being the subject of gossip.

Caroline has a GPS device, but it has led us astray once or twice in the past. This time it is on target, so we find the cabin without trouble.

"There certainly is a lot more stuff for a kayaking trip than a hiking trip," Alice comments.

When Caroline opens the rear door, a couple of paddles clatter to the road.

"Very true," I say. Then everyone unloads the van without regard to whose bag is whose.

Zoey and I carry in the cooler. We stuff the refrigerator with the makings for breakfast and dinner, everyone stacks the paddles by the front door, everyone claims bed space. The rule here is first come, first served. Everyone finds a place for their suitcase, usually on the floor next to their bed. On these trips, we often share queen or king beds. I'm a popular bed partner because I don't move during the night, and I don't snore.

"I prefer the hiking trips. More leg exercise, less servitude to equipment," Caroline half-whispers to me.

After the ritual cabinet survey for where the pots for dinner can be found, we each pour a glass of wine from the bottles that have appeared on the kitchen counter. The screen door slams behind us as we go to sit on the rustic porch, wine in one hand and appetizer plate in the other. The cabin is near the river, so the sounds are as soothing as the best white noise machine; the air is unsullied. The slightly musty smell inside is reminiscent of all cabins by all rivers and suggests the sheets will be clammy.

When the other group arrives to take over the neighboring cabin, they'll join us for drinks and dinner. They'll prepare dinner tomorrow night. Each cabin will prepare its own breakfast. Each individual will have a lunch for the float. State cabins, though rustic, are inevitably well maintained. Clean linens fit nearly new mattresses. Kitchen supplies always cover our minimalist needs: large pots for spaghetti noodles, an eight-cup coffee maker, a microwave, and a dishwasher.

"I followed the emails for the other cabin. Did Melinda ever volunteer to help with a meal?" Alice addresses the question to me.

"I think not." I followed all the emails as well.

Alice purses her lips. "Next time I'm in a cabin with her, I promise to be more direct. I'll just assign her a task."

"Remember the trip to Florida last year? Nancy made her clean up because she hadn't helped beforehand." I roll my eyes.

I had a twinge of remorse. Melinda cleaned up all by herself. I was, however, able to push the twinge aside. I had been annoyed all along too. She stepped over an imaginary boundary the rest of us knew to respect. You're supposed to help until all visible tasks are finished.

I didn't realize it was bothering me until we started talking about it. That's one of the advantages of therapy, same as with good friends. The verbalization of a problem is like a skin irritation—when you pay attention to it, you may realize you have a thorn in your side. Talking about a problem is like first aid. It helps the healing process.

"Does anyone know about Nancy's job? Last I heard, she thought she was going to be fired," Zoey asks the question of the group.

Since I had lunch with Nancy last week, I'm able to contribute. "Her boss fired the lazy coworker. Now Nancy has the stress of two jobs. She's having trouble getting her boss to replace the coworker."

"My husband knows her boss. Maybe he can put a plug in for how good it is for business if you are fully staffed. They golf together." Zoey is ever helpful. The group works together nicely; everyone helps to solve problems.

Over the years, the group has developed its distinct culture. At a January meeting/party, we plan the year's outings. A rule came into existence as the group got bigger and more social. Only one glass of wine until the year's schedule is set. Each person must propose a trip, then we vote to decide what trips we want. The person who proposes a popular trip takes responsibility for the arrangements for housing and activities.

As the air shifts to cold, we move into the living room, plastic wineglasses in hand, cheese and crackers within easy reach.

"How's your mother?" Caroline reaches over to touch Zoey's knee. Caroline buried her own mother last year after several years of being the dutiful daughter.

"It's up and down. Sometimes she knows me, and sometimes she doesn't." Zoey wipes a tear from her cheek.

"I know about that. Hard on everyone, isn't it?" Caroline says.

"Do you think you've recovered from your mother's death?" Zoey asks Caroline.

"These trips, being with friends, being nice to yourself

because you are going through a hard time, do help a lot," Caroline responds.

Alice waves her cracker to call attention to her contribution. "Ron's parents are coming to the point of not being able to tell whether he or his brother are with them as well. It's like the story of the nephew visiting his aunt in a nursing home. He asks, 'Do you know who I am?' She responds, 'No, but the lady at the desk will tell you.'"

When the laughter dies, she continues, "He travels to North Dakota every couple of weeks. I won't go with him, mostly since they are daffy, and the house is drafty. I'm not comfortable there. I struggle with what is the right thing to do. I do fix Ron a special meal when he comes back."

My mother died in her sleep at ninety, several years ago. She was depressed, but her mind was totally good. Despite her blindness, she could correct the totals of her tax accountant, so I stay out of the dementia dialogues.

"Let's start cooking before the wine gets to us." Caroline stands to call a halt to the conversation and heads for the kitchen.

Because dinner is a joint effort, I suspend judgment completely. Thus, I will eat too much of whatever is served. I will be cooking cheese omelets in the morning. Tonight, I brought garlic bread to heat while the spaghetti cooks. Caroline cooks the spaghetti, Zoey is the salad maker, and Alice has dessert ready to serve. The group from the other cabin is expected.

"We have arrived!" Melinda is the first to bang the screen door, then the rest of the group files in. They focus on pouring their wine. The conversation becomes livelier. With years of intimacy, group members feel free to tease each other.

When everyone is settled, Caroline raises her glass to

capture the group's attention. "Angie is super attracted to her divorce lawyer."

Alice of The Four Marriages jumps up, putting her hands in a ward-off-evil sign. "No! No! No!"

Zoey scooches over to hug me and frowns at Alice, whispering "good luck" in my ear. Mostly the crowd is amused.

"How are you getting on with him?" Diane asks.

"This question could be answered in several different ways. One answer is 'we are getting on quite nicely since I never argue with him.' Another answer would be 'we are not getting on at all since he still acts like I'm part of the wallpaper despite my bringing him food and resting my hand tantalizingly close to his. He scarfs down the food and doesn't take my hand. I am mostly patient and determined."

The group members murmur, but no one has anything to add. Soon, plates are out, dinner is served, wine is replenished, and spirits are high. After dessert is eaten and the dishwasher loaded, Caroline brings out a game where we make up proverbs. Group members are smart and funny; I struggle to devise proverb-like sayings.

After several hours of concentration and hilarity, Alice breaks up the party. "We have a river to tackle. How about breakfast at seven?"

"Let's plan to head out by eight thirty." Nancy's excitement shows in her voice.

"Plenty of time for breakfast preparation. I do need my shut-eye. Night, all," I speak loudly over the din.

I head for the upstairs bedroom with its nicer-than-home mattress. Caroline claimed the other side of the queen, which is fine with me since she doesn't snore like Zoey. As I drift, I wonder if Dan snores.

The next thing I know, Zoey's getting coffee ready at six thirty. When I throw back the comforter, the room is chilly, but I can ignore it. I'm pleased I slept well, so I do my early morning stretches and dress for the river trip in quick-drying pants, their coverage winning over the comfort of shorts. My focus this morning is on the omelets. I head to the kitchen.

Lucky for me, the pans are well-seasoned and the cheese I have chosen turns out to be a tasty cheddar. It's a lot of fun to beat ten eggs at one time, especially with the whisk I brought along. These are good eggs with bright almost orange yokes. I'm confident in my judgment of the amount of salt and pepper. I've guessed well with the cooking heat, so the eggs cook thoroughly and remain soft. I slide two omelets onto two plates, and Alice adds bacon and hash browns from the oven. Melinda is standing nearby, sipping coffee.

Alice makes a beeline for her, indicates she should put down her coffee, shoves the plates into her hands. "Take these to the table. Are the napkins out?"

Melinda is cooperative, returns to repeat the operation, and receives a curt "thanks" from Alice.

The smell of browned butter filling the cabin competes with the coffee. The omelets and sides are a success as evidenced by clean plates. Although how anyone can be hungry after last night's feast is beyond me. When the dishes are loaded into the dishwasher, everyone focuses on packing their lunch and putting on their river shoes.

My lunch for the paddle is hummus and crackers, a nut bar, an apple, and a green pepper—no preparation required. My footwear is my new Tevas.

With this group, I have found that one minute everyone is lounging around in nighties and robes, coffee cup in hand, and the next minute, the dishes are off the table, and everyone stands by the door, ready to get in the car. I have learned to hustle earlier than I like.

"Are those new water shoes?" Zoey reaches down to touch my shoes.

"Yeah, they're more comfortable and more foot protective than the old ones. See how my big toes are covered?" I skip to show her how pleasurable they are.

"Won't your feet get cold without any wool socks?" she asks.

"I love cold water on my feet. Otherwise, they get sweaty."

The drive to the put-in spot is less than ten minutes. We drive in three cars, including the two trailers. We unload the trailers. The shuttle is arranged so Caroline and Robbie, who have the trailers, will drive their cars and trailers to the take-out location, then Alice and I will meet them and bring them back to the put-in.

I help Zoey unstrap the kayaks and take them to the water's edge. People concentrate on their preparations. Alice and I complete the shuttle business. The river is wide here and slower than it appeared from the glimpses we got from the road. The forest surrounds the narrow dirt path leading to the small concrete put-in ramp. For an instant, the crisp air lies on the skin of my arms. The small yellow wildflowers embedded in the green beside the path require my attention.

"Come on, Angie, it's your turn. We've carried it far enough, so you can push it in from here," Alice calls to me.

When everyone is safely in the water, the experienced paddlers start off. I am always a little scared. Then, just when I start to relax, we hit some ripples, and I tense again. The water over the rocks mesmerizes. I stay alert enough to see how the experts head around and through the rocks. How do they know the best way?

We are in the North Carolina mountains near Asheville. The scenery is mostly bucolic, but we come to a curve in the river where we can see the grounds of the Biltmore estate and a hint of the castle itself.

When I refocus on the river, I see the highway bridge ahead, where the river becomes faster. It's frightening to see the water pushing against the huge concrete pylons. I watch how Alice and the others start from the right side. They pull hard at one point, and thus, they avoid the white water next to the pylon. With my heart in my throat, I wait my turn. I'm careful about my position, and I don't know exactly how it happens, but I make it fine down to where the water slows.

Shouting comes into my awareness. "Pull, Zoey, pull."

Not enough, or not soon enough. When I turn around, I see Zoey has lost her boat and half swims, half scrambles to the side of the river. I pull to the side downstream from her, where a small eddy allows me, without much work, to avoid being pulled farther down. Caroline is beside me. Most of the group is downstream, circling in a wide, slow spot. They have Zoey's kayak.

I frown to myself. They're the experts. Why aren't they coming to get her?

"Let's go get her." Caroline starts paddling upstream.

I pull in beside her, making my strokes with as much power as I have. We both make slow progress toward the small grassy bank where Zoey waves frantically.

Caroline's breathing labors. "My boat won't allow me to keep going."

"I'll do what I can." I continue upstream. Once I get close to Zoey, the going is easier.

"Thank God. I was afraid I'd have to find a way out of here." Zoey is shaking and pale. "I hit my shoulder. It's going to be okay, but sore. I was so scared to find myself in the water with no boat. The water is really cold. I may have some shock or hypothermia."

"Okay, let's figure out how to get you out of this." I'm

hoping she'll shift her focus from fear to hope. "How about you sit in front of me?"

She makes the shift to practical solutions. "I'll sit behind you. That way you can see what you're doing."

I maneuver the boat close to the shore. She wades in to help. We get the boat parallel to the shore. She moves to lie on her stomach across the back of the kayak, her bending and pushing slow enough that my counterbalance is effective. When she pushes herself upright to sit behind me, she moves so quickly that, when her weight shifts, I believe she is tipping the kayak, and we are both going to land in the river. The fear sticks with me as I paddle to straighten the boat into the river current.

"I'm worried about my legs catching on a rock." She clutches my waist.

"I'll keep the boat as slow and steady as I can. Can you pull your legs up a bit?"

I wasn't aware of an audience, but when we join the group, we are applauded. Everyone helps to get her as dry and warm as possible and settled in her own kayak again. The rest of the float is uneventful by comparison.

The details come out as we sit on the porch rocking chairs in the late afternoon. When Zoey hit the pylon, she was thrown from her boat and tried to pull her kayak around the edge of it. She wrenched her shoulder in the process. Since I had strained my arms working to reach her, we both required sympathy and Tylenol. Several glasses of wine helped us relax as well.

Tonight's dinner is in the other cabin. They have heated frozen spinach lasagna from Trader Joe's. The awful stuff tastes delicious. The too-sweet apple pie is wonderful. This cabin's denizens have built a fire in the big stone fireplace. The smell of burning wood relaxes and energizes me. About half the group likes to mess with the fire, poking, adding wood, and the other half wants the fire to be on its own. The opposing camps fuss at each other.

"Leave it alone, it needs air."

"We'll get embers if I put on this one last big log."

"If it gets any bigger, it will burn the cabin down."

For no good reason, the group sings old songs, Western songs, mining songs, Girl Scout camp songs, songs from old musicals, and popular songs from recent decades. Caroline brought disco music in case there was a boom box. We sing, we dance, we drink. We have a great party. After much laughter and some wild gyrations, we all turn in.

Sunday breakfast is comprised of lox, bagels, cream cheese, and a rehash of Saturday's adventure. I am a heroine in their eyes. Why am I still afraid when I picture the smooth water gliding over the rocks? I've bumped the underwater rocks many times but have never been stuck or imbalanced to the point of capsizing, although I can picture it in my mind.

After breakfast, everyone pitches in to clean and pack. Conversations are more subdued heading out of the cabin than they were on the way in. We stop in Biltmore Village to shop on the way home. I use the New Morning Gallery there as a source for inexpensive craft gifts for friends' birthdays. I am partial to hand-thrown pots. Among the treasures, there are carved wooden kitchen utensils, prints of nature scenes, and other lovely North Carolina crafts. My purchases fill the spaces where the food had been in the back of the SUV.

Caroline drops me off at my house. She keeps the kayaks on the trailer in her driveway between trips. There will be another trip in three weeks.

"Thanks for driving." She accepts my heartfelt gratitude. We exchange a light hug of parting friends.

"See you tomorrow night at the salsa lesson," she says.

"If I can move by then," I call after her as she drives off.

When I get inside, I'm lonesome, so I check the mail.

Dan's first invoice is in the stack. I look at the number at the bottom of the second page three times, then I sit down and look again. The number is way too high. Because I like him so much, is it possible I thought he was going to work for nothing? I find my smartphone in my purse where it usually hides.

"Rachel! I can't afford to see Dan or call him or have him do anything more for me. He's too expensive! Does he eat money?" I shout into the phone.

"Mom, calm down. You knew he would be expensive. Whatever the bill is, I recommend you pay it cheerfully. I believe he will prove to be worth every penny."

"We're not talking pennies here," I say.

"Take a deep breath. Let me hear you breathe," she tells me.

"Okay, that doesn't help."

"Take another breath. Let me hear it."

I do as I'm told, and the hysteria fades slightly.

"Now tell me about your trip," she murmurs.

"You are changing the subject."

"Yes. I'm also interested in the trip."

"I still get scared when I see rocks coming in front of me or just under the water. I did, however, accomplish my first river rescue. Zoey hit a bridge pylon and lost her kayak. She got to the bank of the river after scrambling over the river rocks, although I don't know how she did it. She was scared shitless when I saw her. I managed to go back upstream and get her."

"Why in the devil do you still get scared? Maybe you could consider the feeling a combination of excitement and caution?"

"Nice reframe." I nod even though she can't see me.

"Was there an envelope with the bill?" she asks.

"Yes."

"Just write the check and send it," she orders.

"We'll all be in the poor house. Bye."

My hand shakes as I write the check. I didn't tell Rachel what I was really thinking. I am not myself because I am so hurt. True, life is not fair, but he's not scrimping, so why do I have to? He's a nasty man to take advantage of me. He probably has piles of gold coins he runs his fingers through before he goes to bed at night. Oh, the rat, he goes to bed without me.

I cry while I put a stamp on the envelope. I put the evil envelope where the mailman will take it away. Staggering to the kitchen, I toss down a glass of wine. When I gain a little energy, I head to bed where I cry myself to sleep.

I never wake up with a headache, but this morning I have one. I am never in a rage, but this morning, I bang the pans as I fix my breakfast. When I whip my oatmeal into its usual container, half of it lands on the counter behind the bowl. When I pour my glass of orange juice, it runs over. When I start to drink down my juice, I choke, so I throw the glass in my hand as hard as I can into the sink. I'm lucky I didn't throw it through the window. Cleaning up the mess calms me a bit.

"Can you see I'm in the kitchen cleaning up broken glass?" I shout at Caroline when she comes in.

"Wow! You're still in your nightie," she says.

"You're lucky you're not finding the bloody body of a woman who has slit her own throat."

"What's this all about?"

"Dan is a bastard!" I shout at her.

Caroline grabs my wrist, so I don't throw another glass into the sink. "Hey, slow down." She takes the glass from my hand. "I've never seen you like this."

"I've never been so angry at anybody in my whole life."

"What happened?"

"I don't have my money or my divorce. He is going to bleed me dry."

"I take it he sent his first invoice."

"Does he think I'm head of the US Treasury?" I work to lower my voice. "Rachel says I should just suck it up and pay it. I already have."

My head pounds and what's running through it is that nobody knows what a terrible situation I'm in.

"You don't have to like it. He has done a bunch of subpoenas." She shrugs her shoulders.

"Don't go being on his side. Do I ever have to speak to him again?"

"You know the old saying." She half-smiles.

We say it in unison: "You catch more flies with honey than with vinegar."

I can't believe I am laughing at our shared knowledge, our mocking recital of the illogical ditty. Who wants to catch flies? The saying doesn't even fit, but we both knew it was right for the time and place.

"Do I get to have any revenge for this insult?" I ask her.

"We'll see." She wags her finger at me.

"If I make him my sex slave, he'll have to buy me jewels and cars and furs. Then I'd get my money back."

She chuckles. "We'll see."

I follow her into the bedroom and get dressed in my workout clothes. She gives me a pat on the shoulder as we head out to the gym.

CHAPTER FOUR

Three weeks later, I decide to go to an art opening while clipping ivy, that invasive weed. When spring comes, the weed twines around every strand of fencing in my backyard. I delight in cutting it down, although I know it's growing up behind me as I walk away. Ever since I bought this house, I spend almost every spare minute murdering plants. The yard was overgrown with weeds, the fence covered with that phoenix, ivy. Weeds need pulling evermore, and iris rhizomes from the old house must be planted before they dry out.

You should practice being friendly rather than standoffish was the thought that settled my internal debate about whether or not to go to the opening. I don't understand why I feel like I don't fit in.

The garden requires absolute concentration. I love to use the clippers until my fingers quit working. Cleaning spent flower beds when the temperature is mild is like the moral equivalent of writing checks at the end of the month, plus the feel-good pleasure of becoming exhausted in the sun. The garden looks so much better. The view from the kitchen window over the sink has vastly improved with only two hours of labor.

My thinking has led me to believe what I want is company on Friday nights. I haven't been out in the evening for maybe two weeks. The art opening looks like a good thing.

After a quick lunch of avocado on toast with Hellman's mayonnaise, of course, I enjoy my long shower as a prelude to getting dressed up. I perform all the extras. I choose a slim knee-length silk skirt and a blue blouse with my preferred V-neckline. A kitten heel fits the occasion since I'll be standing around. A higher heel could be painful after a while, and I'm determined not to make my bunion worse by suffering with a leg-enhancing spike.

I always arrive early even when I try not to. Oh well, parking is easy. It's a typical local art opening at a contemporary gallery. The art is strange and way too personal. The large paintings are O'Keefe-like in their sexual symbolism. I'm embarrassed to look at them.

People mill around with clear plastic wineglasses filled with cheap red or white wine. They hold small plastic plates while chattering with each other in small groups. They try to figure out whether to put their wineglass on the food table or balance it on their plate. I find I'm standing close to the food table. The food trays are on multiple tiers, large chunks of tasteless cheese, baskets of wilting crackers, plates of roll-ups from Sam's Club, and bowls of green grapes. The grapes are probably from Peru rather than California. Who knows what pesticides lurk in their skins?

Barbara, a woman I'd worked with decades ago, appears. The main evidence of her aging is her hair is black rather than brown. We had shared similar husbands at the time, although she had been married twice earlier. She used to complain about how men never gave her gifts. We would speculate about what women do so the men in their lives bring them flowers and jewelry. We always came to the same conclusion: we were too nice, too adaptable. We didn't know how to be demanding.

She seems on a mission, guiding a man into position beside me. I look up and take in his kind eyes tucked in a fleshy face anchored by a salt-and-pepper beard. He is way too overweight. I picture myself fixing crudités with seasoned lime juice as a dip, no oil. I would remove the skin from chicken breasts before browning them with a side of mushrooms. What else would complete the menu? Steamed broccoli with a dash of soy? Carrot and raisin salad, minimize the mayo? In real life, he holds a plate piled high with cheap food. The vision makes me a tad queasy.

"Jerry, this is Angie Merk."

"Hi," he says. "Haven't I seen you at the senior citizens center? Have you ever been to the Sociable Singles group?"

"I went for the first time about two weeks ago. There were so many people, I didn't have time to pay attention to each person. I didn't go out to dinner with the group."

I turn to my friend. "So, Barbara, you weren't at the meeting. Do you sometimes go?"

"I only go when my friend Sharon goes. She is an irregular participant, at best. I know Jerry through Sharon. They are both members of the camera club."

"You're a photographer?" I become a little interested.

"Yes, I'm a professional."

His pronouncement has a whiff of arrogance. I smile. "Wonderful."

"Will you go next Tuesday? I usually go out to dinner with the group after the meeting. Perhaps we can join the group for dinner," he says. "Barbara tells me you take pictures."

What else did Barbara tell him? "I'll plan to be there," I respond, a result of my thinking I should get out and about now that I'm newly single, lawyer or no lawyer, sex or no sex, even though the divorce itself drags on.

The rest of the art show passes uneventfully. I visit with some friends. I note Jerry has stayed close to the food table, mostly by himself.

During the three days between the art opening and the Sociable Singles group, I consider and reconsider my "plan to be there," my decision hesitating like a roulette ball approaching the red or the black slot. Or the moment at the top of a ski run where you see the tiny figures at the bottom and the tips of your skis, but only air in between. Push off or not push off? You know they'll let you go back down the chairlift, but deep down you know you'll push off because you know how to do the run.

I consider calling Barbara. What would I tell her? *He eats too much bad food. The Sociable Singles go to restaurants I assiduously avoid.* No! This will be a good opportunity to try to fit in.

The Sociable Singles meetings are boring. The meetings consist of discussions among twenty or so people, who all have to have their say as to whether to send a card or a small plant to an ailing member. Then the participants spend too much time deciding on what low-grade restaurant to go to. This meeting promises to be as boring as the last.

When I get there, Jerry has saved the seat next to him at the long tables pulled together in a circle in the undecorated room. The folding metal chairs mean my hip tightening will make it difficult to stand when the meeting is finished.

"What do we want to do for John's memorial service?" Thelma, who volunteers as the group leader begins.

This is going to be worse than I anticipated. It isn't just that someone's sick; a group member has actually died. Turns out John and Sabrina met at the Sociable Singles Group.

A skinny guy, sitting opposite me and far off, speaks next.

His name is Bob. "Sabrina will need a lot of support. We should all take turns visiting her."

This is the same guy who sidled up to me at my first meeting and stroked my shoulder. Now he wants to make time with the widow?

"We should wait a while for that. A card with all our names on it would be the best thing." Thelma tries to control the group.

A woman sitting next to Bob pats his hand, resting her hand on top of his for way too long.

There's stuff going on here I don't want to be part of.

Thelma makes another attempt at directing the group. "Here is a card to circulate. Should we use some of the money in our undesignated fund to send flowers?"

"We don't have enough money in that fund to send a decent bunch of dandelions," comments the self-designated treasurer.

"We could try to collect enough money to send a small spray." This suggestion comes from a guy in a suit seated not far from me.

"That might put a burden on some of our members," says Thelma.

"We don't have to specify an amount," the suited guy says.

"Let's take a vote." Thelma is determined to keep the meeting from lasting until midnight. "How many people want to send a potted plant to the house? That's six. How many want to circulate a box for money and checks for a fancy spray? That's five. If anybody wants to contribute a bit more for a potted plant, just give it to the treasurer after the meeting."

The group has not even gotten to ailing members, nor to the decision about next month's restaurant. I am finished with this meeting, but I force myself to stay. I am so uninterested I don't realize the meeting has concluded until Jerry pats my hand, which, by the way, is in my lap.

Jerry asks me to follow him to the restaurant, and I do. His white Ford van is slow and easy to keep in sight. He opens my car door when I park beside him.

"This is one of my favorite places." He ushers me toward the fake Western door.

We sit together at a table with several other people. He is solicitous, taking my arm and seating me. We chat amiably. He was a professional photographer, now retired. Since I am a serious amateur photographer, selling prints at a weekly craft market on Main Street, I think it is a possible good fit. He tells me he has retired to a place in the country.

The restaurant is the kind I don't care to go to. I try hard to eat the right food. The menu consists of every kind of grilled and fried meat with a side of fries. There are no specialty salads. I order a cheeseburger with onion rings—a vegetable, right? The meal is delicious. I don't even feel nauseated as I'd like to be. The waiter brings Jerry the bill since he indicated he was taking me to dinner.

He fishes in his back pocket with an oversized finger. He has to shift his weight to make room. He pulls out a dirty leather wallet stuffed with many cards.

"I hope they take this card. All the others are useless." He waves his card at the waiter as he smiles at me.

He says "useless" so cheerfully I don't really hear what he says. Then the waiter tells him they don't accept that card.

"That's okay, let me get it," I say after I grasp the situation. He seems like a friend, so it seems the natural thing to do. I pull out my card and hand it to the waiter, indicating I am paying the bill for us both. The man across the table sneers. Has he seen this tableau before?

When we walk out to the car, he tries to kiss me in the parking lot. I give him my cheek and get in my car.

On the way home, I realize my tummy is full from the cheeseburger and onion rings I ate, so I feel cheerful. See, I am attractive. See, I do fit in. Jerry told me he'll get the money to me for the meal, and the shock of having to pull out my Visa wears off. My sleep is dreamless.

He calls at nine a.m. the next day. "How about we take in a movie Saturday night?" he asks.

"No, that won't work for me. I have a party at a friend's house. Would you like to come? I'm sure she would be open to that."

"Absolutely, how about a photo shoot at the zoo on Sunday?"

"The weather is supposed to be a little cooler, sounds fine." We make arrangements to go to the party.

Two days later, Jerry comes to my house in his van. He is on time, which is a definite plus in his favor. When he comes to the door, he gives me a check for the meal we shared.

"Thank you." I am grateful since I didn't want to think money would come between us so early in the game.

We take my car to my friend's party because his van has so much stuff in it, there is no room for a passenger. The view through the dirty window showed papers piled so high an avalanche would envelop anyone opening the passenger door.

The party is in a lovely house with some delightful people. The hostess is slim and lively. She wears a beautiful sari and serves the best-tasting saag I've ever put in my mouth. Her husband is making fresh puri in the kitchen. There's fish curry and a cauliflower-and-tofu dish, perfectly spiced. On the counter are little bowls of chutneys and nuts to add as you wish. Delicious mango custard in individual cups comprises dessert.

Jerry takes large amounts of food from the kitchen. He sits in a cushioned chair in the living room. He looks humongous. He asks me to get him another beer more than once, and I do it. He finally shoves himself from the chair to get two custard cups.

I know a lot of people at the party whom I enjoy catching up with. I like to go to parties at this house, much laughter, delicious food.

I deliver Jerry to his van at my house. Before he leaves, we make arrangements to meet at the zoo. He tells me what a nice time he had, what nice friends I have. Then he comments, "I don't know how a hostess can serve foreign food to a mixed crowd. There weren't even any people like that at the party."

I have the urge to comment I saw him gobble down a large amount of the "foreign food," but I don't. I make certain to keep a car or a car door between us, so he can't try to kiss me again. My maneuvers are successful.

As I am getting dressed for bed, I scold myself. What is the matter with you? Why don't you want him to kiss you? Then I come to my senses. You don't want to make out with him because he is physically repulsive and bigoted. I work to, again, talk myself into fitting into a different lifestyle. *Go to the zoo, Angie.*

JERRY IS WAITING in the parking lot at the zoo the next morning, again friendly and pleasant. "Let's see if the flamingos are showing their colors."

My family zoo pass gets us both in. The park is nearly empty this early Sunday morning as we head for the flamingo enclosure. As we walk along, I think of a photo I've seen of two flamingos making a heart with their curving necks and beaks touching. The image is too contrived for me, but I think a headshot of a couple of the birds might be interesting.

"Lots of good color here," he says and pulls his camera up to his eye and shoots.

I set up my tripod, secure my camera, and start fiddling with the knobs. The overcast sky brings out the vibrancy of the rosy pinks. The air is cool, so the birds move slowly. They look like they're posing. I think of the f-stop I want, then I decide I'll use aperture priority rather than an all-manual setting. I set the camera at four-point-five, knowing that will give me a shallow depth of field, hence softening the background. Any movement will be reduced with the quickest shutter speed the camera can manage at that opening. I look around to see if there are any interesting formations or compositions with the birds' heads. I see three heads close together on pretty much the same plane, potentially a nice shot. I look through the viewfinder, start to get the focus on the eyes of the birds—

"Finished yet?" Jerry breaks in. "I'm ready to move on."

"I'm barely getting started."

He stands beside me, his camera closed down and hanging lifelessly on the strap around his neck.

I figure I'll go with him, so I pull my tripod legs together. I swing my equipment up on my shoulder and follow him as he moves off. I really don't want to, but I do it anyway. *What are you doing, Angie?* What makes you think you have to accommodate him? What would happen if you didn't? Are you afraid he'll be angry?

"Let's go on to the elephants. That's close to the Safari Diner, and I can get a cup of coffee." He lumbers down the path.

On the way to the elephants, I notice a small tree sporting dew-covered leaves and contrasting white flowers drooping in a curve. The trunk has reddish bark.

"Look at the pretty curves in that plant," I say companionably. "I think it's overcast enough the white won't blow out if I cut off the flash."

When I raise my camera, now attached to my folded tripod, Jerry takes a couple of shots then walks on. I don't even try to get a photo. I'll try to remember this plant when I return another time.

We walk right by the elephants, which is okay with me since I'm not particularly interested in them. The only photos I like of elephants are close-ups of one eye with the wrinkled skin around it, but I don't have that kind of power in my lens.

At the Safari Diner, aka McDonald's, Jerry gets coffee, a double cheeseburger with French fries, and an apple pie. I pick up a bottle of water. He arranges the logistics of the various serving centers of napkins and condiments, so I am behind him at the cashier. He takes his tray to the table. Left alone to face the cashier, I pay for both of us. Now I'm starting to keep a tally. The dinner incident was, it seems, a personality trait—*let someone else be responsible*—not just a simple banking error.

"Want to see what I've got?" he says as I join him at the table.

Jerry shows me photos of the birds he has snapped. They are all in focus since he has used automatic everything.

"Nice. How long have you been using digital?" I'm annoyed but not yet clear on why.

"Are you really not using digital? I was an early adopter." He's clearly taken aback by what he sees as my technological incompetence.

He continues talking and bragging and eating all at the same time. I sip my water. My job to be his friend requires effort, but I am able to stay pleasant.

"I confess, I'm still somewhat computer-challenged. A

digital camera is fine with me, the sensor is like film, but the post-processing has never been a part of producing an image for me. Besides, I have been very busy this last year what with my divorce and working full-time. This is the first time in my life I have lived by myself in my own house." How has he thrown me on the defensive? Why do I have to justify myself to him? Maybe I don't have to like him. Maybe he doesn't have to like me.

"The trailer I live in is on my ex-girlfriend's property." He matches my level of friendliness. "I pay my rent to her, so sometimes we argue, just like you'd expect of a renter and a landlord. She doesn't like me to go out most nights to shoot pool, which I love to do. Sometimes I make enough money to support my beer habit."

He is amused by his description. He doesn't seem to realize the impression he is making on me. Some part of my brain decides to call a halt to this meeting.

"Well, I guess it's time to get back to the house. I have some laundry to do before the workweek starts." I pile the several empty packets of artificial sweetener, creamer packets, the papers from his food on his tray. I sort the trash and file the tray. He watches me. What would this trip have been like with Dan? Surely, I would have brought a nice picnic basket. He probably would have been interested in my photos. Maybe we would have ridden the merry-go-round and laughed together.

We amble back to the parking lot. I am tense, but in broad daylight and with lots of people around, he doesn't try to kiss or hug me.

After the zoo trip, I spend two days thinking through what's happened with Jerry and what a friend said a while back. *Old men are interested in a nurse or a purse.* My path becomes obvious. I compose my telephone conversation, and though it's hard, I force myself to dial his number.

"I've been thinking. Our lifestyles are really different," I start.

I didn't say, "I've realized you are a lounge lizard and mooch, while I am hyperactive and a patsy." I also didn't say, "There would be no challenge in cooking for you since anything would do."

"It doesn't make sense to me for us to get together again," I continue.

"Can we be friends?" he asks.

"Oh, sure . . . bye."

In a couple of days, Jerry drops off a CD of his photos at my house when I'm not there. He also leaves a nice message on my answer machine. I wonder if I've made a mistake.

Several weeks later, I am at the Friday night dinner and dance at the senior citizens center. He introduces me to his girlfriend.

"We've gotten back together," he says.

The girlfriend gives me the smile that says, *I'm completely satisfied and feeling superior because you are here with Caroline rather than my date.*

I smile back, the smile that says: I don't believe I made a mistake. I believe I have learned something.

———

CAROLINE and I have a good time together. This dance is typical of all the other situations when Caroline and I go dancing. She always, always, gets invited to dance more than I do, but I dance enough to make it worthwhile. She instructs me to sit on the edge of my seat, tap my foot, and make eye contact. Even when I try, when they approach the two of us, they usually hold out their hand to her. It does seem bold to do what she does. I feel lonely and apart just thinking about those times when I watch her dance.

After the dance, when I am in bed, I wonder what I can do to get social with my lawyer. I'm also determined to show him I know he is after my money. He is a goat gobbling up hundred-dollar bills. Do I have a split personality?

I decide to drop by his office. What can be my excuse? I can ask him if he's gotten the earlier Merrill Lynch or Scott Trade records that he subpoenaed.

I will want to take a healthy snack to share. Fresh hummus and crudités. Yes, that will do it. Then sleep takes over.

When I wake up, I review my cooking project as I head for my favorite room in the house. My kitchen has a lot of white-tile working surfaces. The cupboards on either side of the sink are easy to reach. Windows over the sink allow me to assess the state of the backyard. The cupboards and drawers contain what I use and very few superfluous gadgets. I'm pleased I remembered to stock the makings for hummus. The thought of cooking for Dan cheers and energizes me. I hum as I get out the blender and peel the cloves of garlic.

What if he isn't there when I stop by? What if he's too busy to see me? I'll just leave the food. I put the hummus, the multicolored pepper sticks, and the cucumber rounds into a sealed container. He may or may not know he is supposed to return the container with something nice in it as every woman knows to do. A reciprocal gesture can be the beginning of a friendship, so it's fine if he's there and free, and okay if he's busy or not there. Either way, he gets a taste of me. Angie! Where is your mind?

The day is zingy, sharp-edged, clear, and in the fifties. I have dressed carefully in slim brown pants, just short of being too tight, a beige sweater, just short of too plunging, and amber beads.

"Hi, what can I do for you this morning?" Pam is unusually upbeat.

"I hope you are having a nice week," I reply.

"My boyfriend, who's in the Army, is home for the week," she tells me, smiling.

"I'm thinking maybe you'd be taking off some time."

"I'm only coming in every day until noon, so I don't get too far behind. Jim sleeps in because he is finally relaxing from the stress of deployment."

"Is Dan in?" I change the subject to one more to my liking.

"He's in, but he's super busy. I hate to disturb him. Anything I can help with?" She frowns at me. She doesn't like me. Suddenly I remember—Pam is a male-identified female—a woman who is only interested in men. Could be for power, wealth, or growing up in a family where only the men are tended to. I shared a secretary once in a male-oriented office. She was an extreme example. She wore high heels below a too-tight dress and had a sign over her desk that read, *Don't ask me to do anything. I was hired for my looks.* She was never helpful to me, of course. If this is the correct guess, I can't expect help from Pam.

"I wondered if any of the subpoenaed records have come in?"

"We expect them, but they haven't arrived." Pam's voice is matter of fact, but she still frowns. I wonder, for an instant, if they are in the pile of papers on her desk.

I realize there is no reason for me to try to stick around. I get the feeling Pam is determined I do not visit with Dan, so I put the food package on the counter in front of her.

"Angie, how nice you stopped by." Dan's voice booms down the hall.

I take the package back into my hand. I take a step toward Dan, deliberately turning away from Pam, and wonder where my competitive feelings are coming from. I smile at Dan.

"Come to the conference room if you have a minute. I had a question or two from our talk the other day. I'll get my notes."

I try to keep the triumph out of my smile to Pam. "Have a good week with Jim."

I go to the conference room, where I put the food package close to the edge of the table where I expect Dan to sit. Then I move it a little off to the right, making it easy for him to reach.

When Dan comes in, he sits where expected but unceremoniously pushes the package away and refers to his notes. "Is Steve's pension a standard state pension?"

"Yes, the university pension system is not separate from other state employees." That much I do know.

"Do you know approximately how much it is a month?"

"I believe it's a little over four thousand a month. He has it deposited directly into the Merrill Lynch account. I put a yearly figure into the block on the 1040 that asks for retirement income. It was a little over fifty thousand dollars for last year."

"Seems about right. That was the main question I needed to ask. Gives me a sense of what we're dealing with. Is this package relevant to our meeting?" He points at the food package.

"I made some fresh hummus. I thought I'd bring some for you since I was stopping by."

As I unpack the food, Dan gives me a friendly smile that suggests he can see I made up an excuse to visit him. He takes a red pepper stick to dig into the hummus. The hummus is thick and garlicky. The aroma fills the room.

"This is delicious. It is definitely better than the processed hummus I sometimes buy. Is it hard to make?"

"It's a staple in my household, so I guesstimate the ingredients. It always comes out just fine. It takes only a minute to make once you have the garlic peeled. I make it easy on myself by using canned garbanzo beans."

"Thanks, Angie, this should energize me." He scrapes the plastic bowl with the last cucumber round. "I have a hearing to prepare. I must return to my desk. Those records should be here in a day or two. Just give Pam a call to make sure. It will save you an extra trip. I loved the hummus. It was a welcome break to share it with you." Perhaps he senses my disappointment. Did I pout? "I was out last night at a ball, so I was getting sleepy." He gives my hand a pat, rises, and disappears without a backward glance.

Dancing gives me life. He went to a ball without me. I could cry.

My disappointment carries over into the late afternoon. I need something to cheer me up, and chocolate always helps. I decide to fix my fudge brownies. Even the thought helps lighten my mood. No shopping is necessary because I always have the ingredients on hand. The brownies I fix come from a quality brownie mix except for the nuts and oil. Rather than walnuts, I use hazelnuts. They are as rich as other nuts, but the baking brings out the subtle difference in flavor. Then I use a specialty oil from a new little store near my house. The oil has an orange flavor, making the brownies something extra special.

While the brownies bake, I sit in the living room, having Yogi Skin De-Tox tea, feet up, relaxing under a cozy blanket. I read an article from the New York Times opinion page about Obamacare, including commentary on the new mental health initiatives.

The thought occurs to me the house next door is on fire. I leap up; too late, the brownies are blackies. My spirits plummet as I dig the mess out of the pan. The damn pan can soak until morning. The garbage bag with the burned chocolate needs to go out to the Hurby Curby. A perfectly timed downpour soaks me in the two-minute errand to get rid of the dreadful smell.

My body tells me curling up in bed is imperative, regardless of what the clock says, so I brush my teeth, put on my nightie, and snuggle in.

A dream comes to me in the early morning. I am standing in warm lake water up to my shoulders. Low mountains form the backdrop. I see my two sisters on a wooden platform out in the middle of the lake. They laugh and call to me to come. They want me to join them. I am overwhelmed by fear and sadness and anger. I slap the water and jump and scream for them to come and play with me. They laugh. The platform disappears. They are gone. I'm confused. I wonder if I caused the platform to disappear. Are they lost? I feel I have to get out of the water. Then I'm standing in ankle-deep mud. When I look down, both my legs have white, somewhat luminous casts on them. I can't move and am frightened.

The alarm insists I wake up, but the dream disrupts me for much of the day. I remember my mother once referring to the time I broke my leg. Was I four, or older? I resolve to call my sisters and ask if they have any memory of it. Could this have been an incident where I couldn't fit in? How did I break my leg?

In the evening, I call my sister Denise. She is the oldest of the three of us. She tends to remember details of incidents I think couldn't possibly have happened. She remembers me chasing her with a large knife. She stays on the edge of skinny. When I visit her in her small apartment in NYC, we eat fish and broccoli. When she changes the menu for my visits, she substitutes kale for the broccoli.

"Did I break my leg when I was young?" I start the conversation.

"You had on a cast and couldn't go swimming. One of the

times I regret being really mean to you was when you couldn't come out to the platform in the lake," she tells me.

"How were you mean to me?"

"I yelled, 'You can't come in. You're not fit.' You hated the cast, so in that way, I ruined your summer. By the way, Mother was enraged at me for teasing you. She felt sorry for you, itching and inactive."

"I think I remember her using a chopstick down the cast to help with the itching."

"Teasing you was a way of life for me for several years. I could say I'm sorry, but I suppose it was just a stage of me flexing my relationship muscles."

"How did I break my leg?" I ask.

"I think the neighborhood kids dared you to jump off the garage. You wanted so to be part of the group."

"So, when I tried to fit in with the older neighborhood kids, it didn't work well for me."

"That's one way to look at it. You tried hard, but we were all older and bigger. I remember when we were older, one neighbor girl and I used to cheat on you at cards. We took away your allowance week after week. When you finally quit coming, we stopped playing since the games weren't as much fun as when you were there."

"I don't remember any of that. I suppose it was good training for your climb up the corporate ladder," I say it evenly, and she doesn't get the intended sarcasm.

"I suppose it was. I'm lucky you still speak to me. The people I have climbed over on my way up would prefer to spit at me more than smile."

I tell her I have to tend to something on the stove, then I call my younger sister, Peggy. I ask her if she remembers me breaking a leg when I was about five. She would have been four.

"I don't remember directly but mother told me you were

pathetic. You wanted so much to do what everyone else was doing. You just couldn't. Mother said I felt sorry for you. Mother made us do your chores; Denise and I didn't like that. Thinking back, I remember you didn't like us doing stuff for you either. I was more sympathetic than Denise."

"I guess feeling sorry for a poor struggling creature was good training for your social-work career with children."

"I never thought of it like that, but it fits," she says.

Peggy is agreeable. She's someone who loves to bake. Mostly she gives away her concoctions to neighbors or her bridge group since her husband can no longer eat sweets because he's diabetic. Peggy always photographs a pretty European mountain scene to serve as a Christmas card. She didn't start doing that until I told her about my success as a photographer. I don't hold it against her.

Both my sisters exercise regularly, like me. My mother is to blame. When she took us ice skating, she skated with us. She took us to the ski train in the winter. She sent us to Girl Scout camp in the summer. She even allowed Girl Scout cookie boxes to flood the living room. She didn't complain when we cooked campfire stew for dinner. Campfire stew is a terrible mess of fried ground beef with a can of undiluted Campbell's vegetable soup poured over it. The glop was delicious after an all-day hike at camp, but not so good after being home from camp for two weeks.

After my father died in an airplane crash when I was three, my mother was worried and depressed, but she did a good job raising her three girls. She had energy and determination. She smoked outside in the backyard because she loved the fresh air. She rolled down the windows when she smoked in the car. She had no lungs when she died at the age of ninety.

My mother cooked like her mother, a farmer's wife—lots of meat, potatoes, and vegetables, all put on the stove just after breakfast. This soft food was served with tomatoes and corn from the garden. For special occasions, there was Jell-O. I remember orange Jell-O with grated carrots, green Jell-O with chunks of canned pineapple. Vegetables with Jell-O was salad, canned fruit with Jell-O was dessert. I have moved on, except for her tuna salad. I am a sucker for canned tuna stirred well with Hellman's mayo. I spice up the dish with the tiniest bit of finely chopped onion.

We were trained to eat fish and liver. Although, in her later years, Mother confessed she hated them. We were trained to like fresh air. Denise was trained to keep her eye on the money she could make. Peggy was trained to be sensitive to other people, so she watched over Mother when Mother became weak. What was I trained up for? Feeling sorry for myself and feeling left out?

CHAPTER FIVE

The records request recedes into the blur of late-fall activities. The invitations for my holiday party go out before Thanksgiving. I send out more than a hundred invitations, so we have Thanksgiving, my party, and Christmas to cook and clean for. Rachel manages the invitations.

We have a full-on Thanksgiving feast. Usually, forty friends, relatives, and neighbors come to her house. She fixes a potato casserole with various creams, all full fat. Guests eat until they no longer can. I make my grapefruit-and-kiwi-mix salad. My soda bread with nice cheese is also popular. One friend typically brings a lamb-shaped cake with too much frosting and lots of coconut shavings on top. We used to roast a turkey, but since some people no longer eat meat, we purchase a little sliced roasted turkey instead.

The week before Christmas, I have my annual party. Dan is invited this year too, although since I know him better I'm hoping the invitation is not being too pushy. His acceptance note was friendly:

. . .

Dear Angie,

Thanks for the invitation. I'm pleased to be included; see you on the 21st.

Sincerely, Dan

His handwriting is masculine and of an earlier time, firm, no flourishes, and easy to read.

My days are filled with thoughts of recipes, table settings, and schedules. My nights are filled with dreams of feeding Dan, everything from smearing a cracker with soft Brie and handing it to him to having him lick fresh flavored whipped cream off my finger. As Caroline said earlier, *"We're not ready for the boobs yet."*

Dan arrives at the Christmas party flatteringly spiffed up. Maybe it's his usual way for a party. I take his coat from him, point him in the direction of the kitchen, and head for the bedroom. On impulse, I put the coat to my nose and smell it. How stirring a pleasant masculine smell is! I pause a moment, but the sound of people chatting takes me from my reverie. What the hell am I doing?!

When I get to the kitchen, Caroline is pouring Dan's wine, so I back away. She's taking care of him. The next time I see Dan, he's helping himself to shrimp salad at the buffet. I do put on a nice buffet table. It has salmon sides, accompanied by a mix of sour cream and yogurt overladen with fresh dill. Quite tasty. I cook the salmon baked in foil with thinly sliced onion on top. He looks up from his task and catches my eye. The smile he gives me covers his face. I smile back. Unfortunately, a friend taps me on the shoulder and says the bread is low. So, I turn away from my inclination to move in and head to the kitchen.

"Angie, I can't compliment you enough on the food for this party. Each dish is tastier than the next. Did you do all this yourself?" I'm surprised by Dan's voice. He has followed me into the kitchen, and we are alone for a moment.

"I love to cook for people. It's one of the pleasures in my life. I'm so glad you're enjoying it." I smile at him, and he looks at me. He opens his mouth as if he is going to say something more, but then closes it and just smiles back. Another guest enters the kitchen, and the moment is broken.

Seventy people can fit in my house. They circulate in and out of the kitchen for drinks, which include a full bar, dessert wine, juices, and water. Guests wander through the dining room where the salmon sides, shrimp salad, pasta salad, lima bean salad, and a variety of bread and cheese are to be found. Then they visit the computer room for cakes and cookies. Guests bring wine and other unnecessary but welcomed treats.

The party continues, and I catch Dan talking with several different people. He seems at home in my group of friends. The party thins, and my presence at the front door to say goodbye becomes solidified. Dan is among the last to leave. With a slight bow, he says goodbye. I smile and thank him for coming.

"The pleasure has been all mine." His words are heartfelt and touch me. Is it possible we're getting someplace, or am I hallucinating and mixing my dreams with reality?

―――

CHRISTMAS IS a partial repeat of Thanksgiving dinner but with more focus on family and, of course, gifts. When the New Year comes, I begin to worry. My life is going well, but the divorce is moving slowly. A vagrant thought cheers me. Maybe Dan is dragging this out because every two or three weeks I bring him something delicious to eat on the excuse I am checking the status of the files. He has various sensible excuses for not moving forward. We chat and eat my "snack," then we are often interrupted by Pam, who tells him he has a client on the phone.

As always, my clients take time off during the holidays, so I am home in the middle of the week when Pam calls.

"Angie, we have all the records you requested."

"Shall I come in this afternoon to get a start?"

"Sure." She hangs up.

Gloves in pocket, hat over ears, scarf around my neck, lined boots—my outfit suggests an arctic outing. Thirty degrees and a biting wind greet me as I lock my door and head for the car. The interior of the car is not helpful. The seat is cold on my rear, reminding me to press on the seat heater. The windshield wipers remove the light frost. As I head toward town, the streets are as busy as usual. Why aren't all these people at home, snuggled under their covers, or sitting on their couches in their robes, drinking hot tea? Some trees are bare, showing the strength of their dark trunks and crooked limbs.

Dan's office building is toasty. Pam is behind her desk and doesn't look up as I approach.

"Pam, I'm ready to review the records."

She leads me down the hall away from Dan's office to a room I haven't seen before. This room sports a medieval flair. The chairs are massive with brocaded seats. Heavily carved legs support the thick table. Suffocating drapes deny any sunlight from seeping in. A faint smell of some cleaning product has gotten locked in the room.

Pam points to several cardboard boxes on the table. She gives off the impression she's just short of raging and doesn't want to be bothered with me. The sight of the papers produces the same level of fear and discouragement as a registered letter from the Internal Revenue Service.

"Thanks, Pam. I have wanted to go over these records."

"I still think we need an expert to interpret them." She flounces out.

A million questions run through my mind. Will the papers reveal Steve has skimmed money from our joint account? Would there be evidence he had a secret life? Did he have another family in Guatemala? Are there checks to fancy vacation locations where he took a mistress? Steady, Angie. He didn't have that kind of energy. He didn't seem to have any sexual energy at all. Or was that just me he didn't cotton to?

Maybe he siphoned money into a Swiss bank account when he went to do "research" in Europe. Perhaps a lovely Swiss maiden welcomed him into hidden vaults. Later, he would take her to a Swiss restaurant, where they would have spiced red cabbage and Wiener schnitzel with noodles and exquisite wines. My mind is running away with itself. Stop torturing yourself, just stop it! Maybe Dan and I are having this meal while traveling through the Romantic Road in Germany with a stopover in a castle on the Rhine.

I shake my head and realize the room is oppressive. The chain for the iron chandelier looks as though it was made on an anvil. The table where I sit is so heavy it would take a crane to move it. The door looks to be of triple thickness. It squeaks when Pam shoves her way in without knocking.

She asks if I need water and, of course, has a bottle with her. I ask her about the specifics of the records.

"We do have the records from Scott Trade." She points with her index finger to the box on the left.

"Did the family bank account records come in too?"

"They're all here. Only the museum records have been slow coming in."

Pam reaches over and presents a two-inch file as if she is presenting an anniversary cake to the Queen of England. I had not noticed her flair for drama before. Pam's shoulder-length dark hair is styled in the latest fashion. Her scoop-neck T-shirt plunges, and her low-slung black cropped pants do not quite expose her navel. She shops in Petites, I'm certain. She probably snacks on baby carrots, the worst kind of thin addiction.

"He lost some money at Scott Trade, believing hotels in general and Starwood, in particular, were going down," I say to show how knowledgeable I am.

"Did he trade in options?" Pam looks horrified.

I look into her beady brown eyes. "He did indeed, but I'll look through the papers. I'm interested to see how much he lost in that operation. He told me once he lost about twenty thousand. But I may not be remembering exactly."

"Can you read these statements?" Her sneer unnerves me.

"I pay attention to the pluses and minuses and the totals. The information about anything strange will be there."

"Let's practice with this one since he only used Scott Trade for betting for two years." She opens the file.

"I can see here the thirty-four thousand he lost the first year. But I didn't have any idea he made eighty-six thousand the second year. It looks like he quit betting against hotels." My finger follows the line to the total.

"Here is the final statement. He took out one hundred fifty-two thousand and the balance is zero. See on this line?" I point out what seems obvious to me.

I wonder why she thinks I can't read the brokerage statements. Maybe she thinks it requires a male expert.

"Since he started the caper with one hundred thousand, he made out like the robber he is." I show where the initial investment is recorded.

"Um, let's call him lucky." She rolls her eyes.

"Nice reframe, Pam. What else is here?"

"We have the Merrill Lynch accounts for several years." She shoves a box toward me and picks up another file case. This one is three inches across. She, again, proceeds with the presentation, requiring her to bend at the waist and then straighten and raise her arms toward the ceiling.

Maybe she took ballet for too long as a child.

"Do you have the amount he started the Merrill Lynch account with?" I ask her.

"No, they only sent us records for the past five years." She shakes her head, and when she stops, her hair falls neatly back in place.

"I have always thought the Merrill Lynch account was his retirement account. I suspected he started it when he retired. I supposed the earlier real estate money was stored elsewhere."

"Why don't I call? I'll see if they will just give me when and how much was in that account in the beginning?" Pam shows some interest.

"I appreciate your making the call."

"That is what I'm here for, isn't it? To help Dan's clients." Her curled lip reveals the sarcasm underlying her nice comment.

I understand now why she is so easily ticked off. She doesn't want to deal with females. It's her, not me. I direct my eyes downward. "I'll start in here and see what is important."

I face the mountain of paper. This is just the beginning of the subpoenaed records. They still have to get the records from the museum. I don't know if the bronzes the museum has were given or sold to them.

As I flip pages, I wonder why they made copies of the monthly statement pages containing the rules and regulations. I don't want to know what the various rating agencies think of these holdings. Only two of the forty pages from each month have relevant information.

What is this? Who is Sandra Welden? She gets payments from him for one or two thousand dollars a month for several months. It is too much money for her to do his website.

Besides, she's not here, but in Hilton Head. He wasn't buying art from her. He already has too much art on hand. Were they having expensive meals of lobster smothered in truffles, with a side of asparagus and lemon butter, nestled next to scalloped potatoes? Perhaps they drank Dom with imported bonbons for dessert. Nope! He's too cheap to eat like that. What could it be?

Ahh. She is the agent for the antique shows he goes to. I hope any other mystery is so easily solved.

It will take a week in court to get him to unravel this mess. What's the use? I sigh. Keep going, Angie. It's the money trail, and you don't know where it will end. I'm not seeing any reference to the Merk Family partnership he formed when he sold some real estate.

There's a cautious rap at the door.

"Come on in," I call.

"Angie, Dan told me to check on you. How's it going?"

"What I have so far is a mysterious woman who got thousands from him about four years ago."

"Maybe she runs a private jet service. I wouldn't mind doing that myself."

"Nope, she is an agent for the antique shows where he exhibited for several years. There are also a lot of payments to our son. I knew he was helping Paul with his real estate taxes, but there are more payments here than I expected. Of course, I can't complain because I also helped Paul occasionally with some money."

"I wish I'd had a generous mother like you. My mother kicked me out at sixteen. I joined the circus."

"How did you end up in a law office?"

"I'm pretty smart. I saw there was no future in getting curled up in an elephant's trunk. They're nasty beasts, really."

"I'm sure." My voice sounds sympathetic.

"I went to secretarial school." She looks at me inquiringly. "You're wrapped up in these papers. What else do you need?"

"I would like to see the museum records about the bronzes. They wouldn't give me any information when I called. He put my name on the bronzes too, but they said only he signed the paperwork."

"Dan has asked for that information. What other records do you want? I wasn't able to get the information back to the start of the Merrill Lynch account. I'll ask Dan to see how we can get it."

"I believe there's an account with the earnings from his real estate dealings. He made a lot of money buying and selling small apartment complexes. We lived in a ten-apartment complex he bought outright for fifty-five thousand and sold ten years later for two hundred fifty thousand."

"That's a lot of profit. Taxes would take a chunk," she says.

"He didn't want to pay capital gains taxes, so he brought the children into a partnership. They sold or gave their shares back to him later or something. I'm don't remember the details. That was twenty years ago, but he made a lot of money, and I don't know where it is."

"Banks keep records too, you know."

"The bank he dealt with for the real estate caper was absorbed by another bank. I'd like to find those records too. One of the things he did with the real estate money was help Rachel with a loan to purchase some rental property. He made her pay high interest on the loan, so he made money on every deal."

"I'll talk to Dan about issuing the subpoenas, but I think we need someone who can read bank statements. There's a smart man we use to investigate bank records."

"Pam, I would like to be the one to read the records. I'm willing to put in the time, and I know what would look fishy."

"There are experts in the field, you know." She, again, rolls her eyes at me.

"I don't want to pay for an expert." I'm surprised I'm short with her.

"Well, as you wish." The door closes with a thud, and she leaves me in the quiet.

I flip through a lot of sheets. The reject pile is about three inches high, and the fuzziness in my brain wants me to put my head on the table. I come across a forgotten document, a check Steve wrote in 2006, and on the memo line, he wrote, "1992 Char. Trust."

My mind goes into low gear. I'm finding it hard to focus. It's so quiet, I halfway fall asleep, still believing if anything untoward happens in the numbers I will be jolted to full alertness.

The edge of the table ripples gently, as though something lightweight blows in a soft breeze. Nonsense, table edges don't ripple, or do they? I focus my eyes. It turns out not to be the table edge, but the rug below. Now I'm fully awake and see the ripple effect is an illusion. What looks like the rug heaving is really a kazillion small brown bugs. I've seen it before. They're swarming termites.

The bugs come from a crack near the corner of the room and become a larger and larger presence on the rug. They occupy about a quarter of the room. I believe I can still escape between my chair and the door. I don't bother to pull together the scattered papers before I bolt for the hall. I have that restless, panicky feeling that precedes a scream.

How is one to behave in this situation? Should I just leave and let someone else discover the invasion? Should I set fire to the papers, so the smoke alarm goes off and the firemen come? Firemen? Hmmm. They're supposed to be the hunkiest guys around. I shake my head. I don't have a way to start a fire. I come back to reality and realize I need to get other people involved.

I scurry down the hall, but Pam refuses to interrupt her telephone conversation despite my desperate attempts. She holds up her hand when I sputter for help.

"A disaster is upon us," I tell her when she takes her cell from her ear.

She languorously rises from the chair. "What's the hurry?"

I am so choked, I am not coherent. "Quick," I whisper and scurry down the hall. I step inside the conference room and point. "See."

Pam doesn't respond immediately. I realize she isn't seeing the seething mass. She comes into the room, heading toward the table. The termites have widened their reach, and by the time she sees them, she has both feet inside their column.

She performs a feat of strength and agility I've never even seen on TV shows. Like mixed martial arts or a Cross Fit marathon. She leaps straight up onto the table and then jumps again and wraps her arms around the chandelier. There she is, swinging with the chandelier like a slow pendulum over the table. I imagine the pendulum in Edgar Alan Poe's *The Cask of Amontillado*. She screams, a high-pitched keening noise, something between an outdoor cat being forced into a carrying cage and a jaguar in the jungle announcing his kill.

Pam is not going to be helpful. I leave to get Dan, who, it turns out, is coming down the hall with a "what the hell is going on?" look on his face.

His authoritative presence lowers my pulse enough to tell him. I point to the office door. "Termites are in there."

Dan takes in the scene of Pam screeching above the seething swarm on the floor and raises his eyebrows. "Stop, Pam!" he orders, which she does. Then there is silence in the room as neither Pam nor I are breathing.

"Go get the broom in the back room," he says to me.

I go to see if I can find it, and several doors later, I do.

When I get back to the conference room, Pam has fled. Dan takes the broom and sweeps the termites into small piles, then he crushes them with his Italian leather shoes.

After several minutes of standing there, I get my wits together. "I'll work on the termites. Maybe you can call pest control."

"If you're okay here, I'll go see what I can do." He puts his hand on my shoulder to turn me to face him. His hand is firm but not hard. When I face him, his eyes are soft.

I am barely functioning, but I keep sweeping and stomping. I am getting tired when the pest-control team comes with their tanks. Dan calls me into his office.

"That was quite an experience. You still look shaken." He comes up close and puts his arms around me. "I know a stressful experience when I see it."

"I can't help it." I'm close to tears because my attraction is so strong and obvious.

Dan pulls me close. "I only worry because you're my client."

The phone rings. Pesky Pam announces his next client has arrived.

"I have to meet with this client. We'll talk more soon."

"I hope so." I walk out on unsteady feet.

With difficulty, I pull my mind from the bodily sensations his closeness has engendered to the hallway where I am walking. I make myself smile as I pass his client. I stop in the restroom to compose myself. When I stop by Pam's desk, I am a little confused about how to approach her.

She looks down. "I saw one or two of those terrible bugs last week, maybe Monday or perhaps Tuesday. Definitely not Wednesday, because that is the day I took my daughter to have her tooth looked after. She banged it falling off her bicycle. She was trying to ride down off a curb. I thought maybe she had killed herself. She hurt her knee and her face. I didn't know whether to take her to the hospital or the dentist. Since she could still bend her knee, I decided the dentist would be my first stop. She wails like me when something is overwhelming. She had so much road rash on her face, it was awful to look at. Do you know what road rash is?"

"Yeah, it's what we used to refer to as 'skinned,' as in, she skinned her face."

What is going on? Pam is emptying her mind.

"Right! She's a good girl and does well in school. She takes drama classes, and she was in a recent performance of The Wizard of Oz. She was the Wicked Witch of the East. The girl who got the role of Dorothy is a teacher's pet and a brat. Granted, she does have long blond hair. My daughter's hair is short and black and a little curly, just like mine. I have mine cut about every six weeks."

I want to come back to the here and now. "It must be lovely here and peaceful at this front desk. This is a small building." I try to stop the linguistic diarrhea.

"What makes you say that?"

"Oh, I'm just thinking if I were in your place and it was quiet, sometimes I'd feel like I was alone here. Like there was no one to talk to. There's no music or anything."

"We wouldn't want music. Mr. McCloud would have a difficult time concentrating. I have to be quiet so he can concentrate."

"How long is this meeting supposed to go?" I am aware of my voice brightening at the idea of seeing Dan again before I leave.

"I'll see if his client is gone. He probably doesn't have time to see you."

Pam goes behind the counter and pushes the button on the old-fashioned intercom. She turns away from me and speaks softly. She always speaks softly to Dan. I guess she might have some kind of crush on him. She draws herself up a bit as she turns to me.

"He said he didn't know you were still here. He'll be glad to make time for you."

Do I imagine it or is there annoyance in her voice? I stand tall and scoot quickly down the hall. He sits behind a mountain of paper piled so high they threaten to exclude customers, but I know he has lots of clients.

Dan smiles. "I'm so glad you didn't go away."

I imagine bringing him lunch and spreading a white tablecloth across the pile of papers. I'd arrange for linen napkins and have a good French Merlot on the side. Curried chicken salad would nest in half a melon. I will have to make rye bread because there is no decent rye in this town.

My eyes focus back on him. "At first, it looked like the table and floor moved, and then I saw the termites. It was scary because there were so many. I'm worried they may come back. I hope they haven't done permanent damage to this lovely old building."

"You do worry, don't you?"

"I can't help it. There are so many things to worry about."

"Are you worried about your daughter?"

"She looks just fine, and the mastectomy went well, and she took the chemo and radiation amazingly well, but I can too easily imagine the cancer cells just hiding out, ready to take over again. All the bugs made me think of cancer cells."

The tension I hold eases as I tell him. Tears come to my eyes, and I let my shoulders release some of the tightness in them. I'm too scared to tell him I worry my tension will give me cancer too.

Dan rises from his seat, comes around his desk, and takes me in his arms. I am too full of sadness to appreciate anything but the warmth and strength of his body.

"You'll be just fine whatever happens."

I'm so surprised I don't even return the hug. Dan retreats behind his cluttered desk. I can still feel the hug and the release of my tight neck and shoulder muscles.

"Thanks a lot. Now I feel better, even if I don't believe I'll be okay if anything happens to Rachel."

"It's true you'd never be the same. I loved my wife. Her cancer was aggressive; it metastasized before they found it. It didn't hide. It marched around her body like an unwanted guest at a family reunion. When she died, I thought I would never have a life again."

The phone rings. Dan reaches over and picks it up. "It's your daughter, come to take you to lunch," he tells me.

"I'd forgotten we had a date what with the special excitement we've had here."

Rachel lights up any room she enters, and this paper-packed oversized closet is no exception. Dan greets her, then turns to me as if the earlier intimacy hadn't happened.

"How did the research go this morning?" Rachel asks me.

"I found some stuff I couldn't explain. I made a list of it. There wasn't a whole lot, except for one check I'd like to get a copy of. It refers to a Charitable Trust. I want to understand how that entity works. Can it exist and not show up on taxes? I didn't find evidence of a separate Guatemalan family. I'm pleased about that." Dan smiles at me, then turns away as Rachel interrupts.

"Did you know you and Dan have grandchildren who are classmates? My daughter Sarah and your grandson Mark are friends at school." Rachel looks from me to him.

"I didn't know that," I say softly. This information ties us together in another way.

"Neither did I." Dan's voice is a whisper.

Rachel surveys the scene. A question flits across her face but she doesn't ask. "We need to let Dan get back to his work." She takes my arm and steers me down the hall.

"Where would you like to eat since we're already downtown?" she asks.

"Let's try the new soup and salad shop. I understand they use fresh ingredients. Maybe they won't be crowded yet."

The downtown streets in Columbia imitate a big city at lunchtime. At night, the empty streets and sidewalks show the true size and energy level of the town.

We wind our way through the noon crowd and luck upon a table for two near the front window of the brightly decorated bistro.

"So, what's going on?" she asks, smiling.

I straighten up. "What do you mean, what's going on?"

"You know what I mean. You look cheerful, no, happy."

"Unfortunately, nothing's going on." I slump a bit.

"Do you want it to go on?" She tilts her head.

"Yes, definitely I do, yes."

Rachel laughs. "Well, that would mean you'd be less available for babysitting my youngest."

"You're ahead of the game. Order your meal."

The waitress has hovered for a full minute without any attention from either of us. Rachel orders the vegetable plate with broccoli, mushrooms, and a baked sweet potato. "Butter on the side," she says.

I order the vegetable plate with broccoli, mushrooms, and fried sweet potato rounds. The potato rounds 'float my boat,' so to speak. The difference in our orders accounts for her weighing 125 and me weighing 140. Age difference has nothing to do with it.

Rachel stares at me. "What are your intentions with regard to Dan?"

"Isn't that question supposed to be part of a conversation between two other people?"

"You drive me crazy, Mom. When you don't want to

answer a question, you ask another question. I repeat: what are you thinking about Dan?"

"Nothing much, just that I'd like to cook for him."

"That serious, huh? I'd better pay attention to these proceedings, both the divorce and others unspecified."

"Maybe it isn't your business," I say gently.

"You're right there. Any way you can find happiness in your life, I say go for it. An oft-forgotten lesson to be learned again and again in life." She looks down, and the light in the room dims.

"I believe your cancer will not come back, and we can all be relaxed and secure in that belief."

"Reassurance for my benefit, or for yours?"

"Really, it's for both of us. You tell me your blood work is good."

"It's fine, but my white blood count isn't coming up as the doctor would like."

And I'm not supposed to worry.

"I have an idea for a short outing this evening." Her smile dazzles me. She has always had beautiful teeth. I suspect she uses a whitener, but I've never broached the subject.

"What could you have in mind?"

"Let's stalk Dan."

"What?"

She's amused. "I mean, let's check out his house. What kind of car? More than one? Maybe even go to the library. There have been other McClouds in this town. Maybe we can find some dirt on Lydia."

"We can't be looking for dirt, that's too crass. On the other hand, I wouldn't mind having a better sense of the competition."

"She's dead, for Pete's sake."

"I don't know how dead she is. She still lives on in his mind. He loved her. I think it was a very good marriage. Not like Steve and me living apart in the same house all those years."

Rachel ponders the idea. "I've fallen so in love with DeeDee. I can imagine she would always be with me even if she wasn't."

"Considering the two of us going snooping, does DeeDee mind staying with the children by herself?"

"She delights in it. You know she'll want me to do anything to help you be safe."

DeeDee's image comes to mind. She dresses casually, white shirts tucked into draped shorts or pants. She's a short, thin, powerhouse of strength and energy, plus she's the soul of generosity. She's madly in love with my daughter. Since Rachel's divorce is final, DeeDee has moved in. This arrangement is three months old, and we're all lucky since the grandchildren love her.

"I'll drop by around seven thirty. We should go to the library first. The house drive-by should occur later in the evening so no one will notice us."

———

IN THE SOUTH CAROLINA history section of the library, it is easy to trace Dan's genealogy to an early governor and a more recent US senator. He won statewide awards in high school as a wrestler. He had a distinguished career as an Air Force pilot.

Lydia's profile, on the other hand, was wild. Her obituary showed she had five names, Lydia Forester Wales Stoddard Smith McCloud. Did all the husbands die, or did she go through them like a chain saw goes through branches? She was a debutante and an artist. I wasn't as interested in her ancestors as I was in the art angle.

"So, she was more than a mystic and serial wife. I wonder what kind of art she produced?" I comment.

"We'll have to find out later, maybe through the art school at the university. The library's closing. Time for our drive-by," Rachel says.

A bright moon edges the stray cloud, the air is January crisp. Rachel's Explorer is the only car left in the library parking lot.

She zips across town. We know the street, a short, curved road in an exclusive neighborhood. The mailboxes sport the numbers at the edges of the lawns with no sidewalks. The large houses sit back from manicured grounds and landscaped flower beds.

Dan's house is smaller than most. Only his gray Lincoln sits in the driveway, silver in the moonlight.

"The large chimneys mean big fireplaces," Rachel comments.

"Perfect for cozying up on a winter day."

"I thought you just wanted to cook for him."

"My place or his. I bet he has a very well-appointed kitchen. Since Lydia was an artist, maybe she decorated wedding cakes."

"Your mind is running away with you. I'll do a little more research while you're seeing clients this week. Let's get together some evening. I'll give you the scoop."

CHAPTER SIX

Although only several days have passed, I have warmed myself through the cold, damp weather with thoughts of Dan's hug. A hug can lead to kissing, and then I get to cook for him! I'm tending to paperwork on a slow client day when the phone rings. I recognize Dan's number, and my pulse accelerates.

"Please come to my office, we need to talk," he says with no preliminary niceties.

"All right, I can come now," I respond, puzzled. The half-mile drive through town in midday traffic is quick.

Dan meets me at the door. "I got a threatening letter from your husband accusing us of having a relationship." He takes me right into the conference room. "He thinks we've been together, and that's why you left him; that we are in a relationship."

Dan isn't angry, just stern and straightforward. Our earlier shared sadness and attendant empathy are gone. It's as if the hug hadn't happened.

Here, I've been trying since we met to get more flirting

going. I'd love a relationship. I stare at him and imagine what it would be like for him to put his hand to my boob. My tummy spikes. I try not to smile. Did Dan shut his eyes like he's sorry he said something about our having a relationship? I realize I'm supposed to say something.

"Steve is so damn paranoid. What happens is always someone else's fault."

"Why would he think we are together rather than someone else?"

"I don't think he needs any more information than the fact I have left him, or I can make it on my own. He would likely jump to the conclusion someone else is bossing me around."

"My question to you remains, why me rather than someone else?"

"Maybe you're seeing someone, and someone saw you and reported to him it was me."

"I'm not seeing anyone, so that couldn't have happened," he says.

My spirits lift. "Maybe you spoke nicely of me at the meeting with him and his lawyer. He could be making up some reason why he is in no way at fault with my leaving him."

"At that meeting, I said almost nothing, but I did come away with the view he's either blocking out a lot of things or lying if he doesn't know why you left."

"I've not been in communication with him since our first meeting. Only one chance encounter on the street, where I was surprised to see him going into an Indian restaurant. He would never go there with me. He knew I loved Indian food and claimed he didn't."

"There is usually some germ of something to provoke a letter like this. Mr. Merk also seems to have information neither his lawyer nor I have communicated to him. So, you are not talking to him. Is your daughter talking to someone who is talking to him?"

"I don't know, but I'll do my best to find out."

"He seems to know you were out of town for a weekend. He also knew you purchased an expensive refrigerator. We wouldn't want that brought up in court as evidence of spendthrift ways."

I don't want to go on the defensive. Doesn't he remember my sister bought the refrigerator for me? Be quiet, be quiet! I shake my head to show my concern.

"I don't consider myself a spendthrift." I can't help it, my chin juts out. I pull it back. Then I get up to leave. The other issue jolts my mind. "I thought this meeting was going to be about Sarah and Mark."

"What about Sarah and Mark? I know they're classmates and friends."

"Sarah is hurt. Mark evidently said on Twitter that they are being sexual. Sarah denies it. She's afraid her life is ruined."

"What? Mark is too young to be sexual. He's still into Minecraft. There's been a mistake. He wouldn't lie." For the first time I've seen, Dan's face flushes, his jaw tightens.

"You wouldn't defend him if it was your granddaughter who was weeping herself to sleep at night."

He softens immediately. "That's true. I'll look into it. Thanks for letting me know something is brewing on the home front."

"He may not be the nice boy you think he is."

"That may be. We'll see. Now, do remember to find out how Steve is getting information he shouldn't have."

"I'll check with everyone."

As I leave Dan's office, I run through all the possible

suspects for a leak as big as Texas. What about Paul, my son, who doesn't talk to anybody about anything? He can be trusted not to notice I've left town for a weekend. It's unlikely to be him. What about his wife, Stella? Now she is a talker, but she has never liked Steve. She stays away from him as best she can. When he comes over to their house, if he's in the living room, she's in the kitchen. When he goes to the kitchen, she goes upstairs. When they all sit down to dinner, Steve dominates the conversation, so there wouldn't be a time either Paul or Stella would have a chance to reveal my actions, even if they did it unknowingly. When I stop by, I'll ask them not to tell Steve what I'm up to at all.

Then there is Bill, my daughter's ex-husband. He's too busy to bother with what I'm up to. He was always tolerant of Steve at family events, but that was because they would both drink quite a bit. One time, Bill shucked oysters for a solid hour. Steve downed them all in about five minutes. They were both weaving as they walked. Bill didn't seem distressed. He just kept on shucking. Who could be spying?

―――――

THE NEXT MORNING, Caroline and I walk. The air is the closest it ever comes to crisp in Columbia. The humidity is unusually low. When Caroline comes in, I usually judge by her gear whether I need a jacket or not. She has on a sweater and earmuffs. I pull a wool hat over my ears. We walk faster when it's nippy. Despite Dan's scolding, the weather cheers me.

"Someone is leaking information to Steve he is not supposed to have," I say, catching her up. "So far, it's been minor stuff, but Dan doesn't want him to know what his strategy might be for Steve's deposition or the mediation. I've checked with all the children. They don't discuss anything with Steve. What do you think?"

She hesitates only a microsecond. "I don't think, I know."

"What? You're joking." I stop with my hand on her arm. She stops too.

She laughs, then looks me in the eye. "He's reading your emails."

"No way!" My cheeriness dissipates as we start walking again.

"Sure, you send emails to friends, thinking you can tell them anything, and he reads them. I've never read anybody else's emails because the opportunity hasn't come up. If it did come up, then I would do it. That would be when you could really find out what people are thinking."

"I can't imagine reading someone's emails. They're private. I did tell my sister I have a crush on my lawyer. Could he be reading outgoing as well as incoming?" I pause while I think back. "I do remember I looked on his computer for my emails once. I told him my password so he could get into my Yahoo mail account. At the time, I wondered if he should have my password."

Caroline laughs so hard she can hardly walk. "Reminds me of when you told me you were appalled someone at a party would check the contents of the host's medicine cabinet when they went to the bathroom."

"Well, I've never, ever done it!" I couldn't be more indignant.

"You're the only one. So, what are you going to do?" she says.

"I guess the first thing is to change my password. Then I'll see if the leak stops."

"Hmmm. I've got another idea. Is there a way to set him up? To expose him?"

"What do you mean?" I ask.

"I mean something where you send a message, maybe to me, and provoke him into doing something really dumb."

"It would have to be something he has a stake in."

"He has such a strong sense of entitlement. If he feels he owns something and someone else is getting it, he might be moved to action," she says.

Caroline puts her head to the side in thought, but I know him and what would be a siren call for him.

"I'll tell you what pops into my head. His birthday is this Friday, and I always made him a deluxe cake. The cake was regal. It had four different layers with different liquor-flavored whipped creams between heavy chocolate layers. I used Tia Maria, Godiva Cream, Limoncello, and Amaretto. Then I covered it with ganache and embedded raspberries in a spiral design. He loved it and wouldn't share it with anybody. I never got to taste any part of it except the batter. It's like it belonged to him exclusively. He froze the part he didn't eat right away, so later, he could taunt the children again."

"Okay, so you could tell me you're making this cake and going to share it with a bunch of people but not him."

"He would believe other people should not have a taste of his cake, but what action do we want him to take?"

"Maybe you could provide him with an opportunity to steal the cake." Her excitement level rises.

"Let's think a minute. I could say I'm glad I have portable window screens in the kitchen so the cake can cool easily without being refrigerated. The cake isn't as good after refrigeration. Nobody wants cold cake, anyway. If he steals it, I'll call the police and make them go get it for me. If he doesn't steal it, we enjoy the cake. At least we'll be closer to knowing if he's reading my emails."

"I can offer to help you with it on Friday morning after our walk. We could have a movie date with Alice and Zoey and plan to return for cake and wine later."

"What makes it likely to provoke action is that Friday is, in fact, his birthday. I don't know if he would steal a cake."

"We both know he has no respect for your personhood. I believe he would have no qualms about reading your email or stealing a cake he believes belongs to him."

"I'll shop for the ingredients tomorrow and set up the timing for the movie and party on emails to you."

I always have the requisite liquors for a party since I live by myself. When I lived with Steve, we drank whatever was in the house daily. If we got a bottle of Amaretto as a gift, it was gone in two days. Now, I don't think about alcohol unless I'm being social. The bottles I purchase stay full.

My mind goes to the cake and its ingredients. I will need whipping cream. I saw fresh raspberries at Whole Foods. I wonder where they come from, Central America? Australia? You never know. Hopefully, they'll be organic.

From: Angie
To: Caroline
CC: Alice, Zoey

I am fixing a lovely cake, the one I used to fix for Steve's birthday. After we see a movie, I would like to have a small party at my house and enjoy the fruits of my labors. The cake will be fresh and cooling in the evening breeze because I have portable screens on the kitchen windows. The screens will keep the bugs from getting to it. I will have appropriate libations to accompany the main course. Let me know if you can come. I think we can get together to go to the movie at 7:15. I can't wait to see everyone.

From: Caroline

To: Angie
CC: Zoey, Alice

You know me and chocolate. I'll be at your house at 6:30, so we make the movie in plenty of time.

From: Zoey

To: Angie
CC: Caroline, Alice

What a great idea! I know the cake will be special because you have the Midas touch with chocolate. How about I pick everyone up at your house at 6:30? We can all go together.

From: Alice

To: Angie
CC: Zoey, Caroline

I'd love to get together with the three of you on Friday night. I'll bring a nice Pinot

Grigio we can chill while we're at the movie. See you at 6:30 at Angie's house.

———

"Here it is—Party Friday! Here is the vanilla you missed when you shopped." Caroline does a fancy two-step as she speaks.

I butter and flour the cake pans while Caroline measures flour, sugar, butter, eggs, and chocolate. The recipe requires melting the chocolate in a double boiler. After beating the ingredients to fluffy perfection in the recommended order, we fill the cake pans and put them into the oven.

While the cake layers bake, we sit and have our snack of nuts and dried fruit. Caroline watches me rinse the raspberries. I still have the whipped cream layers and ganache to make.

"Your soon-to-be ex-husband will steal the cake. He'll take it to Paul and Stella's house and tell them he made it for his birthday. He'll kindly offer to share," she says.

"He knows no one would believe he made it. He'll steal the cake and invite several of his buddies to come and share it. He'll say, 'It's my birthday, come over, and bring a bottle of expensive liquor to share my cake with me.'" I mock his fake enthusiasm. "Maybe he'll only take half and leave me a thank-you note."

"Fat chance! I don't think I've ever heard of him sharing voluntarily," she says.

"You're right. He runs on his own time for his own agenda. We tried to be companionable early in the marriage."

"I can imagine that worked out well." Her voice drips with sarcasm.

"Of course, it didn't. If I had never commented on anything, it might have."

"There you go again, blaming yourself for everything. Face it, his unpleasantness was not your fault."

"When I tried to stand up for myself, he became more difficult. I didn't know how to stop it. He easily escalated to where I would back down."

"He escalated until you were frightened and backed down," she says.

"He's smart and determined. He got his way every time we had a disagreement, so I learned to go my own way. Mostly it worked for me. I have had my own career."

"A very successful career it has been. You have a great reputation in the community as a super therapist."

"This is a small town," I say.

"Wow, you don't know how to accept a compliment, do you? Isn't that assertive behavior one-oh-one?"

"I'm going back to working on the cake." I turn away, recognizing the truth in her scolding.

"I'll let you escape this time. One time soon, I'll make you admit you're good at something." Her voice softens.

"Hey, I confess to making a great chocolate cake. I hope I don't over-flavor the whipped cream layers."

Caroline rolls her eyes. "I can't wait to see what happens this evening."

———

AT SIX THIRTY, Caroline, Zoey, and Alice arrive at my house. The four of us contrast in every way. Caroline, my plain-speaking blonde, is dressed in jeans and a designer T-shirt with spangles. Alice, with silver in her dark hair, wears a long-tiered skirt and peasant blouse. Zoey, the tall redhead, has on nicely fitted yoga pants and a hoodie. I haven't changed since coming home from the office, so I have on black pants and a cowl-neck, lime green silk blouse.

The four of us set off to see *The Devil Wears Prada* as a rerun at the discount movie house. I forget about the setup and look forward to chilled wine and a small slice of the great cake. Caroline and I keep Zoey and Alice oblivious to the potential drama. We discuss the movie on the return home.

"I love the scene where Anne Hathaway is sitting behind a counter, and the director shows Meryl Streep coming in, again and again, throwing one designer coat after another on the counter," I say.

"She's portrayed as such an arrogant witch," Alice comments with delight.

"Wasn't it wonderful how well she played the part?" Zoey joins in.

"I don't think she's nasty in real life," I say.

"She's supposed to be a down-to-earth person," Caroline adds.

As Zoey rounds the corner to my street, the neighborhood looks like a movie set. Three police cars with flashing lights and big searchlights play over the front of my house. A fire truck is across the street. An ambulance is backed into my front yard with lights blinking. Sirens blare from all the emergency vehicles. Every neighbor on both sides of the block either peers from a window or stands outside under the streetlight.

"Should we just keep moving and pretend it isn't happening?" Zoey slows the car almost to a stop. We all have our noses to the windows, peering at the tableau.

"We can hide out at my house and read about it in the newspapers tomorrow," Caroline shouts over the noise.

I point to a space down the street. "We have to face the music. Just park over there. This is pretty exciting."

"It's too late to worry about what the neighbors are thinking." Caroline sneers. "They're imagining everything from a drug bust to the apprehension of a real live terrorist."

My son approaches the car. "Welcome to Planet Oz," Paul says, shaking his head as he opens the car door for me.

"What happened?" I force myself to keep a straight face.

"As I understand it, Dad brought a ladder to get into a kitchen window to steal a cake from you. He got in the house okay, but the delicate matter of the cake's exit didn't work for him. He fell off the ladder, and the cake fell on top of him."

I am torn between thinking it serves him right and hoping he isn't seriously injured. There is a lot of the city's finest in attendance.

"The medical people tell me he has a couple of cracked ribs and a possible concussion, although I understand that requires brain matter. I can't see where there was any brain matter involved. He evidently began screaming and hollering, so several neighbors called the police, and the result, you see before you. I guess he knew you would be baking his birthday cake because it's his birthday," Paul tells me.

"The unprincipled lout has been reading my email, and I hate to confess it, but this scene is a sort of payback," I tell him.

"Wow! He's been reading your email? Is that legal?"

"I think it's legal, but given the circumstances, certainly morally and ethically questionable."

Paul moves away toward the ambulance.

The stretcher carting Steve's body emerges from the darkness at the side of the house. He is indeed a mess. His arm is over his eyes. He seems to lick the cake from his hand even as they move him into the ambulance. Paul climbs in with him, Stella leaves in their car, and the ambulance screams off.

One by one, the searchlights extinguish. A policeman addresses the crowd with a bullhorn. "Okay, everybody, back to bed. This drama has reached its conclusion. Everyone, back to your home, please."

The blue lights turn off, and the sirens quit screeching. I thank the police officers for their late-night work, and the four of us troop into the house.

"Are they all gone?" Zoey asks.

"There goes the last one now." Caroline peeks through the curtains. She grins.

"I could use a little of that chilled wine. The movie was great, but can someone explain the drama occurring here?" Alice had been in the back seat and had not heard the conversation between Paul and me.

"Well, the man on the stretcher is Angie's estranged husband. He was trying, or, in fact, did break into the house while we were at the movie," Caroline says.

"This is suspiciously timed. Did you know he was going to break in?" Alice asks.

"We suspected he might," I chime in.

"You told him you were going to be away, and he should come or what?" Alice says.

"No! He read my email," I exclaim.

"So, the movie was a setup. Why did he want to break in?" Zoey asks.

As we talk, in typical womanly fashion, the wineglasses and wine are taken out and made ready to share.

"Angie! Do you see what I see?" Caroline slings her arm and finger.

There, on the counter by the window, is half the cake with a note next to it. Caroline reads the note: *Thanks for making my special birthday cake. In a break with tradition, I have decided to share it with you and Caroline and Zoey and Alice.*

"So, you're telling me he read your emails and broke into your house to steal half a cake?" Zoey's eyes widen with astonishment.

"The black substance all over his face and shoulder was chocolate?" Alice's voice shows how disgusted she is. "What a waste, and then he's pleased with how generous he is being in contrast to his usual selfishness?"

Caroline shakes her head. "Let's move from the subject of the robber. Although Angie and I do get a second to congratulate ourselves on the close-to-perfect setup."

We high five, and she takes my fancy cake knife by the handle and waves it around. "The cake hasn't dried on the knife, so we can still use it. Who wants what?"

"I'd like a substantial piece, but not a quarter of the half," Alice says.

While the portion discussion is underway, I get four plates from the cupboard. Caroline plates the slices, Zoey uncorks and pours the wine, and I scatter napkins and forks around the kitchen table.

Caroline takes her first bite and licks her lips. "This cake is delicious."

"Thanks. I used to make it with my heart in it, now it's a skill. The cake is great either way," I say.

"Right. I did see him sucking his fingers," Zoey comments.

"I can picture the nurses trying to wash the whipped cream out of the hair he still has," Caroline quips.

"Maybe he'll get a plaque for the hospital wall—Most Unusual Patient." Alice makes a square with her hands.

"Or maybe, Highest Drama Patient of the Year." Zoey puts her hand over her heart and bows.

"Maybe, tastiest mess this year, so far," Caroline licks her lips in a sexy way.

The picture of Steve carried through the searchlights as if it was a red-carpet moment amuses me, and I laugh. I snort a bit of white wine, and we all become hysterical. Each of us saw a different detail.

"I flashed back to the blinking lights in Star Wars," Alice says.

"The dark goo made me think he had been tarred and feathered, but without the feathers." Zoey sets us all laughing again.

"Will you prosecute him for theft? I can see him in chocolate-and-cream-striped prison garb," Alice says.

"I think broken ribs are fairly painful, and I don't want to pay any more lawyer fees than I am now. He is pretty predictable, isn't he?" I say.

"Speaking of divorce lawyer fees, since I've paid for several now, I have found the fees vary a lot. The service provided doesn't necessarily relate to the amount of the fee. Other factors inflate the fee, like the stylishness of the lawyer's clothes or the location of his office." Alice shakes her head.

"Angie is not only having difficulty with his fees. She's struggling with his availability." Caroline winks at me.

"Sometimes he's available, and sometimes when I really want him, he's not."

"What kind of a lawyer is that?" Zoey shakes her head sympathetically.

"Sensible and ethical." This time, Caroline winks at Zoey.

"Oh, that kind of availability."

CHAPTER SEVEN

Several weeks have transpired since the cake robbery. The new computer passcode will not reveal email secrets to Steve's prying eyes. Dan has run into a bureaucratic snag, blocking some records. "No need to call, I'll give you a call when I get some satisfactory answers," he told me.

After a frantic search, I find my new smartphone in my satchel. If it's so smart, why does it get lost in there?

Rachel's number is pleasant to see. "What are you up to this evening? Any chance DeeDee and I could get a night on the town? I don't have anything planned. I just thought maybe we'd catch a movie. I know we were going to research on Lydia's art but that can be done later."

"Sorry I didn't let you know, but I have a dinner invitation. Zoey has invited a group to dinner, partly to be social and partly for me to meet Red." I wiggle my eyebrows even though she can't see me. "He was widowed two or three years ago. According to her, he just hangs out with old friends. Zoey is interested in matchmaking two lost souls."

"You are not a lost soul! So, you are not saving yourself for Dan?"

I imagine the twinkle in her eye but ignore the Dan comment. It brings a flash of sadness and discouragement since I have received another outrageous bill. Maybe Dan can't be brought around.

"I'll be glad to sit with the boys tomorrow evening, but I'm looking forward to meeting Red."

"Great. We'll feed them supper. If you can come around six thirty, we'll have plenty of time to catch a seven o'clock movie."

"See you tomorrow."

―――

I REPEAT the story about tonight's dinner with Red to Caroline as we leave the senior center.

"Lost soul! What kind of crap is that?" She stops in the middle of the road to put her hands on her hips. She gives me the frown of horror she is so capable of.

"Move, there's a car coming." I grab her arm. We skedaddle across the intersection.

"Are you trying to get us killed? Then there would be two lost souls." My voice is loud.

"Even then, I would not be a lost soul. I would haunt you forever." She raises her arms, makes a ghostly face, and sways. "Oooooo, ooooo."

"Okay, okay, so lost soul is too evocative. How about pathetic single?"

"How about proudly independent?" she retorts.

"Terrific attitude adjustment, I'll go along with that."

"So, what are you going to wear? How about I come over around four and help you out? We'll see what will help you look hot."

"Thanks. You always know what to do."

"What are you thinking might be right? What will be the level of casualness?" Caroline cuts to the chase.

"The dinner will be informal. I haven't decided, maybe jeans and a sequined T-shirt. See you later." I wave goodbye and head home, knowing Caroline has a magic touch.

Later, when she comes to my house, she lets herself in. I call to her from my bedroom.

She comes down the hall. "This house suits you so well. The sparse furnishings show off the artwork. Is the quilt the one your friends made?"

"Yes, he dyed the fabric, and she made the quilt. I'm so fond of it. I hope it lasts as long as I'm here."

"You planning on going somewhere?"

"Nope, I'm here for the duration. See this stack. One of these shirts will be chosen to go with my jeans." I toss several shirts onto the bed.

"Don't discard the pink shirt yet. Pink is nice with your hair and skin."

"This shade of pink is too forward. It might clash with his hair. To be honest, the neck is not cut low enough. A deep V-neck makes me look taller."

"Do you know how tall this guy is? Maybe he's short. You don't want to tower over him."

"I'll wear flat boots with my jeans. I just want to look as tall and slim as possible."

"What about this blue sweater? He'll be mesmerized by the blue in your eyes. He won't notice what the V-neck points to."

"The eyes have it. If eyes are the windows to the soul, do I want him seeing I have one? However, I don't want him to see I wish he were Dan."

"Fixated, are you?"

"Fixated is one word, attracted is another."

"Here, this blue is light enough to be perfect with the black jeans, shows off your eyes, has the required V-neck." She holds the shirt to my chest.

"Good. Now for earrings," I say.

"You have only two pairs of decent earrings, the heavy gold, and the filigreed gold. The heavy ones are too formal for dinner at a friend's house."

"My silver dangling balls are flirty." I am partial to them.

"Yes, but they look cheap. You want this guy to know you can hold your own. You're not looking for someone to support you." Caroline wags her finger at me.

"Sometimes, we take in information even when we're focused on something else. Maybe I'll know right away if Red is the right guy for me even if he will have to be someone special for that to happen."

"You're right, sometimes you just know."

A NICE MERLOT encased in a party sack in one hand, a black leather clutch in the other, and I'm tempted to push the doorbell with my nose. Amused, I transfer the clutch to under my armpit and press the button. A form floats into view behind the leaded glass panes. "Let the party begin," I say to myself.

The door opens, revealing a smiling tall man. His hair is not red, but dark brown with red highlights. His dark eyes focus on mine.

"You must be Red. I know the other cast members for this dinner."

"Come in, come in." He guides me down the hallway by the elbow, not being pushy or rushed; rather, nicely supportive.

"Our honored guest has arrived," he announces as we come into the living room.

"It's not my birthday." I manage a subtle mix of surprise and scolding.

He chuckles softly, appreciatively.

We sit side by side on the couch while Zoey passes plates of cheese and crackers. The tiny triangles of warm spinach spanakopita have come from a Costco box, but they're tasty if a little greasy.

He holds plates for me, and in turn, I hold plates for him. When Zoey offers him food, he passes the attention on to me. Zoey serves my favorite blue cheese. Delicious.

I turn to him. "Do you like this cheese?"

"I don't eat much cheese. I like fairly bland food."

I keep my spirits up by rationalizing I can always add pepper and spices at the table.

"Have you seen *Lincoln* yet?" Zoey interjects. "The movie clears up the different political battles leading to the war. I enjoyed it."

Puzzled by the abrupt change of direction, I join in the discussion of recent movies. All six of us discuss the good, the bad, the acting, the scenery. The banter is light, the disagreements amusingly handled. Aided by a glass of merlot, I am having a good time.

Zoey gets up and heads for the kitchen, signaling dinner is ready to be served. I rush to help her move hot dishes to the dining room table.

"He's a nice guy. Thanks for inviting me. I love the color and attention of his dark eyes," I tell her.

"You're a good match for him. I can see you are lifting his spirits. He finds you enchanting."

"What more could a woman want?"

Red and I sit next to each other. The dining room light is soft and flattering. I know I look just fine. I give him lots of eye contact; he is attentive and reciprocates. I notice he takes a large helping of potatoes lying sickly white in the Wedgwood bowl. They are only boiled, without even any visible pepper. As Zoey passes me the bowl, she notes that butter, sour cream, and grated cheese are available so we can doctor our own as we please. After the first taste, I add a lot of saturated fats and salt as the potatoes are not salted much, and the end result is that they are, of course, delicious.

The Charleston-style crab cakes are superb, but I notice he doesn't have one. The asparagus was perfectly marinated and broiled, but he doesn't taste even one stem. By the time dessert is served, I'm vigilant and confused. What does he live on?

"Do you exist only on potatoes?" I ask him with a smile and lightness in my voice.

"I have to eat something. Good tasting food is overindulgent." His mood shifts, tinging his voice with sadness.

"Overindulgent?" I'm not able to keep the astonishment out of my voice.

"Yes, it's wrong. You're not supposed to have things that taste good. It's sinful, really."

I have to relax my eyes and mouth so I don't reveal my thoughts. "That's certainly worth thinking about."

"You're kind and generous. Most women say, 'That's crazy.'" His laugh is forced.

Now I understand the earlier change of subject away from food. Zoey's difficulty in getting Red paired off is transparent. Did the sin thing apply to everything that felt good? *Wow!* No wonder he has no children. Maybe that's why I have four. My philosophy is, if it feels good, go for it.

"So, has this always been the way for you?" I stretch to understand what has gone so wrong.

"As long as I can remember. Sometimes, when I'm distracted by music, I can relax enough to eat what I'm served. Tonight, I could feel myself wanting to be normal, but it didn't work."

When Zoey sees me out, she tries to be chipper.

"I'm so fond of him. He's a sweetheart," she says.

"I enjoyed the evening, and we'll talk later about his difficulties."

———

THIS TIME, the phone call comes to me. "Angie, this is Red."

"How nice to hear from you."

"You were kind last night. I saw how much you enjoyed the food Zoey served. The contrast between us is too stark. Seeing someone enjoy their food like you do is too painful for me. I like you, but the differences are too great."

"Thanks for your call. I will be thinking about you."

"I appreciate that."

It's possible if Red and I talked more I would hear about his therapy and his therapist since he undoubtedly has one. She probably specializes in eating disorders. There are a lot of eating disorders out there, but his case is a bit unusual. I zone out a bit after the stressful call and reflect on some of my old clients and how I see their issues mirrored in some of the new people I meet.

My phone rings again. "Hi." Zoey's voice is unmistakable.

"Zoey, you know me better than to think I'd like a food avoider."

"Angie, I'm sorry. I knew better, but I'm so fond of you both, I couldn't help myself."

"The party was delightful until he didn't eat any crab cake. I wish I'd had the chutzpah to eat his."

"I should have warned you."

"Don't scold yourself. He called this morning and took me off the hook. He is sweet. Sadly, it just makes me more interested in Dan. If he and I had been at your dinner party together, you wouldn't have had to go to a special menu."

"Let's hope it comes to pass."

I get occasional clients who confess to purging, usually with high stress. The serious younger ones who don't want to eat end up in the hospital since the line between fashionably thin and dangerously malnourished is porous. Purging leads to feelings of relief, so it's addictive, and addiction leads to strange thinking. I have had several clients who stand out for addictive behavior.

John, an early client, was a cocaine addict. It is well known that addicts rarely stick in therapy. He was distressed because his girlfriend, in the guise of helping him make tea, poured boiling water over his hand. It turned out he worked for a family business and was having sex with the daughter and, separately, with her mother. He believed neither knew of the other. He was mystified by his girlfriend's aggression. He complained the burn was painful.

I never did it before then and I have never done it since, but I laughed out loud when he asked me if it could have been purposeful. Not a good therapeutic technique on my part as he never came back. At least I kept my cool with Red, despite my horror.

Jojo, another addict client, had an affair with her psychiatrist. When he caught on to her manipulations and didn't give her all the pain pills she wanted, she tried to ruin him. I listened to the secret recordings and phone calls supposedly proving he had ruined her life. She moved to another town when she found a wealthy new boyfriend. I was grateful not to have to deal with the trouble she stirred up.

When Lois, a smart, alcoholic woman, became afraid of her guns, I made her bring them to me in my office. I kept them in my file drawer under lock and key. That was an interesting—no, nerve-racking evening, waiting for her to return from her house with the guns. I later learned she had kept one.

Mostly, my clients are ordinary people with commonplace suffering from their losses, their guilt, and their nasty experiences, and usually, I like them. They want me to help them, so I am sympathetic to their issues. When I understand how they think and behave in detrimental ways, therapy moves ahead. I would be jealous they have me to look after them and be interested in their lives if it weren't for Rachel.

Since Rachel is my youngest daughter, she is, statistically speaking, first in line to care for me in my old age. I'm lucky she calls regularly and keeps up with things I would let go. This evening, when I am reflecting, she calls.

"Mom, do you want to know more scoop on Lydia?"

"I'll be right over."

This is a simple process of grabbing my keys from the bowl by the front door, locking the door, and walking across the street. I bought my house shortly after I left Steve when Rachel was diagnosed with breast cancer. We could both imagine me raising her children.

I like to sit in Rachel's kitchen. Expensive upgrades occurred just before she learned about her cancer. The gleaming large appliances surround a black marble-topped island. People sit at the island on high stools and drink wine while she cooks. The cheery recessed lights welcome me. This evening's tasty herbal tea is honey-bush. She hands me a large mug. The drink is smooth and easy to sip because it smells so sweet.

She pours herself a mug and turns to me. "I do good research."

"What did you find?"

She has scrawled notes on several sheets of paper. "Lydia divorced three men in six years, then she married Dan. Dan had an early, short-term marriage, but evidently, he and Lydia were well-matched since they were married for thirty-plus years. Brent, their oldest, has a different father. Sally had another mother who died giving birth to her. They had Phil together. All the children were raised by Lydia and Dan. They were social, I gather, since there are lots of photos of them in the society pages of the old newspaper. They entertained senators and representatives and judges, even President Clinton once. Mostly Democrats, you'll be pleased to know."

"That may be more information than I want to know. When did they stop entertaining?"

"I didn't see anything after about eight years ago," Rachel informs me. "Maybe she got sick then."

"I do feel sorry for them having to go through the cancer thing while still raising children and grandchildren." I sigh.

"Just like us." Rachel's eyes are bright when I face her. The parallel is too true.

I know Mrs. McCloud died following her sickness. I try to turn my mind to something else, but I can't help my mind going to Rachel's illness and the fear—no, terror surrounding it. Mostly I can squash it down, but not when another breast cancer victim comes to mind.

"Reminds me, I haven't heard the latest report of your blood work. ¿Qué pasa?"

"You have to know my tumor markers went in the wrong direction this month."

"Oh, honey, what does it mean?"

"We don't know yet. They'll do some more checking in two months rather than three."

I don't want to put any pressure on her since I know stress is not helpful. I will not scream or cry. I'll be able to put it in the background after two or three sleepless nights. The plans for me to raise the children will ping around in my head until I'm exhausted.

"I'm sure it will be just fine." My words belie the tremor in my voice.

"Not to change the topic, however, I'm going to change the topic. How was dinner with Red?"

"He's a good fellow but not right for me. He only eats boiled potatoes. Too close to his Irish ancestry, I guess. Where his notions came from is a mystery. He believes anything tasting good is from the devil. Like I said, he's not for me."

"I'm sorry. Was the evening a total bust?"

"The dinner and the company were great, just the one anomaly."

"While you're here, I've got another issue, nothing we can do anything about." For Rachel, lack of control is not usually the way she rides. "Remember I told you about Sarah being in a Twitter mess with some friends at school? The group includes Mark, Dan's grandson."

"You told me, and I mentioned it to Dan. It was a day or two before Steve's birthday-cake debacle. He said he would look into it, but he probably hasn't had a chance, or anyway, I've not heard from him about it."

"Let's review. Mark put out on Twitter Sarah had been intimate with him. Sarah denies it. She's horrified and sad. She's sure she's been ruined for life; although I have been able to get her to go to school."

I have had fantasies about taking our grandchildren on water-park adventures. Once again, I have gotten ahead of myself. Now I have to deal with Dan's son and daughter-in-law about their fourteen-year-old son. Will he turn out to be some kind of sexual monster? Luckily, I don't have to deal with it. Rachel does.

"What are you going to do?" I ask.

"I'll start with research on Mark's parents. If they look all right, I'll ask for a meeting with them to make sure they know what's happening. I'll have Mark and Sarah at the meeting so we can confront the thing straight-out."

"Would it make sense for me to be there as a buffer?"

"I'll think about it. If you came, Dan would likely be there too as they might need a lawyer."

Rachel's call comes later that afternoon. "It's all arranged. Movie night has been transformed into a 'Let's have a confrontation' evening. Everyone will come around seven."

"So, I have three hours to ratchet up my anxiety?"

"Dan is coming. I want you here."

I SURREPTITIOUSLY PEEK around the edge of my curtain when I see the gray Lincoln glide into place in front of Rachel's house. There they are. Dan, his son, Phil, daughter-in-law, and Mark. My tummy is tight. I am quite frightened, but I try to saunter across the street. I have been in a quandary for hours. The awfulness of Dan's defense of his grandson sits in every tightened muscle, head to toes. The idea of seeing Dan in a setting besides his office gives me some relief. I stewed over how to dress for the showdown. I decided on casual khaki pants and my best blue-and-white-striped T-shirt.

Rachel is not doing the formal thing in the living room, so I join the group in the kitchen. Introductions are made with no chitchat. The setup in the kitchen is strange for a confrontation. Rachel has Sarah and Mark seated next to each other. Dan hovers near Rachel at the stove. I head over to see if I can be helpful. Mark's parents stand at the counter, looking tense. The black marble counter is laden with Rachel's go-to snacks—a bowl of popcorn, cheese and crackers on nice plates. Her fancy wineglasses almost suggest a celebration.

After the wine is poured, Rachel begins: "I know something the rest of you don't. I know what the Twitter feed said." She pauses. "I also know what Mark meant. The Twitter feed said, 'I like Sarah. I even like it when she comes down on me. I think it's cute.'" She grins.

There is a moment of silence, then Dan laughs, a belly laugh. He is delightfully, hysterically amused. All the adults join in. What a relief that Mark thinks Sarah is cute when she's annoyed. What a dumb misunderstanding. Then I notice Sarah and Mark are not laughing.

Sarah is angry. "What's so funny? Why did everyone get so upset because Mark thinks it's cute when I fuss at him?" She looks around. No one makes eye contact.

Mark joins her protest. "Why does everybody think I accused her of a sexual act? All I did was say she comes down on me. I do think it's cute."

I cannot look anyone in the face. It would be cruelty added to torture to laugh again. I press my lips together.

Dan turns to Mark, takes Mark's chin in his hand to force eye contact. "Your father is definitely going to have a private conversation with you tonight . . ." He looks across the counter. "And Rachel will have a conversation with Sarah."

He looks around the room. "Now how can we right this wrong?"

Laughter relaxed me. "How about another tweet clarifying what Mark meant to say? Maybe 'I think it's cute when Sarah fusses at me.'"

Dan gives me the twinkle smile. "I like the idea of a correction without an elaborate explanation. Any other ideas?"

Mark stands up. "I haven't done anything wrong. I don't know why you all are laughing at me."

Mark's dad looks at him sternly. "Sit down and be patient." He turns to his wife. "Let's go home, so we can get his cleared up."

Dan turns to Rachel. "Thanks for your help with this." He leads the way to the front door.

Sarah sidles up to Mark. "I don't mind at all that you like me and think I'm cute. I think you're cute too."

Mark smiles at her. When she smiles back, his shoulders visibly drop.

After the McClouds are gone, I escort Rachel back to the kitchen. "How the devil did you find out the truth?"

"Knowing Roscoe would be in on the Twitter feed since he and Mark are best buddies, I asked him to send it to me. Mind you, I had to get on Twitter when I had sworn I would never do it."

"I'm hoping we have seen the end of this."

Rachel cocks her head. "What do you think when Dan gives you that special smile?"

"I call it his twinkle smile. It relaxes me down to my bones."

"Ah, so . . ." She smiles knowingly.

I shake my head and kiss her cheek in goodbye. I walk across the street. Dan and I have been through some difficult times—the email fiasco and now the Twitter misunderstanding. I'm feeling extreme relief. My anger at Dan for his sympathy to someone who made my granddaughter cry and my fondness for him made me tense this evening. I decide the experience was enlightening. Dan kept his cool at first and then immediately saw the humor. Even though it's early, my bed beckons, and I sleep soundly.

When I awake the next morning, I do my back stretches and smile to myself.

CHAPTER EIGHT

I resolve to take Steve's deposition seriously. There are four boxes of files lined up against the wall in Dan's conference room. The smell of a recent cleaning is faint but clear.

Dan comes into the room where I have been asked to sit by myself. I see he has a twinkle in his eye. "We have survived the Twitter adventure together, and you were able to find the culprit of the information leak. Congratulations!"

Despite my nervousness, I smile.

"So, the ambulance driver's report includes the statement that the frosting was the best he'd ever tasted," he continues. "I interviewed him in preparation for this deposition. What a clever way to prove Steve was reading your emails."

He looks at me with wide, thoughtful eyes. Then he bursts out a deep-throated laugh that throws back his head and brings tears to his eyes. I have to join him. He has a beautiful laugh. When he stops, his chest heaves several times. I don't swoon, but I'm close. *The frosting could be yours for the asking.* I give him as big a smile as I can without looking like a cartoon chipmunk.

Dan indicates my chair for these proceedings. He sits next to me.

"Steve has a Band-Aid on his forehead, but other than the head wound and the cracked rib, he's just fine." Dan indicates where the bandage is placed.

"The window isn't very high up, so he didn't fall far. I do regret the loss of the cake, but I feel it was in a good cause." I straighten my back. I slowly shutter my eyes.

Dan shakes his head. "Let's both take several deep breaths and see if we can give this deposition the weight it deserves."

"I can! My money is at stake, right?"

My mood changes to anxious with the rap on the door. The court reporter enters with Steve and his lawyer. Steve is dressed in his ancient tweed jacket, laundered white shirt, old-fashioned wide tie, khakis, and polished loafers. He looks thin and scared. Steve's lawyer, Mr. Castro, is a step up in his attire. He has on an almost shiny, well-fitted black suit, patterned shirt and tie, and short boots. He is tall and nice-looking, and he carries a big black leather file case. I recognize him though it has been a long time since we met. He nods at me as if there is recognition on his part as well.

The large Band-Aid covers half of Steve's forehead. *No sympathy. He was robbing you.* Reality kills the last remnants of mirth sitting in my chest.

The preliminaries of who is here and why pass quickly, and Dan begins.

"Doctor Merk, may I refer to you as Mr. Merk?"

"Yes, please."

"And then I'll call your wife Ms. Merk."

"Yes, that's up to her."

"That will keep the record clear as you both would be addressed as Dr. Merk otherwise."

"Uh-huh."

"Would you tell me the date of your birth?"

"October 18, 1942."

"And where were you born?"

"In a hospital near Detroit."

"Detroit?"

"Uh-huh."

"Have you ever been told you're selfish?"

I'm pretty calm until this question. I look down to see my quivering hands. My stomach is tight, and I'm suddenly hot. Is it the extra protein I had for breakfast? I know what Steve had for breakfast because it did not change for decades. He had oatmeal he took out of the refrigerator and didn't heat up, not even in the microwave. He bought the beat-up microwave, used for the occasional leftover, at the flea market, then I spent two hours scrubbing it to make it sanitary. He puts milk and honey on the cold mush and occasionally makes it even more attractive with uncooked raisins. God forbid, he should add fresh blueberries. The children called the oatmeal, "daddy's gray mixture." He would sometimes slather either sour cream or full-fat yogurt on it and claim it was delicious.

"Possibly," Steve responds after a short pause. "But I can't think of the specific reason."

"Don't remember the particular reason?" Dan asks.

"It just hasn't occurred to me. I don't think about these things."

"Say again." Dan leans toward him.

"I don't think about this. I don't remember. Maybe so."

"Maybe so?" Dan asks.

"Yes." Steve nods in agreement.

"All right. How do you define selfish?" Dan sits back.

"I think someone who's overly concerned with their own interests at the expense of others."

"Would you repeat that, please? I didn't hear all of it." Again, Dan leans forward.

"Someone who probably is overly concerned with their own interests at the expense of others."

"Okay. Do you fit that definition?"

"I pray not," Steve says softly.

"You pray not?"

"Yes," Steve says.

"Do you feel that you do?" Dan matches Steve's soft voice.

"I cannot say. It's an appraisal I cannot fairly make of myself."

"Okay. Have you ever been told that you want or demand what is not yours?"

"I can't recollect it."

"Okay. Now, you and Ms. Merk separated on what day?"

"The departure—I think her desertion was August 16, 2018"

Desertion? He deserted me two years, make that one year into the marriage. He wouldn't let me get involved in collecting textiles. He forced me to find my own way. Not the worst solution to the problem of an ill-matched marriage, but not the most companionable.

"August 16, 2018?" Dan seems interested.

"That date or either side of it."

"Okay. And you had been married at that time forty-five years."

"Not yet forty-five. Forty-four, I think."

"The date of your marriage was what?"

"December 28, 1973."

"Have you spent or sent one dollar to her since the separation?"

"No."

"Have you spent any money for any bill for her benefit since the separation?"

"No."

I don't know where this notion that Steve should take

care of me or pay any bill of mine comes from. Is it Southernism?

"When you married Ms. Merk, what education had you already received?"

"I had a bachelor's degree."

"And what education had she received when you married her?"

"She had a bachelor's degree."

"Where did you receive your degree?"

"Wayne University in Detroit."

"Now, beginning with the time of your marriage, I believe both of you received further education. Is that true?"

"Yes."

Uh-oh, I have a chin hair, a thick one. Is it black or white? Now how do they expect me to concentrate? Angie, do not move it back and forth. Put your hands in your lap. Damn! I don't have tweezers in my purse. I wonder if the secretary has some. Will I remember to ask her? Is this a woman's life? First, the worry about zits, then the embarrassment of the sweaty armpits of menopause. Now, chin hairs. *Oy vey!*

"Was Ms. Merk employed at the date of your marriage?" Dan asks.

"I can't recollect," Steve responds.

"Okay. How soon after your marriage did you begin further studies?"

"Just about at once."

"And where did you begin your studies?"

"University of Colorado."

"And were you employed while you were going to the University of Colorado?"

"No."

"Okay. Was Ms. Merk employed while you were going to the University of Colorado?"

"I think no."

Mistake there. I had a research-assistant job with a research institute. I can't remember the name of the place. It sat on a hill near the campus. I remember the pleasant director and the fun we had as staff members making undergraduate students respond to flashing lights for course credit. The point of the flashing lights escapes me now.

"All right. What was the means of your support and/or her support after you were married?" Dan asks as if they are old friends.

"After the marriage, she had the G.I. Bill from her father's death in the war, and we lived on that for about two years."

"For two years?"

"Modestly."

"Do you remember the amount you were receiving—she was receiving for that?"

"No, not specifically. It was very small."

"Did you receive a degree from Colorado?"

"Yes, a master's degree in history."

"And, at any time during that two years, were you working other than studying?"

"No."

Not true, we were dorm advisers in a freshmen dorm, although we only lasted a semester. The beefy freshmen tore the telephones from the wall. One poor drunk threw a bike from the second-story window. Unfortunately, it landed on a police car. There was quite a ruckus.

"Okay. Was Ms. Merk working at any time during those two years?"

"I can't recall, but she was working after we got to Berkeley."

"And did you go there for further studies?"

"Yes."

"Were you still living on the stipend due to her father's death?"

"And she worked."

"She worked?"

"Yes."

"Where did she work?"

"She had jobs in San Francisco."

"Okay. And what period of time did she work in that area?"

"I think she always worked."

I'm suddenly extremely tired. Was I always tired? Did I get enough to eat during those years and those pregnancies? Of course, I did. I gained a lot of weight each time. What I remember most about Berkeley and San Francisco were the heavenly bakeries. The one on Shattuck Avenue in Berkeley had puff pastries that included fruit and chocolate and sometimes chicken. They were unbelievably good.

"After you left Berkeley, where did you go?"

They talk about the year we spent in La Jolla, where Steve was a librarian and wrote his dissertation. The image of the beach there, the stone seawall, the crystal-clear water comes into my mind. I had an obsession with California grapes. I ate them daily for a year as they were a staple for taking babies to the beach, those and Triscuits with cheese.

Dan and Steve move on to our time in Toronto. Steve is not getting the time sequences straight. In Toronto, we had a Jewish bakery around the corner from the house. I took the children there every day for a snack. The lady who served us believed it was their breakfast. She slathered cream cheese on the fresh bagels. I took warm rye bread home, and butter melted easily into it. A pregnant person could devour half a loaf in twenty minutes.

"Okay. Was she primarily taking care of the children when you came to the University of South Carolina?" Dan shows incredible patience.

"Yes," Steve responds.

"And how long would you say she was the principal caretaker of the children here?"

"She was mostly."

"Mostly?" Again, the friendly clarifying questions from Dan.

"She did more than I did."

"What degrees did Ms. Merk have when she was here? When you arrived in Columbia?"

"She had an MA."

"All right. When did she receive her PhD?"

"I can't recall exactly, but we knew it was coming, and it wasn't a big event. We celebrated; we were pleased. It was something over with. I can't recall the exact date."

I realize Steve may be getting tired. His vague responses suggest he didn't review dates before he came here this morning. Did his lawyer not prepare him, or did Steve not listen when his lawyer tried?

"Yeah. Okay. And when did she begin employment then after the birth of your four children?" Dan asks.

"Strangely, very quickly after each one."

Damn right, I'm a healthy female. We needed money, and I had statistics skills. University research jobs in the Bay area were flexible. He doesn't remember I took a year off with the second baby when we were in La Jolla. I worked on my PhD after he got his first university position.

"After each baby?" Dan is incredulous.

"Yes." Steve is definite.

"All right. What was the date of your retirement?"

"Let's see. December 31, 2002."

"And your retirement fund or pension, or whatever it is, is how much per month?"

"I get just under three thousand a month."

"And that's been drawn by you since December 2002?"

"It was less in the beginning. It's more now."

"And when you . . . when you began to draw your pension, you had an option, did you not, about how much you would draw early on?"

"Some option. Yes."

"All right. And the option you took was if you drew more, then Ms. Merk, after your death, would draw nothing. Is that right?"

"Yes."

"And so, the option you took was the one that would pay you the most?"

"Yes."

The banter continues about Steve's money and his income. I can't believe he doesn't see where Dan is going with this whole selfish thing. Steve doesn't even protect himself when he can. He did some childcare, after all. We had a nanny when the children were young. I couldn't have done the whole thing myself.

They get around to the art collections and bronzes. What will he say to the data we have?

"I have bronzes," Steve says with pride.

"And you've collected them for quite a number of years?"

"In the year 1997."

"Was that when you started?"

"And pretty much finished."

"In one year?"

"Yes."

"Tell me how many bronzes you acquired."

"About seventy. I probably have about twenty-five now."

He's underestimating, just like he underestimated their value on the asset form he filled out.

"Did you claim a value on each one?"

"Yes. I think you have some records of that."

Does he think we are depending on the rinky-dink amounts he put in the legal discovery? Those amounts were like buying a prostitute for a dollar. What do prostitutes do that men like?

Where is your mind? Back to business, please.

"Did you have some bronzes delivered to the National Art Museum of Sport in Indianapolis?" Dan, again, with the friendly questioning.

"They borrowed some."

"They borrowed some?"

"Yes."

"Borrowed eight?"

"I don't know. Maybe you do. I don't know. I don't recall."

"They belong to you?"

"Yes."

"Where are they now?"

"In my house, in my storage building in back."

"What value would you put on them?" Dan's questions come quickly.

"I don't recall."

"Did you put a value on each piece you sent there?" Now Dan's getting to the heart of Steve's rapaciousness.

"I may have for insurance purposes."

"Alfred Boucher—is that a name you recognize of a bronze?"

"Alfred Boucher." Steve smiles.

"Did you have one of those?"

"Yes."

"And you put a value of twenty-five thousand dollars?

"No! I couldn't! It doesn't seem likely. It was a mistake."

Wow! He's hanging himself. I wish there had been third-party observers to see what was going on in the marriage. No, I don't. I'm embarrassed I let his manipulation go on so long. When he fussed, I just adapted.

They spar about the value of the bronzes. At least my story about them has held up quite well. Steve's valuation of the bronzes at $250 each in his discovery paper shows how worthless his statements are. Luckily, the papers subpoenaed from the museum came this morning. That sheet with the inflated values on it will be like gold in court.

"All right. Now, let's go down the list of the bronzes there with the figures you had by each one as to the value." Dan is relentless.

"They are all too high."

"I didn't ask you that." Dan remains friendly in demeanor, but the statement is clearly meant to keep Steve in check.

"Okay. Yes."

"You put twenty-five thousand on it, didn't you?"

"It must have been for insurance purposes. It's not worth that much money."

"You wouldn't be false with insurance, would you?"

"Yes, I would. I have done so."

"Where else do you put false things out?"

"I don't do it. I'm not sure I actually did it with the bronzes. Maybe they are imaginably more valuable . . ."

"You wrote those numbers down?"

"I did indeed."

"Nobody else wrote them down?"

"You're quite right."

"Nobody had a gun at you to tell you to put the figures down?"

"No.

"And you sent it to somebody?"

"To the curator."

"And you expected him to rely on it, didn't you?"

"I guess."

"You didn't send it to him so he could just throw it out the window?"

"No."

"I'm asking you again, read them and the price you put by each one."

Steve looks defeated. He had been pretty perky up until now. He reads the list of bronzes and their dollar figures. He looks sick to his stomach. I don't have much sympathy for him since he has lied about a bunch of stuff. He has done it deliberately too.

"Thank you. Mr. Merk, in view of what you've just said—"

"Yes."

"Should I rely on anything that you've written and signed?"

"Try your best, please."

"Did you ever form an LLC or a partnership or a joint ownership or corporation that was called 'The Merk Family'?"

"Yes."

"When did you form that?"

"Let's see. I didn't . . .this was so long ago, and I haven't thought about it since, but it had to do with the ownership of the James Edward apartment building."

"I see, and was Ms. Merk a shareholder in the business?"

"No."

"It was called 'The Merk Family Partnership'?"

"Yes."

"But you cut out the family? Who was it?"

"The children."

"The children?"

"Yes."

"And when you sold the James Edwards apartments, did you distribute the money to your children?"

"No."

"Did you ever give one of your children some money which you then asked that the child give back?"

"No."

"Remember that question."

"Just a minute, just a minute. If you can possibly—if you have an incident, can you remember something? Do you have any incident?"

"I'm asking the questions. So, Ms. Merk never had—"

"Just a minute. I can't think of how or why I would do it."

"But Ms. Merk never had any interest in The Merk Family Partnership?"

"No."

They go over the details of tax payments, household expenses, and travel expenses. I get bored. Oh, back to the partnership.

"There was a trust created, The Merk Trust. Are you familiar with that?" Dan asks.

"Please tell me more about it." Steve, puzzled, turns to his lawyer.

Mr. Castro turns to the recorder. "Well, here it is. It's a copy that was furnished to us right here. It's a terrible copy, but that's all I have. I would like to ask, on the record, that when you go back, at your convenience, you furnish us with a clear—"

"That's all I have." Dan is short.

Mr. Castro retreats, sits back in his chair, and assumes the bland face he has shown throughout the proceedings.

"Tell me, what it is, Mr. Merk. What is the trust?" Dan reasserts his authority over the room.

"It was twenty years ago. I don't know if I paid much attention to it afterward and what the purpose of it was."

"Is it still in existence?"

"I think not. I don't know."

"You don't know what was in it?"

"It had to do something about the ownership of the James Edward apartments."

"Well, it's extremely difficult to read."

"Indeed." Steve shrugs his shoulders.

"I've not been able to read it. I'll try to decipher the original," Mr. Castro murmurs.

"Now, there's a Merk Family Limited Partnership in existence as well. Are you aware of that?"

"I can't recall. I don't—maybe . . . maybe I neglected it since it occurred."

"Well, the South Carolina Secretary of State has it listed. Merk Family Limited Partnership." Dan points to a paper on the table by his side.

"What's the date of it?" Steve seems curious.

"The status is given here as of June 20, 2013. I don't know when it was created. What can you tell me about that?" Dan asks.

"Let me see it, please." Steve holds out his hand.

"Here it is, right here." Dan hands the paper to him.

"This was created in 1990. I think it may be another version of what you have there. I paid no attention to it since that time. I don't know what my obligations are with it." Steve shakes his head.

"Do I understand from your statement there's nothing owned now by The Merk Family Partnership?"

"No, I believe not. No."

"Nothing?"

Steve nods his head.

"And the trust, you don't know what that's all about now either?"

"It doesn't seem relevant to my life now at this moment."

Is he lying, or does he really not remember anything about the partnership? The lady at the Secretary of State's office was as pleasant and cooperative as someone hoping for a big tip. Should I have tipped her? No, she is a state employee. The only ones you tip are the guides at state parks. Or do they refuse? She made me a copy and didn't charge me. Maybe she would like some cookies or a small carrot cake?

"What does the official partnership copy say in the third paragraph on page two?"

"It says, 'The silent partners Mrs. Merk and the children will have no say in the decisions regarding the partnership.'"

"So, you've been telling me something different than what is stated in the official document."

"I don't remember much from that time."

Mr. Castro, who has only occasionally shifted his position in his seat, finally comes to Steve's rescue. "I believe this is a good time to take a break for lunch." He rises to his feet.

Dan looks at him. "I'm not finished. We'll continue after lunch and then proceed to my client's deposition." He waves toward me, finally including me in the proceedings.

"I no longer want to depose Mrs. Merk. I think you've covered just about everything." Mr. Castro looks sad.

Dan shrugs his shoulders. He stares at Mr. Castro. "I have enough."

Mr. Castro helps Steve to his feet. They disappear, and I let my shoulders drop.

"You now have your afternoon free." Dan grins.

I grin back. I want to hug him, but no permission has been granted for a level of gratitude beyond the grin. No deposition for me. What magic has he performed?

"I didn't exactly follow all the last part. Why doesn't he want to depose me?"

"His client gave enough information about what a hard worker you have been. It's also clear you were a good mother and a good wife to someone who didn't deserve it. He knows you are competent in court. At this point, he'd agree to anything to avoid a trial."

"You did a great job. I was surprised when you asked Steve about being selfish." My smile shows how grateful I am.

"I've never met a man so poorly disposed toward others.

You gave me all the information I needed to reveal his character."

"And, to think, I wasn't trying to reveal anything, just give you the picture of what the marriage was like from my perspective. Lots of times over the years, I was enjoying myself, you know."

We walk down the hall. I so badly want to put my hand on his sleeve and ask him to lunch. Despite the thousands going out in monthly checks, I'd gladly buy him lunch.

"Yes, I know you have a lovely capacity for fun and adventure. I'm glad Steve wasn't able to squelch that in you."

He turns to me, hesitates, then continues down the hall. "Have a nice afternoon." His voice warms me.

"Thanks. I was anxious about my deposition."

"You weren't the only one." He disappears into his office.

What was that about? Maybe he didn't want to see me raked over the coals, or maybe he didn't quite trust my version. Now he has every reason to believe anything I say since I almost always tell the truth.

CHAPTER NINE

How does one dress for a post-midnight visit to a graveyard? Shall I pretend I'm just coming from a party? Would heels, a sexy little shirt, and a Marilyn Monroe skirt be required? The heels might catch in the gravestones, or Lydia might not like me to look good.

Perhaps I'm out for an evening stroll in running shoes, long Lycra pants, clingy short-sleeved tee. No, I mustn't be disrespectful. Besides, I haven't run in so long, the outfit might not fit.

Angie, put on your dark jeans and a dark shirt. Get out of here.

Now the issue is, what purse to take? The purse has to be big enough to hold a flashlight. I won't need my credit card unless Lydia takes plastic for her séances. *Stop it!* You're just going to see if you can find the gravestone. Dan said it was right across the street from his office.

"Truly," he had said, "she's right over there." I hope he didn't notice I jerked in my seat, expecting to see her hovering outside the window.

The purse can't look like I have burglary tools in it, so

midsized black will be best. Okay, working flashlight, paper and pen for taking notes, driver's license, cell phone.

I call Caroline even though she will tell me not to go. She answers on the second ring.

"I know you're a night owl." I don't even say hello. "I think someone should know I'm going out for the evening. I can't bother Rachel since she gets up early to take the children to school," I whisper.

"You're headed for the churchyard, aren't you? To see her grave?" Caroline probably knew I was going to do it before I did.

"How the hell did you know?" I'm annoyed, but I refocus on my mission. "No matter. The night air is warm and seductive. I have to go."

"As long as you don't have any expectations, I think you'll be safe."

"The bad guys don't spend time in graveyards since there's nothing to steal." I know I'm trying to make it all right to go.

"There are bad guys wandering everywhere, but not many."

"I'm betting on statistical improbabilities. Wish me luck."

"Thanks for letting me know. Do carry my cell phone number on you. If anything looks wrong, call earlier rather than put it off."

"I appreciate your support. See you Wednesday."

I stick a baggie with a few of the fresh lemony butter cookies in my purse. Cooking kept me from being anxious while I waited for midnight. Everybody likes these. I'll include a fold of tin foil with some of the chocolate-dipped ginger slices. They are good, and to complete the evening's repast, a bottle of Auslese. It has a fruity flavor to mesh nicely with the lemon and ginger.

Angie! Stick to business. Can Lydia tell you anything about hidden accounts? No, she can't. Can Lydia tell you what

Dan likes for dinner? No, she's dead. Can Lydia tell you what Dan likes to do for sexual pleasure? No, she can't. She's dead.

As I wander around the house, pacing really, I picture Dan with me, hiking, traveling, having wine with dinner. When I try to picture myself with Dan, in his life of formal events with lawyers and judges, I feel scared. What would I say to Chief Justice Sullivan? What would I wear? I would want to take food to fancy catered dinners. I wouldn't fit in. This line of thought weighs me down. Here I am, on a nighttime adventure, putting myself down when what I want to do is quit this line of thinking and remember that I love to be out and about at night. Why can I still find ways to make myself sad?

Keys. Don't forget your keys. Leave the wine, it's too heavy, and this isn't a visit to the Queen of England. I wish it were a visit to Dan.

I drive across town with little traffic, allowing myself to daydream.

Dan comes into my house with a big bouquet of irises. He knows they're my favorite flower. He has a big smile on his lush lips and that darn twinkle in his eye.

He sweeps me into a full-body hug. "I can hardly wait," he says.

I put a finger on his lips. "We have to sample my wares first," I say, and we both laugh.

Give it up, Angie. Why should I? Daydreaming is partway there. The greatest athletes imagine themselves winning. I can imagine myself attaining my goal as well. Let's stick with the program.

What is the program? The question is, does Lydia answer questions? Does she have the final say for Dan? Does she rise from the dead to talk to him? The answer is no, no, and no. Then why the heck are you doing this? Just to make sure.

Nice night, a crescent moon, and no clouds. Now where

to park? Close by? Or somewhere a little farther from the main drag? How about in front of the church? It will look like you are someone with a big problem just waiting for the doors to open in the morning.

The city is so well lit at night, I don't need a flashlight. I'll just leave this weighty object on the front seat. On the other hand, if there is a bad guy, I could bean him with it. I'll take it with me.

Is this a delaying tactic? Get on with it.

I leave my car and head for the cemetery, opening and closing the gate without noise. There, you wouldn't want to wake the dead. Quit being so nervous, you ninny. Stealthy goes it. This graveyard's bigger than it looks from the street. If this path were any longer, the people who make bricks would be billionaires rather than just millionaires. What's your excuse now if a policeman comes down the path from the other way? I want to leave cookies on my mother's grave. That won't wash.

What's that noise?

"Lydia, my dearest Lydia. I still miss you terribly."

Oh no, he's here. He's in black, sitting on a little bench. Listen to him. You'd think he was putting down his favorite hunting dog, not grieving a long-dead wife. He is still passionate about her. He turns his head to look down. I can't hear what he's saying. *Give it up and go home.* I'll just move over behind this stone, then I'll be close enough to hear.

A hand reaches out of a grave and takes my ankle. *"Eeiia!"* I throw myself to the side to get away and go down. A sharp pain shoots up my leg.

"Who's there? Speak up or I'll shoot."

"Dan, it's me, Angie." My voice is the squeak of a sneak rather than the calm voice of someone who feels they belong in a graveyard at one in the morning.

"Come over here so I can see." Dan's voice is tight.

I pull myself up to lean on a gravestone when I really don't want to touch it. My right foot refuses to touch the ground.

Dan has a flashlight too. The light is fierce in my eyes. I hang my head to avoid the brightness and to avoid looking at him. I blink tears of pain and humiliation.

"What the devil are you doing here? Never mind, I can see you've hurt yourself. Is it your foot?" His voice turns sympathetic.

"I'm all right. This isn't what I want. I want to get out of here." Really, what I want is to leave town.

I put my foot down but the pain makes my leg give way. I crumple to the ground, and this time, my head hits something solid, maybe a gravestone, and darkness descends.

―――

As I come to awareness, I recognize Dan's voice but not the man who is questioning him.

"Whatever were the two of you doing in the graveyard at one in the morning?"

"We weren't together." Dan's voice is firm.

"Right," the deep male voice says with sarcasm. "You have talked more about her than any other client you've ever had."

"You know I visit Lydia sometimes at night. I don't know if Angie is stalking me or if there is some other reasonable explanation. I've never had the feeling she was dangerous."

"I'm not stalking you, and I'm not dangerous, except evidently to myself."

I try to sit up and realize I have a cast to the knee on one leg. Considerable pain races up and down the same leg. "What happened? What did they have to do?"

I cannot hold back my tears, and they run down my cheeks. When I brush them off, I realize my hands are covered in slick red clay. My jeans are cut off at the thigh on one side, confirming my realization: I am a total mess. The image I've tried to have around Dan is shot to hell, and I didn't even get to talk to Lydia. My crying is entirely out of my control.

Dan comes over. "You'll be all right." His voice is not sympathetic, but rather, a little rough. It's as though he's performing—not his usual warmth. "Your daughter is on the way. She'll help you. I hope you will be all right for mediation. That's three days from now. We don't want to put it off if we don't have to."

He turns and heads to the ER door with the man he is clearly close with. They walk with identical strides and posture. It's his other son Brent, and he pretended like he didn't see me. What a night this has been.

I lay back down on the gurney and try to relax some of the pain away. I can't stop crying. I sit up, thinking maybe that will help me be more comfortable. Down the hall, Rachel comes in as Dan and his son go out the wide sliding doors. They talk to each other, looking amiable. Is he reassuring her I am okay despite the bandages? Is he wishing her luck with rehabilitating me? Is he telling her to take me to a mental institution? Is he wondering why I can't cure myself since I'm a psychologist?

Oh! The pain eases. I guess the pain medication is kicking in. My brain goes fuzzy.

Rachel approaches my gurney. "Mom, don't go to sleep on me here. I have to get you home."

"I'm so tired. Dan hates me."

"Look! Sit up if you can. Here comes the wheelchair. I'll help you in. I've got the car at the door. Let's get going. We both need some sleep."

"What did Dan say?"

"You mean as he was leaving you with me in the emergency room?" Rachel sounds annoyed, but I know she's worried.

"Yes. What did he say to you?" I sound like the proverbial broken record. Can one say broken CD?

"He said he was sorry you got hurt."

"And what else?"

"Mom, you sound fixated on him in a strange way."

"What did he say?"

"He said you were a nice lady. He said he will be glad when your divorce is final."

That could mean anything. Tonight, with the drug-induced self-loathing, I believe it means he will be pleased to have me out of his way.

"Mom, please quit snuffling. The noise has me worried we will have to talk, then I won't get any sleep at all." Her voice softens. "I'm sorry you got hurt. I'll help you get settled. After a good night's sleep for both of us, we'll talk and make some sense of this."

"I'm sorry to be so much trouble." I try to stifle the hiccups.

"In the grand scheme of the world, you are so much more helpful to me than any trouble. We'll talk about it later. Move your good leg over here and put your weight on it."

"That hurts."

I find a way to get into the wheelchair. Rachel wheels me out to the curb, and I make the slow transfer into the car. With the crutch she hands me, I am more stable than I thought I would be. The cast feels strange, but I can bend my knee.

Rachel comes around, settles in, starts up the car. She turns to me. Her deep frown says it all. "Whatever were you up to?"

"I wanted to get a sense of Lydia's spirit." I say it definitely, as though it's true, but I sense she doesn't understand.

"It's been a while since I needed to be rescued. I remember how angry you were when the group left me behind after a long hike in the mountains. I had a wonderful day, but when I got back to the parking lot, the cars were gone. I had stopped to take some photos, and I figured they would be back to get me soon. I remember you driving me home late that night too."

"It still annoys me they didn't do something as simple as count. Every teacher or group leader of any kind knows to count the number of people to make sure everyone is back. I know what you're going to tell me. 'There were four cars, and everyone thought I was in a different car.' Still, there's no good excuse for what happened."

"I guess tonight's little adventure will mean you'll have to put a leash on me if I want to go out."

"Not a leash, but I am going to make sure you have an ID bracelet for when you run or go out anyplace by yourself. You never know when you're going to break an ankle, and Dan might not be there next time."

"I'm sure he won't be next time. He'll never see me again except for the mediation gig, which is three days from now."

She turns into my driveway, and I realize my car is in front of the church and tomorrow is Sunday.

"My car is going to need to be rescued. What a bother I am."

"Don't worry. Dan and Brent have parked it across the street."

"So, it was Brent. Dan didn't even introduce me to him." I wiggle off the seat and on to my crutches.

Rachel comes to steady me. "Dan said he'd call me tomorrow afternoon to see how you're doing."

"He just wants to make sure we don't have to reschedule the mediation. He wants to get rid of me." The tears start again.

"The idea of mediation is making you cry. I'll help you get in bed with a box of Kleenex. I have to go home and get some sleep. Tomorrow is a school day for the boys."

"Nobody loves me."

"See if you can handle the pain. Please try not to take any more of those pills. They depress you."

I cry while I get into my nightie. I cry while I scrunch my pillow. I have the foresight to put the phone by my bed.

It rings at 9:30 in the morning. Caroline's on the line.

"How did last night go?

"Total disaster is not a strong enough phrase."

"What happened?" Concern infuses her voice.

"When I got near Lydia, her ghost friend grabbed my ankle and broke it. Dan took me to the hospital."

"Whoa! I need some detail. Is it a bad break? Do you have a cast?"

"It's not a bad break, but I won't be walking to work out for a couple of weeks. Maybe I can do some of the arm machines. This cast will definitely not walk around the block, much less a mile and a half to the center."

"Do you have crutches?"

"All the working out we do is paying off. I discovered last night I'm a whiz on the crutches."

"It's supposed to be raining tomorrow morning, so I'll pick you up by car at eight. We'll see what you can do with your arms. When do you see the doctor?"

"I'll see her this afternoon. I think they put this cast on to keep me immobile. In a week or two, they'll give me a walking cast if the X-rays show I'm starting to mend."

"Have you started on extra calcium?"

"I will as soon as I get to the kitchen."

I FEEL SO MUCH BETTER the following morning. I am pleased I can drive, although it took a couple of slow turns around the block, getting used to using my other foot for the controls. After my time at the gym, where I got the same amount of attention Ms. Jackson received with her "wardrobe malfunction" at the Super Bowl, I go get yogurt and cheese and extra-strength calcium supplements. I also indulge in my favorite chocolate truffles to help raise my spirits. Everyone in the store is solicitous because of the cast, so I get cheerier as the morning wears on. The pain medication must be wearing off because I am feeling less fuzzy.

Caroline calls in the evening. "What else are you going to do to help yourself?" she asks.

"I did the chocolate thing."

"That helps nothing. Are you trying to keep the ankle elevated?"

"I'll work on that tonight."

"I hate to be nosy, but—"

"What am I telling everyone was the reason I was in the graveyard after midnight?" I interrupt.

Everyone asks the same question: was it a tryst with my lawyer? I wish it were so.

"I've told everyone I had a dream about Aunt Helen. She's there, so I could have been visiting her. You know, because of the dream."

"Pretty pathetic for an excuse."

"I wanted to commune with Dan's dead wife."

"Commune?"

"You know, get to know her."

"Whatever for?"

"I thought if I explained to her how lonely he must be without her, she'd be in favor of Dan and me getting together."

"Did it work for you?"

"No, by the time Dan saw me, I was filthy and crying in pain."

"Uh! Dan saw you?"

"Yeah. When I broke my ankle, he rescued me. At least, I think he did. I knocked myself unconscious for a while."

"I'm going to need a video to make sense of this. *Midnight Madness*, we'll call it. Was Dan also visiting Lydia?"

"Yes. Now you have it."

"So, Lydia gets more visitors at her grave at one in the morning than the Pope does at Easter. I'll have to go see for myself."

"No! I mean, I wouldn't recommend it."

"What! There's more?"

"A hand reached out of a grave to grab my ankle. That's what caused my fall."

"Was the hand Lydia's hand?"

"I don't think so. It felt masculine and strong."

"Maybe it was Lydia's dad, jealous of all the attention she gets."

"Don't make fun. I think it was a friend of Lydia's. I won't go back."

After lunch the next day, Rachel and I circle the church block until we find parking. The gate swings easily with a squeak. The brick path is clear to the bench where Dan was sitting. A thick root partially covering a hole adjacent to the path explains the ghostly grab. Oh darn! I'd like it to be real.

"Mom, you have a terrific imagination. A masculine hand? Where is the grave?"

"I never got that far. The way Dan waved his hand when he told me where she was indicated we should be able to see his office window from it. It's fairly new. Is that it?" I point.

The gravestone has roses carved on it. After the birth and death dates, the writing states: *Here lies Lydia, beloved wife, mother, friend. Gracious in living, remembered in death.*

"Gracious." I shake my head. There have been a lot of words applied to me during my life, but gracious is not one of them. Although thinking back, there was a neighbor when I was about twelve who said, 'Gracious me, what has she done now?'"

"I'll never fit into Dan's life."

"You're a ninny to think like that. If he decides you should be part of his life, the people around him will accept you. Is that what not fitting in means? People won't accept you?"

"Yes. That's how I'll know I don't fit in. People will be mean to me."

"You're lucky I have a dental appointment. We could be all afternoon figuring out how you got such a crazy idea."

Later, I head to my office to see clients. The building is wheelchair-accessible, so I swing myself up the ramp to the door.

I have three clients today. Melinda is a wild child. She complains how everyone is so mean to her. I sympathize, and she tells me what she does to pay back these awful people. I'm horrified. She lets me in on her original victimization. I want to go home and cry.

Maryann brings in Jason, who will go to school next year for the first time. She is worried his tantrums won't go over well with the teachers. Jason hits his mother because she won't give him candy. She tells me her husband only watches TV when he comes home from work. I wonder where to start.

Tara, who is fifteen, tells me she doesn't fit in. She's teased at school because she has a foreign last name and large breasts. I can see she has outsized boobs for a fifteen-year-old. I didn't get breasts until after all the other girls in the tenth grade, so I didn't fit in either. Some mean girls would comment about me when I was in the bathroom. I encourage Tara to think well of herself. I work to persuade her the opinion of others doesn't count. Why can't I be personally confident in who I am? Is "why" critical in this instance? Okay, Angie, time to think about supper.

CHAPTER TEN

*D*an and I stand in the parking lot behind his office building. He puts his file folders in the trunk of his car. The number of files is greatly reduced since Steve's deposition. We are headed for mediation, and I am not looking forward to it, although I have been reassured there will be no meeting or confrontation with Steve. I look up to distract myself. A flock of black birds lands in a nearby tree. Are blackbirds a good omen or a bad one? Since it's early spring, daffodils cluster at the edge of the parking lot, and a yellow pollen fog blurs the sky. I wouldn't mind spending a little time here with my camera, but not today. I have tried many times, but the perfect daffodil photo has escaped me.

"We both had quite a night on Saturday. I must tell you, Brent and I enjoyed the cookies and ginger. I took your other belongings to your daughter. What were you going to do with the food? Share it with Lydia?" With that statement, Dan's eyes go sad. "It's hard not to treat the deceased you loved as if they're alive."

I ignore his sad eyes. "I baked the cookies in the evening. I like to carry emergency supplies. I wasn't really thinking of trying to have tea with Lydia." I am trying to be light, but not quite making it. He was there to commune. And truly, if it had worked out, I would have happily communed with her spirit.

I will be resolute. I will not cry. He is being nice to try to make it as though we were both there for Lydia. I made such a mess of it.

"I see you have supplies for this mediation too." Dan gracefully moves from Lydia to now.

"I don't like to leave the house for the day not knowing where I'll find food." I try to smile. Birds or no birds, daffodils or no daffodils, I'm near tears.

He opens the door. "Let me store those crutches."

The panic handle is helpful. Despite the gym work, car entrances and exits are awkward. I do appreciate the smell and softness of the expensive leather I drop into.

He does not drive his gray Lincoln like an old man. The big car moves smoothly in and out of traffic. I can relax now that I know the fantasy about the two of us getting together was just that. The upside is I get to focus on the money rather than holding hands. A wave of unhappiness sinks in my chest. He saw me at my most disorganized, disarrayed, and dirty. I was actually dirty. The last several days have seen a flood of self-recriminations. He has not scolded me, but my thoughts of disgust with myself have run rampant.

The drive is longer than expected. I looked up the mediator's address because I like to know where I'm going. I understand Dan is taking the long way around to avoid the campus streets. This time would be ripe for students to be walking or driving to class. The long way will be shorter.

The center of the campus is brick buildings with brick walkways. Evidently, when they spiffed up the university many years ago, the provost owned the local brickyards. More recent additions are of stucco blocks, fascist in style, and ugly. I guess the earlier idealists gave way to the business factions.

Dan parks in front of a modern three-story office building. He retrieves my crutches from the back seat, opens my door, then removes his files from the trunk. His attitude seems to say, 'you got what you deserved.' He is polite but not solicitous.

The April sky has turned a bright, heavenly blue, known in these parts as Carolina Blue, and the pollen has dissipated with the stiff breeze. My preference would be to leave this place and picnic at a table by the river.

On a day like today, the menu would reflect the midpoint between winter and summer. Chicken or fish rather than beef or pork. Tuna fish is too prosaic, although it has overtones of childhood. Maybe turkey instead of chicken salad. Craisins and nuts would be a nice addition. I would roast the turkey breast smothered in butter. After chopping it finely, I would add a little mayonnaise cut with yogurt. Should I add a small amount of curry powder? The spice addition depends on my mood. But my fantasy is not to be.

Dan waves his arm, indicating I should go ahead, so I pull myself away from devising the menu for a picnic lunch, even though I hadn't gotten to dessert or drinks. The sandwiches are in a sack I can carry if I wrap the handles around my wrist.

The sounds here by the office building are of the busy street, not the gentle ripple of the river. The river would be high and fast with so much rain the last two weeks. I take a deep breath. Maybe I can keep the outside air with me.

Dan follows me up the path to the building. Before I can put my crutches in position to open the door, he is by my side.

"Thank you," I say.

"I was on crutches once. I know it's awkward to handle

doors." He sounds more sympathetic. My unhappiness must show on my face.

"Cheer up. This will be over soon." He nods at me, then the receptionist, who gives him a big smile. He indicates the way down the hall. He knows which door hides the conference room.

The room for this mediation event is luxurious compared to Dan's conference room. Modern leather sling chairs circle the chrome-and-glass table. The geometric-patterned carpet reminds me of a Miro. Vases of supersized pink and white Asian lilies with yellow Gerber daisies and fern-like greens brighten the room's neutral colors. We settle in to wait.

"What happens next?" I ask Dan.

"As soon as Mr. Merk and Mr. Castro settle in the other conference room, the mediator will come in here. She moves between the rooms, trying to get an agreement." He is slightly amused for no apparent reason.

Rat-ta-tat-tat, tat-tat comes the rhythmic knock at the door.

The door flies open, and our mediator presents herself, blond hair swept up, bright red lipstick, tall, and skinny. How do women keep their lipstick color like that? I would have to reapply mine every five minutes.

She hesitates only a second, then sprints into a full-body slam with Dan, who has risen to receive the onslaught. After he extricates himself from the armlock, she makes a sound like a mouse caught in a trap.

I watch, mesmerized, and realize my lip is curling. My mediator is clearly not a Zen master but a drama queen. At least she appears to be favorably disposed toward Dan. Look on the bright side, Angie.

Our mediator has one mode, rush-and-gush. I'm the next victim. First, she rushes over and embraces me. "Dan's told me all about you."

Then she skewers me with intelligent large blue eyes. I instantly succumb. I want to be her friend. I want to do what she wants me to do. Will she like the sandwiches I brought for her? What are her favorite chips? Maybe she lives on watercress and organic cheese. I'd be thin like her if I were brave like she is.

"Angie Merk, this is Dolly White. Dolly, this is Angie." Dan is amused by the introductions. Does he know I'm smitten with her?

She pulls a clean yellow pad from the Coach briefcase she flung onto the table. "I've reviewed the financials. A half-and-half split of marital assets is called for. Dan, I see you've excluded the value of Angie's new house because it was paid for with her mother's stocks and bonds. What about the debt on the house?"

"We had put the house in a separate category. I do apologize; I hadn't been concerned about the debt since she purchased the house after she left, but you're right, it was before the legal separation started, so the debt is marital property."

"We may be able to use that at some point." She turns her full attention on me. "Ms. Merk, do you have any questions?"

"Why the heck didn't he accept my first lowball offer? What was he thinking when he flouted his inheritance appreciating at eight percent?"

"He has the strange notion you abandoned him for no reason, so all the marital assets are his. On the second question, he has reduced the suggested appreciation to five percent. Your son has a more balanced view. He wants the division to be fair, and Mr. Merk is allowing your son—Paul, is it?—to speak for him."

"Remember his inheritance was commingled with other income in his Merrill Lynch account. When he got it, he put it right into what he considered his account," I tell her.

"Right! I'll go down the hall and see what their concerns are." She pats my arm, throws the yellow pad into the briefcase, and rushes out.

Dan looks at me expectantly.

"I've never seen a mediator before. Is she typical?" I turn to face him. My mood is more upbeat than at any time this morning.

"She has a style honed by the big city. She lived in New York for a while. But she has a bleeding heart. She'll focus on what's important to each side, so she usually gets the job done in record time."

"What happens now?"

"We sit here until she comes back. We have no idea when that will be." He hesitates. "Do you have plans for the weekend?"

"Are you suggesting we'll be here for several days?"

I get the big smile and twinkle eyes. I'm aware just the two of us are sitting next to each other in this quiet room. I can smell his masculinity.

"We'll probably be finished around lunchtime. Did you bring enough sandwiches for both sides or just for us?" he asks with a smile.

"I don't *not* feed people. Besides, the other side includes my son. I probably have enough sandwiches to include the secretary since I always plan a little extra. Paul eats plenty, so I planned on that . . . I'm grateful you'll still talk to me after the graveyard debacle."

"You frightened me more than anything. I have been reluctant to adopt cell phone technology, but I was so relieved to be able to contact medical help immediately. I was afraid you were dead."

"When I woke up in the hospital, I had enough sense to wish I had died. I hate to cause so much trouble."

"I've lived long enough to see real trouble, and that wasn't it." He hesitates. "When I was in the war and we were on patrol, people got badly hurt. There was no cell phone and no helicopter, so people died. Some of them were friends. When I was a pilot, it was easier because you didn't see what was happening on the ground."

Tears come to his eyes. "But enough of that. I'm here, doing work I love. I'm enjoying my old age and grateful for it. Even last weekend, I went quail hunting with friends."

People tell me what comes to their minds. Do they do it because I'm a psychologist, or am I a psychologist because people empty their brains when I look at them? I try to avoid looking at people, but you can't flirt by avoiding someone's eyes.

"Where do you go hunting?"

"I have property near Chester on the Black River. It's been in the family for generations. There's a lodge there. Sometimes I invite friends to come, sometimes I enjoy the lodge by myself. The best month to go there is October. Reliably, the trees have color, and the stream is clear. When you breathe deeply, it feels good. I love to get out in the woods early in the morning when it's clear and frosty."

"My friends and I have kayaked on the Black River. In some places, the trees form an archway almost enclosing the water. I couldn't tell you if we were near Chester or not. The other thing I remember about the trip was the amount of wildlife. A great blue heron took it upon himself to fly ahead of us down the river. There were turtles galore on every downed tree. The trip was near perfect with slow, deep water and an easy-to-find place to take out the kayaks."

"It's a wonderful place to hunt."

"Do you really shoot the quail?" I ask him.

He smiles. "You're a city girl, aren't you?"

"Yes and no. I live in the city, but I also love to be out traipsing in the woods, morning, noon, and night. Our kayaking and hiking trips are important for me to feel right with the world. I shoot animals too, but with my camera. You'll have to see some of my images. I don't want to be critical, but some of the prints you have in your office are pretty faded. I'd be honored to supply your office with up-to-date nature prints."

I tilt my head and raise my eyebrows. I want him to understand I love our conversation. Do any of my machinations make any difference?

"We're about to redo the office. I'll keep your offer under advisement. Do you sell your prints? Are they all nature prints? I'll bet they are since the woods and rivers are your natural habitat." He gives me the twinkle smile.

"I display framed prints in a gallery on Duncan Street. I sell some prints at markets and festivals. I'm having trouble switching to digital technology. The camera isn't the problem for me. It's the same except there's a sensor instead of film where the light falls. I just don't want to sit in front of a computer to learn the system everyone is using now. I just can't get myself to fuss with each image. In the field, I fiddle around until I get the image I want."

When I check in on his eyes, they are softly focused on me.

"One of the reasons I took up photography," I continue, "was to spend time in the woods looking for beauty. They say you have to start with a good photo, even with a digital image. I know Ansel Adams worked on each print, but I personally would rather spend time seeing the beauty, the symmetry and asymmetry of flowers and trees and skies, and work on a photo there to obtain classic balance and interest."

"How do you get time to look at flowers if you're still working, tending to your house, and having parties? Thinking back on it, I did enjoy your Christmas do. It was exceptional. People were so friendly, and the food was unbelievably good."

"For me, the secret is not having a television. I'd rather cook for friends than sit. I know I miss important stuff, and I'm never up to date on celebrities. I try to catch a summary of the news in an occasional *New York Times* Sunday issue. I sometimes try the recipes in the Sunday magazine. Did you try the vegetable terrine at the party? That was a new recipe for me. It came from the *Times*."

"Was the terrine only vegetables?" he asked.

"The combination of mushrooms and cashew butter makes it taste rich, doesn't it?"

I love his smile. I almost reach out to touch him. Instead, I smile and try to look at him with soft eyes.

He takes my hands in his. All thoughts of where we are and what is at stake disappear.

"Dan, you know all about me. Tell me about your children."

He looks at me and sighs. "No, I don't know all about you." A faint blush comes over his face. Am I imagining he's physically attracted to me?

Rat-ta-tat-tat, tat-tat.

Dan pulls back and drops my hands. Strangely, the trust and the partnership and the mystery around the real estate money pop back into my head.

"Here she comes," he says.

Dolly performs the same flouncy entrance. Not startled this time, I enjoy her grace. She gives me her undiluted attention.

"What do Paul and Mr. Merk say about accounts other than the Merrill Lynch account?" I ask, thinking they probably told the truth if she threatened them.

"I asked them if there was anything not on the table. I pretty much threatened them with long prison sentences if there was. They both said there was nothing else. I sympathize with your worry there might be."

"I guess there isn't any place to go with that. If it's hidden, it's hidden. What about other stuff?"

She pirouettes into a chair. "Okay, they are agreeable to splitting all the artwork. Paul will take responsibility for being fair, he says he can do it. Do you trust him?"

"Yes, I do. Besides, I don't want to bother with all that stuff. I'd rather split the value, but, no doubt, agreeing on a valuation would be impossible."

"Angie! It's half yours. Find a way to deal with it." Dan's voice is stern.

"Okay, okay, I'll find a way."

"Now with regard to the Merrill Lynch account, Mr. Merk has agreed to split it if you recognize his inheritance in some way." Dolly watches my reaction.

"What do you think of adding twenty K to the eighty K he claims his mother and his aunt Dorothy left him? I'm willing to take that off the top," I respond.

"A generous offer, his inheritance really is commingled." She glances at her notes before her eyes meet mine. "One item Mr. Merk is adamant about is the issue of alimony. He says, and I quote, 'This is not a fucking alimony case.'" She tightens her lips and frowns.

"Has he agreed to split his pension?" Dan asks.

"He's not having any problem with his pension. The idea of alimony enrages him. I guess it implies he has done something wrong."

"I always thought of half his pension as alimony. I don't think I've ever even used the word," I say.

"Since I didn't see it on the list, I mentioned it. He steamed a bit, but his lawyer was able to calm him down. Mr. Merk claimed it was a deal breaker."

He wants to get away with his stance that he has never done anything wrong. Give it up, Angie. Keep it civil. What he thinks is not your problem. Get the money.

"We can give him that one and the inheritance add-on. Did he accept half the debt on my house?" I ask.

"He doesn't want to accept any debt. But he's willing to add that in if you'll accept the tax-assessed value of the marital home."

"So, the value of the house will be added into the pile of money before the split?" I had gone with the fiction the house was his.

"Yes." She nods.

"What do you think?" I turn to Dan. "I'm satisfied."

"Let me talk to my client alone while you carry this back to them. We reserve the right, at this time, to change our minds about anything."

"Right, I'll carry this to them and see where things are." She rushes out.

I take Dan's warm hand in my chilled one. "So, what do you think?"

"I think you will be a wealthy woman after the court hearing."

I will be able to help my children. Maybe I'll buy myself a spiffier car. "So, the next step is a court hearing? Will the divorce be final then?" I ask.

"I'll see if we can get an early date since this has lasted long enough. I'm glad I convinced you not to worry about hidden money. The Merrill Lynch account split will do nicely for you."

Rat-ta-tat-tat, tat-tat.

I didn't get a hand squeeze in. I push myself back in my chair.

Dolly enters and raises both arms above her head like an Olympic track runner winning the gold. "Ta-da! We have an agreement. Let's have lunch. I'm having my secretary type up my notes in a more legal format."

She turns to me. "Pass out the sandwiches and chips. I

told my assistant to bring sweet tea and paper plates. What kind of sandwiches are they?"

"Meat and cheese, as in gourmet prosciutto and perfectly ripened Saga. I used the best bread I could find."

"Toss one over here and give me a few corn chips."

I made the sandwiches last night, but they are still super fresh. I didn't brag to her about the secret topping I use since it's a trade secret. I put the tiniest amount of peanut butter in the mayo. It adds a little richness and the taste is undetectable unless you think about peanuts. The mayo and the peanut butter don't want to mix, but they do with a little effort.

We pull chairs close to the conference table, and I set out napkins. When I pass out the sandwiches and chips, I consider taking the Olympic position of hands held high, but sanity prevails. As often happens, there is a lull in conversation as we unwrap our sandwiches. The rustle of chip bags tickles my brain. I'm fond of chips of every kind.

Dolly falls right in line. "This is perhaps the best sandwich I've ever eaten. The balance of all the elements is just right. The taste of the meat, cheese, and slightly altered mayonnaise go together nicely. Since I lived in New York City for years, I know a superior sandwich when I come across it. Congratulations."

Dan stops chewing for a second. "I concur." Then he takes another healthy bite.

Skinny Dolly reaches for a bag of chips. "I suppose I should take the rest of these sandwiches down the hall to the other group. Anybody want a second one before they disappear?"

Dan sheepishly puts out a hand. Dolly drops one into it and scoops the rest of them into my bag and heads toward the hall. "Mr. Castro said he wanted to talk to Steve and Paul for a minute, but now they've had their minute. I'll be right back."

"She has had some rough times." Dan chews thoughtfully. "When she first came to Columbia, she couldn't find a job. The old firms didn't want to take on her kind of energy. So, she started her own firm and has been quite successful. I was sorry she never applied to my firm. She would have enlivened the place. Old men who run things have made long-term disastrous mistakes by trying to shut out women. I've seen a lot of it during my time. I have had women partners over the years and been fond of them Have you ever run into blatant discrimination?"

"Oh yeah! Those incidents are too numerous to go into. Worth noting, however, some have been life-changing. The group of psychologists I'm with is an all-female group, as is the kayaking and hiking group. We are not anti-male, far from it. The groups are a mix of married and currently single."

Dan smiles. "I like the use of 'currently.' You have mentioned kayaking several times. Do you kayak white-water rivers or swamps and slower water? I've never kayaked myself, but I do see an occasional small group on the Black River."

"We kayak a lot of swamp areas and slow tidal rivers near the coast. Once in a while, we see a little water over rocks. Some of the group members are skilled enough for white water, not me. When I retire shortly, I will—"

Rat-ta-tat-tat, tat-tat. The knock comes just as I am about to offer to take him on the outing we use for newbies, a lovely millpond and quiet stream near Camden. When Dolly comes in, I see her in a new light. Despite her vulnerabilities, she's strong beneath the blond hair and perfect makeup.

I smile at her. "I am impressed by your energy. Where do you work out?"

"I use the same gym Dan does. I don't use his trainer

though. She's a drill sergeant disguised as Doris Day." She and Dan laugh together about the gym scene.

I decide I don't want to feel left out. "The gym class I attend is around the corner from my house. Our maestro is Ted Jackson. He was famous as a pro bicyclist."

"He owned the bike shop, didn't he?" Dan asks.

"Yes, you know the shop? Do you ride?" I ask.

"I rode with his team for a couple of years. Do you like to ride?" His eyes laser on mine.

We have a tête-à-tête. The rest of the world falls away.

"I'm still hungry. Do you have any cookies stored away in the bag?" Dolly asks with amusement.

I give her two large chocolate chip cookies to which I have added some candied ginger. Dan and I settle in with our dessert. Dolly takes cookies to the others.

I turn to Dan. "I don't know anything about your other children. I feel I know Phil because we had the Twitter exposé. You have a sense about Valerie, Paul, and Rachel."

"I have three children. Brent, the middle child, is a corporate lawyer. His wife and three children are too good to be believed. I think when their youngest child is a teenager, they will have their hands full. She is pretty and bright and she does well in school but is a tad willful." He rolls his eyes.

"That, of course, is the problem," he continues. "She's so delightful she gets away with murder. My two grandsons in that family are serious students and athletes. I take them all hunting with me. My oldest child is Karen. She and her mother had a difficult relationship when she was a teenager. Often, when I'd come home from work, one or the other of them would be in their room crying. I couldn't fix it."

"Of course, someone on the inside of the family can't fix something like that. Did they get on better before Lydia passed?"

"Oh, yes, they found out they had a joint passion for

clothes shopping. They didn't buy much, but when they spent the afternoon at the mall, they would both be extremely cheerful. Karen now manages a women's fancy clothing store. She's divorced and has custody of her fourteen-year-old son. Then there's the grandson Mark with the sexual prowess." He flashes the twinkle smile.

"My third child, Phil, Mark's dad, was more problematic. He spent time managing an upscale restaurant in Charleston. He didn't graduate from college because he was using too much marijuana. He moved to Columbia to manage a restaurant here and now is more settled with a lovely wife and Mark"

"You've had as much action with your children as I have with mine. It is nice when they stabilize. Valerie, my oldest, sounds like Brent. My son sounds like your Phil," I tell him.

"I met Valerie when she was in town for your big shindig. She lives in Colorado if I remember correctly." He grins. "She came and talked to me at the party. I think she wanted to check me out."

"You passed her test with flying colors. I do keep her informed about our progress here."

Somehow, I know he wants to take my hand. He gives his head a little shake. He rises and hands me my crutch.

"I was so sure we would be finished here by lunch, I made client appointments this afternoon," he says.

"I didn't know how long it would take. I'm up to date on my invoicing so . . ." I let my voice trail off. I give him a big smile with lingering eye contact. I am trying to flirt.

When he doesn't break, I continue, "I'm going to indulge in a little Lydia therapy. I'll take the freeway out to Columbiana Mall."

He takes the reference well and gives me the twinkle smile. "Have fun."

The spell is broken, but I can tell his mood is as upbeat as mine. He drops me off in his office parking lot where my car is. When he opens the door to his building, he turns and gives a cheery wave. I am afraid I will faint. I am tempted to run across the parking lot and practice the full-body slam that worked so well for Dolly. I want his body next to mine. Since we have talked intimately, I know he likes me. I can just tell.

When I get home after my wandering in the mall, another invoice is tucked in the mail slot. This one is scary. Worse, the fee for the mediation is yet to come. I curl up on the couch and dial Rachel. "Sweetie, why is he doing this to me?"

"Doing what?"

"He was pleasant at mediation. Then he sends me a bill that would buy me a full-length mink coat."

"Just pay it. You don't need a full-length mink coat—this is South Carolina."

"True, but didn't you just get a second bill from your oncologist?"

"No, it was the plastic surgeon. He did such a good job of restructuring my boobs, I'd pay him anything. Let's both work along. We'll find a way out. Hopefully, the grant I'm working on will come through," she says.

"You need that grant to live on. Medical debt sinks a lot of middle-class folks, but if the results of the mediation hold up, we'll have more money to work with," I say.

"I'll find a way. I'm only a little desperate. Besides, DeeDee has said she will help with whatever insurance doesn't pay. Did insurance cover your emergency-room bill?"

"Luckily, they don't look at whose fault it was for a broken ankle. Insurance paid almost all. I do like the convenience of medical availability. The ankle is almost as good as new."

"I know you're going to the museum-opening gala next month. Do take it easy."

"No one will invite me to dance. I'll eat too much snack food. I'm sure I'll have a great time."

"Good things happen when you improve your attitude."

My sarcasm doesn't get to her. "At least I'm not holed up, and I'll have some money as soon as the divorce has been accepted by the court."

"When is the court date for the final hearing?"

"I don't know. Dan said he would try to get an early date."

"When you become wealthy, maybe some man will be interested in your money."

"I won't have that much after I pay Dan's bills."

"You'll have plenty," she says.

"In fact, I will." I nod and smile.

CHAPTER ELEVEN

I watch for uneven sidewalk as we head toward the gym, but my mind is on alligators. I don't want Caroline to know I have major concerns about our weekend trip with the group. "You know how Zoey is afraid of bears, I wonder where that comes from."

When we're in the mountains, Zoey is very careful where she sleeps. If it's a big tent, she sleeps in the middle. If it's a cabin, she sleeps away from a window. She is afraid a bear will come right to where she sleeps and get her.

On an earlier trip, I had a can of tuna as part of my lunch. When I opened the can, she panicked, "No! Angie! Put the tin in a plastic bag! Bears have a super sense of smell, and they love fish." She accompanied her screech with a dance over the leaves. I did what she asked, and she calmed down a bit. "We don't ever bring tuna or salmon on a hike," she had said. "It's too dangerous."

Caroline laughs. "You want to know about alligators, don't you?"

Bears don't scare me like alligators do. Alligators have

enormous teeth and jaws so tough you can imagine them clamping down and devouring your leg or arm. They have been known to eat dogs and two-year-old children. "Will there be alligators on our paddle in the low-country this weekend?"

"Sure," she says without a blip.

My heart rate and blood pressure rise and I begin to sweat. "We won't see the alligators, will we? They won't try to overturn our kayaks so they can drown us and eat us, will they?" I try to keep my voice steady, but it squeaks.

"We will probably see one, but no, they won't try to eat us. Usually, they're sunning on a sandbar. Occasionally, you see their eyes just about the waterline. When I see their eyes in the water, they are hanging out in a lagoon area, not near a river. If I see their eyes, I try to paddle slowly away from them."

"You've seen their eyes above the water and you just paddle away? You don't start screaming for help?"

"They're so interesting, so prehistoric looking. It's true, I wouldn't want to find myself swimming with them."

"I wonder if I should go on this trip. The cabin is on the edge of having too many people."

"Don't be silly. We'll be in the river, and the alligator will be on the sandbar. There's plenty of room in the cabin. The cabin sleeps eight, and there are eight of us going."

"Does anyone else worry about an alligator attack?"

"Not that I know of. Even our bear-phobic member isn't concerned about alligators. They pretty much stay where they are in the sun."

"Whoa! You say, 'pretty much.'"

"Right. I did see one move once. It took a baby alligator in its teeth and moved it up an embankment. Most unusual to see one in action."

"So, they don't always just sit on a sandbar?"

"They're animals, just like we're animals. This animal is sweaty and hot. I can't wait to get inside where it's cool."

Her distraction suits me, and soon, we are in the weight room, lifting whatever weight we can manage. I am left with the assumption I will go on the paddle.

Friday morning comes quickly. Caroline and I settle the equipment, the food, and the other members into the truck. We head east toward the Low Country, gossiping easily. Not quite two hours on the freeway toward Charleston, then north on Highway 1, and with careful looking, we find the one-lane dirt road leading into the woods. It seems like we go a long way through the pine forest before we come to the two-story structure described as a primitive cabin. Luckily, it sits in the middle of a clearing, or we never would have seen it.

Every trip is different, and every cabin is different. At the front of this one, narrow wooden stairs lead to a main room and kitchen. A large wooden platform for bedrolls is over the main room and accessed by a ladder. A short path behind the cabin leads to the outhouse, which is going to require focus in the middle-of-the-night trips to the bathroom. We haul in the food and water, our sleeping bags, and backpacks. There is running water in the kitchen and electricity for the apartment-sized refrigerator in the narrow galley kitchen.

Since it is still early in the day, we decide to pack a lunch and hike farther down the road to see if we can get to the river. It's fresher here than in the city, with a slight breeze and shade over the trail.

I make an effort to walk next to Zoey because I have a question for her. "Do you worry about alligators? Caroline tells me they are not scary."

"One of the reasons I am particularly interested in this trip is to see the wildlife on this undeveloped stretch of the river."

She has not answered my question, so I persist. "When I think of wildlife, I think of a deer bounding through the woods or a turtle or a blue heron or a butterfly, not an alligator."

"I think of alligators as part of the natural scene here. They're not elusive but generally not active. They're more like the turtles, just sitting there in the sun. I have seen them move into the water, and they can move fast."

"What do you do if one comes into the river toward you?"

"I guess you bop it on the head with your paddle. Of course, it's likely to bite off your paddle." She smiles broadly. "I guess that's the origin of . . ."

I join in: "Up the creek without a paddle." Even as we laugh, my breakfast feels unsettled.

The group ahead of us waves and shouts, and when we look, we can see the river and the road's end. The broad river is so slow you have to see something floating on it to realize it's moving. The cleared area between the road and river is large enough for vehicle turnaround. We will paddle upstream and then return to this place. No other vehicles are parked here, so maybe we will be the only people on this stretch of the river tomorrow. In a moment of silence, only the cicadas are noisy. We eat lunch, sitting on a downed log, and return to the cabin. The afternoon is quiet as everyone reads or naps.

There are burners but no oven for the dinner crew. The uncooked potatoes get peeled and fried, the uncooked frozen fish is poached rather than baked. The coolers yield salad makings and tomatoes to be served with basil and vinaigrette. Caroline and I shuck and boil the corn. A typical summer meal.

Tiki torches keep the mosquitoes at bay as we eat outside at the picnic table. This evening's game is Spoons. Everyone else has played it except Linda and me. We sit around the table with seven spoons for eight people and three playing cards dealt to each. When a player gets three of a kind in their hand, they take a spoon.

I am so focused on the cards I don't notice the spoons are gone until everyone laughs. The game is repeated. I soon learn to pay attention to the spoons as well as the cards, but if I lose focus for a second, the spoons disappear. Since we want to get an early start to beat the heat as much as we can, we turn in.

"Will you please stick by me tomorrow?" I whisper to Caroline as we settle in our sleeping bags. "You're my friend; you're faster than I am, but please stay by me. Promise you will or I won't go on the paddle."

"I'll do that." Her voice is serious.

In the morning, the sky is overcast as we head to unload the trailer. "That was my favorite breakfast—lots of fresh fruit, yogurt, and granola," Zoey comments. "We'll get a good early start since no one is delayed with cooking a breakfast."

Although I nod in agreement, I wonder if there is an alligator in the woods near the sandbar where our kayaks now line the edge of the water.

I turn to Caroline beside me. "You promised."

She smiles. "I do try to keep my promises. What was it now?"

"Don't joke with me, it's not funny."

I pull my kayak halfway into the water and get in. After I'm settled, Caroline pushes my kayak into the slow dark water. Then Zoey pushes Caroline into the river. Lazy paddling keeps us near the sandbar until everyone is in the river. We pair up and chat and paddle. The woods come to the edge of the river for a while. On a wide curve, the water flows a little faster on the far side of a sandbar.

"Let's not get hung up in the shallow area by the sandbar. Come this way." Caroline waves to show me where to go.

Since the last thing I want is to get stuck on a sandbar, I

paddle frantically toward her. Then I see it. The alligator stretches out at the end of the sandbar. The humongous monster is resting with its eyes closed, the great mouth smiling, and the armor-plated body reminiscent of a dinosaur. It looks prehistoric, yet here, in this bucolic scene, it is all too real. When I become curious, I stop paddling. I forgot to ask if they're sensitive to sounds. If I yell at Caroline, will it come at me? She points to make certain I see it. I nod away my trance and begin paddling again. I'm pleased I have seen an alligator in the wild. The animal didn't attack, so I survived and now have a story to tell.

The several hours of the paddle are immensely satisfying for me. Blue herons, cormorants, osprey, ducks, turtles, a snake, and several deer keep the photographers among us happy. We pass several sandbars, but no other alligators, making me doubly pleased I did see one. The river in the part we're paddling is special since it is slightly tide-dependent. Water pushes uphill with the incoming tide and downhill when the tide goes out. We have timed it well, so the paddling is easy all the way.

As is typical after a morning outing, my peanut-butter-and-fig-jam sandwich is delicious. We have returned to the picnic table at the cabin and share chips and cookies.

"Did everyone see the alligator on the first sandbar we passed?" I'm uncertain what answer I want. I want them to have seen it because it was so interesting, and I want them not to have seen it so my viewing stands out.

"I've seen a lot of alligators near the coast of South Carolina," Zoey starts, "but that was one of the biggest."

My chest expands with pride. "Do they all have a disarming grin like this one?"

Caroline laughs. "Underneath the grin is a set of choppers unmatched in land animals. Did you know you can guesstimate the length of an alligator by the distance, in inches, between their eyes? His eyes were about twelve inches apart, so don't you think about twelve feet?" she asks Catherine.

"I made a similar guess," Alice pipes up. "Twelve or thirteen feet. It was a big one."

Before other stories can start, I push in. "Let's give it a name. How about Frank?"

Other names are proposed—Jack or Mortimer—but the final decision is Tony.

"All the names proposed have been male names, but I guess Leslie or Monica just doesn't fit," I note.

Caroline segues into the practical matters at hand. "This has been a wonderful trip, and I could sit here and ham it up with you all forever, but we do need to clean up the cabin and pack and get on our way. How about we celebrate our outing with a meal at the fish place near the stadium? Let's aim for five thirty."

There is general agreement, and we all head into the cabin to start the process. The unspoken rule is no one heads home until all the work is accomplished; the cabin should be cleaner than when we arrived. If someone has a valid excuse, they can exit early.

The restaurant is casual and comfortable, and spirits are high. I enjoy the grilled salmon and grits and refuse a second glass of wine.

"I would love to truly relax, and I am not driving, but I want to review the official mediation papers before I meet with Dan on Monday, and tomorrow is a family-picnic day. I want to make sure I am prepared for the meeting. Is this a good time to leave." I turn to Caroline.

Caroline looks at me with a twinkle in her eye. "So, you are meeting with Dan. What's on the menu?"

People around the table are puzzled. However, I am determined Caroline will not best me. "The menu is a secret, but it does, in part, involve food."

She hoots with laughter as she rises to go. I smile at her and we leave. There may be telephone gossip this evening.

Monday turns out overcast with rain predicted later in the afternoon. As is usual, I am early for our meeting, and I sit in Dan's conference room and think about feeding him. Am I in love with Dan, or am I in love with the idea of feeding him? The thought amuses me as I conclude it doesn't make any difference.

I have brought some slices of homemade zucchini bread; it is dark and super moist. I have some room-temperature cream cheese, a knife, two paper plates, and two linen napkins, the perfect balance of casual and formal for a meeting about divorce mediation.

I wonder if people eat alligator meat. I suppose they do, but is it tough and have to sit in a marinade for, what, days? Do you have to pound it like abalone? Do you have to grind it with lots of spices to make it "palatable?" What do you serve on the side?

Dan comes into the room, smiling. "How are you?"

"I have to ask . . ." I pause. "Have you ever eaten alligator meat?"

He is visibly taken aback. "I presumed, evidently wrongly, we were going to discuss the mediation final report this morning." He gives me the twinkle smile.

"We can get to that in a minute. I'm wondering how people eat alligator."

"You have to catch and kill one first. In South Carolina, there are raffle tickets and a lottery to even be able to hunt one. I was on a hunt once."

"Please tell me about it. I know the topic for today is different, but I want to know about alligators since I saw one in the wild last Saturday and I was impressed."

He cocks his head, as a good storyteller does. "About a decade ago, a friend of mine won a lottery ticket to engage in a hunt. He had been in the lottery for a couple of years, and he had a better chance that year. The Department of Natural Resources somehow weighs persistency into the chances, and he finally got a ticket. Bob, the ticket holder, needed two sidekicks. He asked Will and me to join him, and he told us where to be and what to bring. Bob has a boat and some land a little closer to the coast than my property. I am inserting that information so you will know I have never seen an alligator on my property." Dan settles himself in his chair. "We arranged to meet on his dock at seven in the morning since we were going to hunt in the daylight rather than at night. A nighttime hunt seems a little spooky to me, even though everyone has flashlights in order to see the alligator's eyes above the water. I understand they shine green and luminescent.

"The weather was overcast on the day of the hunt," he continues, "even foggy, with rain predicted for the afternoon. Bob's boat was rather small for the three of us and an alligator, but not knowing what was going to happen, I didn't ask the obvious question. When I got in the boat, I saw the loop, the snare, the fishing line with the snatch hook, a jab stick. All, I suspected, would be critical pieces of equipment. As we motored into the river and headed downstream, Bob turned to me and said, 'I know you carry a gun, so you get to shoot the animal once it is close enough and has the jab stick in it. The recommended placement of the bullet is at the back of the head, just behind the bony ridge into the brain. If you have to shoot it more than once, go ahead. We want it to be quiet for transport back to shore."

"Wow. So, you have to shoot the alligator in order to kill it and get the meat. I'm interested in how it worked out."

. . .

"Angie, I must confess, I was tempted to tell him I wasn't up for it, but I was with two buddies who were cheerfully contemplating the morning's adventure, what could I do? I went along. We arrived at a kind of cove area, maybe an oxbow, where the water was quiet. Bob told us he had seen several large gators in the area over the last years. We saw two alligators and decided to go after the larger one. Bill, who does a lot of fishing, cast the snatch hook; he was accurate, and the big animal hooked to the line."

"You must have been close to the animal to be able to hook it."

"We could see it clearly under the water with its eyes watching us above the water.'

"Will and Bob talked back and forth. Slowly the huge beast surfaced and was pulled toward the boat. I was scared, but I knew I had to do my part, and I pulled my gun out. Things moved fast. Bob used the jab stick and pulled the gator, who thrashed about, close to the boat. I moved into position, got a sight on the bony ridge, and pulled the trigger. We hooked the mouth and put a lot of electrical tape around it. Bob insisted we tie the legs, telling us he was once on a hunt and the gator wasn't dead after the gunshot, and the crew almost went swimming. We put the tag on the tail and headed home."

This story was accompanied by hand and body gestures while I watched and listened with rapt attention.

"Unreal," I exclaim. "And I think I've had adventures." Then my original question returns. "What did you do with the meat?"

"Bob took the animal to a processor, and we got carefully wrapped and frozen parcels. I believe I still have some packets in my garage freezer. You're welcome to them if you're interested."

"I'll do a little research and see if the meat is worth the

trouble. I did like the story of the hunt." I put my hand on the bag where I have the zucchini bread. "I do have something here I know is tasty."

"This is very kind of you to bring me homemade treats when you come to see me. I appreciate it more than I can say."

He busies himself spreading the cream cheese. If someone looked into the room, they would see me looking fondly at him.

After our snack, he turns to me. "We are still going to have a meeting about the mediation report."

"I have looked over the report with care, and I believe it is just fine, better than I would have expected. You and Dolly did a great job, so I will have plenty of money. I'll be able to help Rachel with her medical bills. I couldn't be more pleased and grateful."

"I guess we have had our meeting as I am also of the opinion the report is ready to go. The next stop is the divorce court. I'll see how soon we can get on the docket. It can take weeks. I'll give you a call as soon as I know."

He gives me the twinkle smile and leaves. I put the remnants of our snack in my bag and head to the office as I still have clients this afternoon.

CHAPTER TWELVE

My meeting with Dan slips to the back of my mind. What comes to the fore is the Columbia Museum of Art gala. The museum galas are a substantial social event in Columbia. I go every time they have one. Zoey and Frank have invited me to go with them.

Caroline, who doesn't go, is going to help me dress for the event. I'm going to her house for her take on my clothes. She lives in a four-bedroom ranch in a good part of town. She's lived there all her life. It was her mother's house. She took care of her mother until her mother's death, then it became Caroline's house. From what she says, the upkeep keeps her poor, but she isn't in a position to make a change.

Along the driveway, she has hostas in pots. The variegated leaves with the spiked flowers give me pause.

I give a knock on the back door and push it open. "Hello, hello," I shout down the hall, passing the kitchen.

Her kitchen is white, clean, and refurbished. She had her laundry room redone too. A large dryer sits on top of a large washer. I suppose convenience is enhanced, but it doesn't look right. I expect the washer and dryer to sit beside each other. The table for folding clothes has a couple of sweaters ready to put away, and the rack for hanging clothes has matching hangers. How can she complain about money?

"Be with you in a minute." Her voice comes from the room she uses as her office.

I sit down in the family room, with the lounge chair and TV, to wait. The room smells vaguely of cat, so I look around. Sure enough, the ancient tabby is curled on top of the couch.

Caroline comes quickly, holding fabric in front of her. "I found it this morning. I'm not convinced it's the right shade."

She hands me a big paisley shawl in shades of pink and mauve. I pull the long skirt I plan to wear out of its protective covering.

"Wow! It's perfect," I say.

"That skirt is slinky." She whistles. "I see you're walking well enough. You appear to be over the ankle injury. Will you be able to dance?"

I straighten in my seat. "All the walking we do makes my legs okay. Besides, the slit only goes to my knee. Believe me when I say, if I can walk, I can dance."

"You'll look great. What's the blouse like?"

I pull it from the hanger. "See, it's pink, a drapey material, with a low vee in front, no sleeves, hip length. It has all the perfect characteristics. The shawl will pull it all together exquisitely."

"Will you wear earrings?"

"Yes, gold dangling ones." I get up and gather the items into the bag.

"Sounds lovely. I hope you have a great time. Do you expect Dan to be there?" she asks.

"I don't know if I've ever seen him at a gala. But I wouldn't have noticed. He would have been with Lydia, so I wouldn't have paid any attention to him."

We get up and head to the back door. Caroline accidentally lifts up her purse by one handle. Without its balance, the elements of her personal life rain down to puddle at her feet: several colors of lipstick, eye shadow, a comb. The Trojan condoms stand out in the detritus.

I raise one eyebrow. "I see you are prepared for whatever might come your way."

"Here, take a couple. Look at you, so surprised. Who knows, maybe you'll get lucky."

Now that I have Caroline's blessing, my spirits rise. I have not thought sex could happen to me, but you never know. I have new lipstick, and although it was expensive, it's a perfect pink to go with my outfit. She gives me a hug, yielding nice support and inflating my confidence.

When I pull into my driveway, the rain starts. A warning not to get too confident? The dark clouds drift on. Inauspicious weather could spell difficulty with my outfit. The one fancy umbrella I have—the only one without a Nature Conservancy theme—has red roses when I'll be dressed in pink. What the hell, it will hold off the rain.

My house is always just as I've left it: dishes done, or not; paperwork on the coffee table, or not. Today, I've carefully cleaned the clutter so the bed is nicely made, the underwear and blouse for tonight are laid out. My warm shower heats the bathroom. It's soothing and refreshing, which leads to my relaxing routine of oil application and makeup. I'm pleased to see the fit of the blouse will cover the bra straps. The deep V-neck encourages a look of tallness. The mirror shows my excitement—pink cheeks and sparkling eyes.

I peek through the curtain at the slam of a car door. Frank, Zoey's husband, resplendent in his tux, comes up the front walk. I'm pleased he didn't sound his horn; the civility of his walking to the door sets the tone for the evening. He's a man of few words, but his low whistle is a high compliment. He offers his arm, which I appreciate, though the walk to the car is short and the four stairs easily managed despite the long skirt. At the car, he makes certain my shawl won't get pinched by the door.

"I haven't been to a museum gala for a while." Zoey gives me her toothy smile. She has been careful with her makeup, and the silver gown sets off her dark hair so she looks glamorous.

"Where is the casual Zoey I know so well? You look great," I tell her.

She nods in thanks. "I hope they do better than last time with the food. I can't imagine what the theme of the food will be. What are the specialties of Vegas? Do casinos even have food? I've never been to one."

"The restaurants I've been to in Vegas specialize in glut. They offer huge amounts of every national tourist item. Whatever Italian, Mexican, or Asian food might come to mind is what they have."

"Excess would work for me. I'm starving. I've restricted myself for three days in order to get into this dress."

"The rain is getting heavier," Frank intervenes. "How about we use the valet service?"

Zoey turns to him. "It's more expensive. You know my mother's nursing-home expenses are draining us."

"Let's let it go just for tonight." Frank smiles and pleads simultaneously.

"You're right. I'll focus on having an evening off."

Caroline was spot on. They stress about her mother, and they have the skill to manage it.

The valet service is handled with aplomb. The darkly dressed students have grand umbrellas. When we enter the museum, Frank places Zoey's hand on his right arm and mine on his left. The room is lit up like a Vegas hotel, with flashing lights illuminating the interior. The casino theme is done well, with blackjack tables scattered in the atrium. Scantily dressed croupiers look like a mix between cocktail waitresses and table operators. The exhibit consists of black-and-white photographs from the 40s and 50s of celebrities galore. I love the emotional hijacking of the photos. We wander through the gallery, where the museum members' clothes are at least as interesting as the photos, with lots of long, fancy dresses.

"Would you like a ticket for wine or for a more serious drink?" Frank is solicitous.

I dig in my purse for cash. He shakes his head and puts a hand on my arm. I give up easily since I am enjoying being taken care of.

"I'd love a splash of bourbon on ice." Zoey has returned to her cheerful self.

"Bourbon goes with the glamorous image you have. Since I have svelte on my mind with this slit in my skirt, I'll go with a chilled white. You know I'm picky about my food; however, any wine will do. Thanks for being such a gentleman." I give Frank a pat on his arm as he turns to go.

Zoey and I do the southern thing of giving hugs and air kisses to everyone we know. We meander toward where we think the food tables are. Frank engages with another architect after he brings us our drinks.

"Do you know who's catering tonight?" I ask Zoey. It doesn't make any difference to me, but Zoey sometimes knows these things.

"I think Villa Tronco," she tells me.

"How can they kill a theme with such flair?" I ask her.

The ice-sculpture centerpiece for the long table is, I finally decide, a slot machine. At the bottom of each side of the four-foot-high block are black ribbons representing the lines of the roller behind the machine's glass. Different foods represent the cherries and symbols of an actual slot machine.

I look over the offerings. "Luckily, there's not much edible here." I lower my voice. "The ravioli is dry, the salami comes from packages at Publix, and the olives have been dumped from cans. The overall effect is dreadful."

Zoey chuckles. "The cheese is probably acceptable—real Italian from the names on the bricks. I guess they are not going for anything but Italian, no Mexican, no Chinese, no Japanese."

"The cheese selection looks great. Since I could live on cheese alone, I'll dub the food a success." I smile at her.

"Are you willing to try the tables? Doesn't that sound sophisticated, 'the tables'?" Zoey asks.

"I bet the house take is a high percentage. The museum needs money," I respond.

"How much do you have in your little purse?" she asks me.

"I have two twenties and a ten and my debit card. If I drop thirty, I'll consider it a donation to the museum," I say.

"I can throw away a twenty. Any more than that, I would cry in my pillow tonight."

We laugh at our meager contributions.

We avoid several tables where the croupiers are shuffling with excessive concentration and find a place where the croupier is handling the cards with skill. Watching people gamble has always fascinated me. Gambling is addictive; you can see how the victims lose all sense of the outside world.

Even here, where the chips are one or two dollars, people determinedly lose significant amounts of money. I notice one man, very heavy, fiftyish, sweating in his tux, and pushing quantities of his chips forward with every round. Then, something's wrong. With a groan, he curls in on himself, one hand to his chest, the other flailing to catch the edge of the table. He slides to the floor as people around him back up.

"Is there a doctor here?" The croupier looks around.

"Somebody, call an ambulance," a voice on my right shouts out.

"You have a phone in your purse. Call nine-one-one," I

mutter to Zoey as I move toward the man. I kneel beside him.

"Do CPR," a voice from far away calls.

First things first, size up the scene. No danger, no blood, one person. Is he dead or alive? Living. As my mind whirls, I straighten his body. How is his airway? I check his mouth. How is his breathing? Rapid. How is his pulse? Slow.

Now people are shouting at me to do CPR.

I look up, very annoyed. "He's breathing," I say loudly. "Did nine-one-one respond?" I ask Zoey.

Zoey keeps people away. "They should be here now."

The crowd parts as the EMTs make their way through the throng of party attire. A uniformed lady helps me to my feet.

"His breathing is rapid. His pulse is slow."

"Thanks, useful information," she says.

The uniforms roll him onto the stretcher, which is lifted immediately onto a gurney. A petite lady insists on accompanying him. They include her in the parade, and within seconds, the siren starts. Luckily, the downtown hospital is close by.

"He will be just fine," I address a nearby group. Then I congratulate myself on doing the right thing regardless of what others say. Well, well, your confidence is growing. Being away from Steve is enabling your sense of capability, of being all right when in charge. No need to second-guess yourself.

Zoey and I move away from the tables. We indulge in several minutes of silence.

"How did you know what to do?" she asks.

"I told you I took a renewal weekend with the Wilderness Medicine Institute of NOLS," I tell her.

She shakes her head as if to rid herself of the whole upsetting incident. "You're amazing."

"Let's go toward the music and see who else is here." I

give her a sign to follow me. I am interested in only one person. Is Dan here, and if so, would he dance with me?

"Hey, Angie, come meet my boyfriend," Pam calls from thirty feet away.

One of the people I would not have placed at this art gala is tiny Pam. If she'd been on a multiple-choice question of attendees that also included Elvis, Houdini, Mary Magdalene, the President, I would have answered "none of the above" and been sure of myself. Her minuscule sequined skirt stands out from the conservative getup of most of the gala participants. With yellow and orange swirls, the effect echoes her circus background.

"This is my boyfriend, Jim." Pam winks.

Jim belongs here. His tux fits well, is relatively new, and not rented. He stands tall with his deep red cummerbund and displays a rare lack of tummy for a man over forty. He turns sympathetic green eyes on me. "Pam tells me you frequent the office where she works for her cousin Dan."

"I'm not his cousin. I'm Lydia's cousin, so far removed it doesn't count," Pam corrects him.

I'm quick. "Her untimely death was a blow to all her family members, I'm sure."

Graceful in a time of social astonishment, I do okay this time.

So, Pam and Dan are distantly related? Hang on to your sanity. Does that explain anything at all? You know if you go back three generations with South Carolina natives, they are all related. They also love to figure out the details.

"Oh look, there's Dan and Marguerite." Pam points with her itty-bitty forefinger. The sight of the two of them delights her. She pushes Jim with both hands. "See, I told you. Dan is a great dancer."

The feeling I have is reminiscent of when I once roller-skated down a steep driveway at age ten. I missed the turn at the bottom, flew off a curb, and landed on my back. I had no breath or any likelihood of it, and the feeling scared me shitless.

A search of the small dance floor reveals Dan and the aforementioned Marguerite. Dan looks great in his tux. Marguerite is young and lovely. A little short, perhaps. Blond hair, a full, graceful dance skirt, and eyes only for him. They waltz like professionals. After an eon, the music stops, and when Dan sees us, he brings Marguerite toward us with his arm around her waist. He introduces us as if we know of each other. I am grateful Caroline doesn't go to museum galas. She would have known how I felt and called the ambulance to come back.

Marguerite's pleasure at dancing is clear. I cannot hate her for being where I wanted to be. Not her fault he prefers young blondes to silver-haired old women. We shake hands and smile at each other. The handshake is firm on both sides, showing Marguerite does not lack confidence.

The music starts again, but this time, Dan turns to me, hand open in invitation. "May I have this dance?"

A nod is the best I can do. I take his hand, warm, encasing mine gently.

"You look spectacular in pink."

"Men in their tuxes are beautiful." I remind myself to breathe.

He smiles, and we position ourselves for a waltz. I hadn't allowed myself to dream of anything like this. Not true, I'd actually imagined sex with him. Could sex be any better? I relax with just enough counterweight so he can easily lead.

"You're a great waltz partner," he says after a few turns.

"I only follow." I lower my eyes to show I am only partially modest about my dancing.

"Very nice retort. Let's see if I can do some fancy stuff."

He puts me into the cuddle position, and we strut side by

side. Then, after a turn, he goes into a side-step routine with a lot of flare. Just as I am aware of the crowd staring, I'm aware of my seam ripping and the air on my upper thigh where the slit isn't supposed to go. Dan understands my dilemma before I do. He turns me, so my slit is against his side rather than exposing my leg to the audience. I am so high from dancing, I am amused rather than humiliated.

"Let's go find your table." He holds me close.

I have trouble getting the grin from my face because I am so hyped from the music and dancing. I feel a giggle coming on.

"You two looked professional until the mishap—quite a flash of leg." Pam smiles broadly, clearly enjoying the disaster.

Marguerite holds my scarf. "Here, put this around your waist. See, you can knot it on the side. No one will know what happened. It looks very fashionable." *Why is she being so nice?*

"I enjoy seeing the two of you dance together," she goes on. "Both of you are good dancers. Your pleasure is palpable."

She smiles broadly at me while Pam frowns.

"Go, dance some more. I love to see it," Marguerite says.

Why is she not jealous of our dancing together?

"Shouldn't she go home now?" Pam's voice wobbles.

Dan ignores her. "Come on, let's try this foxtrot. The problem was with the dips, the lovely dips of the waltz." Dan steps close, his arm encircling my waist as he leads me back to the dance floor.

The ludicrousness of dancing with a wardrobe malfunction tickles me. I laugh. "Sure, let's do it."

At that instant, I realize I don't fit in, and shit, I don't care anymore. I am who I am. I can do what I want.

Dance after dance, he leads well, and I follow well because I am in paradise. We take a break and go sit on an outside bench to cool off in the sensuous breeze, the noises of the bugs suggestive of their nighttime activities.

He sighs deeply. Even though it's dark, I sense he is smiling and relaxed. The joy of dancing suffuses my body.

Interesting, the wonderful feeling is not sexual or connected with eating. When have I ever felt like this? Maybe after a strenuous hike to the top of a high peak in Colorado; maybe the time I snorkeled in a bay in Hawaii where every fish in every National Geographic magazine sparkled and floated beneath me. They call it a peak experience. Sitting here, relaxed but energized, is enough.

I turn to Dan. "Dancing drives away tension. I focus on the music, the beat, mostly, and my feet do the right thing. I love to dance, and you are, without a doubt, the best dancing partner I've ever had."

"Thank you. You express the joy it brings very nicely." His voice is soft against the noise of the screwing toads. "I hate to break the magic of this minute, but since we are together, our next step comes to mind."

Even though I don't turn to see him, I know he gives me the twinkle smile, and I understand he is taking us out of our trance.

"So, what is the next step?" I hope he understands, as I do, there are several possible next steps.

"We now have a court date for the divorce itself. I want you to know I hope to find another dance evening with you."

"Do you enjoy taking care of nearly divorced women?"

"Not as much as dancing with you," he says, then adds, "I do enjoy the challenge of being helpful to people who are in bad situations."

"That's like me, although I don't have court to get nervous about."

"Once I've decided on a strategy to use in a case, then I'm home free, and I can relax."

"What do you mean, 'strategy'?" I ask.

"Remember when I asked Steve if he was a selfish man?"

"I almost fell out of my chair."

"I knew I could get him to hang himself, and he did. You were looking at Steve, but I kept glancing at poor Mr. Castro. He knew what I was doing."

"Mr. Castro was way more cooperative after Steve's deposition. Fascinating! Do you have another example of a strategy?" I ask him.

"A case on my desk now is puzzling me."

"Tell me about it." I push since I am truly interested.

"A fifty-plus-year-old woman was a longtime caregiver to her uncle. She was kind to him when his two sons were too busy to visit. The woman had been attentive and kind to her mother, whom she adored. This was her mother's favorite brother. Doctor's visits, food, bill-paying, keeping his house—she did it all for several years."

"I can see where this is going," I say.

"Maybe not. The uncle put five thousand dollars in his will for her and five thousand for one of his sons. The other son got everything else: the big house, the big boat, and several million in investments, for starters. Now the son, who was mostly left out, wants my client's support to say his father was not in his right mind. He wants to break the will. He would still only include my client for a small amount. He says, 'I'm his son, after all.'"

"Nice boys," I say.

"When big money gets involved, niceties go out the door. The uncle had purchased the woman a nice car, as well as retired the debt on her house," he elaborates. "He also fixed the house to a high standard. She is fine with the exchange they arranged. The problem comes in that the younger son wants her to testify his father was not in his right mind when he made the will. She knows her uncle was demented and persuadable when presented with the paperwork the scoundrel of a son presented him with."

"So, her course is clear. She has to help the lazy son break the will so both lazy sons profit unjustifiably from their father's hard work," I tell him.

"The solution was not clear until just now. When I explain it out loud, the strategy is clear: help the woman prove the uncle was demented." He is definite.

"I love to hear the stories of complicated cases."

"I could do this with Lydia too. She would listen well, and the course would be clear."

We sit still in the darkness, listening. The bug noises are almost gone. I wonder why he doesn't try to kiss me. Then I remember Marguerite. Is he so nice to everyone? Am I just one in a group of women pining after Dan?

"Let's go dance." He takes my hand to help me rise.

"You're on, for sure. I love it." I readjust the shawl.

Toward the end of the evening, I realize I don't know who Marguerite is or what she means to Dan.

Don't ask, don't ask, don't ask. "Is Marguerite another client?" I blurt out.

"Oh, I thought you knew. She's my dance instructor. I take a few lessons a year to keep up. She's fun to dance with, but not like you. You're the only client I've ever wanted to dance with. I've enjoyed this evening."

"Not as much as I have." I look him full in the face.

He laughs. "This could constitute a first argument, but I'll just concede. Maybe you did enjoy it more than I did, but I doubt it." His smile fades. "One other thing I wanted to mention, I was at the back of the crowd when you knelt beside George."

"You know him?" I ask.

"Yes, we were in law school at the same time."

"I believe I did the right thing. I hated to take over, but nobody else was moving toward him."

"Your being coolheaded might have saved his life. CPR could have done him in."

"I never thought I'd have to use the information from the NOLS course I took." The memory of the incident gives me a shiver.

"You took a NOLS course? Will wonders never cease? You dance like a dream too." He shakes his head in mock astonishment.

Zoey comes up beside me. "Frank and I enjoyed dancing too, but it's getting late."

"I was having such a good time, I lost track of the hours," Dan says as he gives a short bow. He turns away and heads for the door.

In the car, we review the evening. "Pam and her boyfriend look like an interesting couple," Zoey starts. "She's Dan's assistant? She's strange. Did you see how she shoved her boyfriend?"

"She's evidently a distant cousin of Lydia's, as well as Dan's assistant."

"Who is Lydia?" Frank asks, all innocence.

"She's Dan's deceased wife."

"And so, Pam is related to her boss, Dan?" Frank asks.

What could it mean for Pam to be related to Lydia?

I turn to Zoey. "So you noticed the way she treated her boyfriend in public was out of bounds?"

"It would be out of bounds anywhere." Zoey's voice is firm. "I also noted when she wasn't aware anyone was looking at her, she stared at you with a look like she wished you were the dead one."

CHAPTER THIRTEEN

The city is in full bloom. The governor's committee on development should run tour buses through the neighborhoods. The ancient gardens in Europe are rarely as splashy as streets in Columbia rife with azaleas and dogwoods. Maybe the tulips in the Netherlands or the lavender in Tuscany can compare. After the buses tour the neighborhoods, the restaurants in town could up their game and vie for the tourists.

However, even the pink double azaleas and the full white dogwood in my front yard cannot lift my spirits today. I'm grateful we have only passed two people on our walk because, in our town, reflexes kick in. When someone smiles and asks how I'm doing, I have to smile and say, "Just fine, thanks." We cannot *not* do it, and it doesn't matter how you feel.

Most cities require people to tend to their own business; not here. The ritual greeting is cousin to a more advanced form of social involvement. When people in Columbia are introduced, they always try to form a connection. Once, in an office, I turned my back on two people who had just met. While I filled my coffee cup, they had figured out the woman's grandson and the man's daughter had attended a birthday party together a decade ago. Could there be any place else where the governor requires all state employees to answer the phone, *It's a beautiful day in South Carolina.*

Today, I want to turn away from the strangers, but I can't.

Caroline stares at me. "You really took it on the chin."

"I don't want to talk about it."

I can't erase the image I saw in my mirror this morning of a pale, hollow-eyed version of myself with a big red contusion on my jaw.

"You don't have a secret boyfriend, do you?" Caroline asks.

"You know me better than that." Her question makes me sadder.

"It's going to look a lot worse before it gets better. I'm thinking yellow, green, and purple."

"I know." I'm sure my face reflects the horror of that knowledge.

"Is your final hearing this afternoon or tomorrow?"

"Tomorrow. I plan to use a lot of cover-up."

Caroline snorts. "All the drug stores in this town combined don't carry enough cover-up for that one. How did it happen?"

"I'm not going to tell you."

Caroline faces me, calling attention to the exaggerated shock on her face. "You're not going to tell me?"

"No!" I manage to sound resolute.

"You know you can't keep a secret." She starts walking again.

"This time I can."

Caroline always gets more information from me than I want to give her. I don't know where my reluctance comes from. She is kind and teases gently.

"Let me speculate. I believe you when you say you don't

have a secret boyfriend. You'd never be able to keep a male friend a secret from me."

"You might be surprised."

"Now it wasn't an accident caused by someone else, was it?"

"You rat, you're guessing. It wasn't."

"So, it was an accident caused by something you did. If it weren't kind of foolish, you would give it up. What did you do?"

"Let's change the subject. I promise I won't do it again," I say.

"Why don't you just tell me?"

"I'll tell you at the next Christmas party when we're both a little tipsy, and I'll find a way to put a humorous spin on it."

"Doesn't look funny to me, looks painful, eye-crossing painful. You didn't break a tooth, did you? Do you have hidden bruises?"

"My teeth are fine. My ego is the only part of me seriously crushed."

"So, what is it you prize yourself on that would result in a bruised jaw like that?"

"I told you, I'm not going to tell you."

"I guess you're not."

We walk along quietly for several minutes.

"You're going to give me the silent treatment, right?" I can't help myself since I don't want her to be annoyed at me.

"No, I'm waiting for you to change the subject because I can't get rid of the image of you trying to do push-ups against the sink, slipping on the rug, and banging your jaw against the stainless-steel sink set in tile."

My teeth clench with annoyed surprise. I hate she knows what happened, and I'm relieved to have the truth between us. "I wasn't standing on the rug. My foot slipped. Am I really that predictable?"

Caroline laughs. I know she's laughing at our conversation, not my crazy efforts to blend exercise into my daily life, so I join her.

"I'm more into cosmetics than you. I have some thick stage makeup that will do the trick," she says sympathetically.

"How did you do that?"

"What?" She radiates innocence.

"Get my secret out of me?"

"It's done by instinct. I have no plan. I just let my mind go to a place where images come. Then I know what it is. If you had fallen, you would have other bruises. It had to be some kind of controlled fall."

"They could use you in international diplomacy. This country can't tell what other nations are up to with any accuracy. The Far East may be inscrutable, but the Near East, Africa, and South America come up with surprises on a regular basis."

"They *could* use some help." She mimics looking into a crystal ball. "I see a divorce in your future."

I take the imaginary ball from her. "Let me look. I see a visit from your boyfriend soon. He is bringing flowers. His mother has died, so he doesn't have anyone to go to. He is looking into your eyes. He is asking forgiveness for his failings, and you are fixing him breakfast," I say.

"That ball is a fake. I would never fix him breakfast. The rest is likely to happen."

I toss the ball away since someone's feelings could get hurt. I don't want it to be mine.

"I hate to see the destruction of a nice ball. Let's return to the present. What time do you want to come over so we can practice covering up the facial abnormality?" she says.

"Will four o'clock work for you?"

"Fine."

In the late afternoon, she pulls out a suitcase-sized

cosmetics case, and we look over her arsenal. Then she gets busy.

"You're close to making me look like someone who is not accident-prone."

"You have good bones. With proper care and skill, you could look sensational all the time."

"That's not me. I've never had the time or inclination to spend money and energy on cosmetics."

"Sad, but true."

I want to cheer her up. "I do know enough to use pink lipstick in the summer when my skin is brown and red lipstick in the winter to contrast with my pale skin."

"What a pleasure to hear your knowledge about your skin tones. Do you ever consider lighting?" She curls her lip just a little and tilts her head.

"What about lighting? Either the sun is out or it's not."

"You're a better photographer than that."

"True, when I think about taking a photo, I know light has different colors, with different effects on different objects. I've never applied it to myself as an object."

"If you were into cosmetics like I am, you would consider where you want to look your best and what the lighting would be."

"Caroline, you are a master of the ways the world works." I smile my admiration.

While we are talking, she finishes her work. I look good. With the slathering, she was able to make me look almost normal.

She stands back. "Here is a bunch of tissue. Wipe off the outer layer, smear this oil around, and then wipe off the oil with the rest. Don't scrub, wipe gently. While you do that, I'll get us a glass of wine."

We have a glass of wine and giggle over her latest bouts with the board members of the local dance club. They can't agree on who should do what, and when, so nothing gets done until she goes ahead and arranges everything. Then they complain.

She gives me a pat on the back. "Is ten a good time for you to come by, and we'll do it again for the court?"

"I'll see you in the morning around ten." Her good work on my face will be critical for tomorrow's public appearance.

Several times a week, I wake up thinking it's raining. The regular soft swoop is the train going through town. Is Columbia the only capital city in the nation where trains cross major streets? Cars can be stopped for an hour. There is a shared sense of *c'est la vie* when you glance at the other drivers lined up next to you.

Luckily, the trip to Caroline's is uneventful, with no trains blocking my way. The application of undesirable chemicals softens the look of the bruise. Although I look like a Geisha, I like it. She has done a good job.

Worry usually furrows my brow, but today, even in the car, I practice maintaining unwrinkled skin, knowing the thick makeup will crack like plastic.

I meet Dan, as scheduled, on the steps of the courthouse. He greets me in a normal fashion. I am surprised he can keep his face under control. He is graceful about opening the door, although the wind requires him to strain against the heavy glass. The inside of the building smells stale.

I've been through my share of evil scanning devices, starting with the childhood X-rays showing how feet fit in new saddle shoes to a recent and misguided MRI to show my heart pumping perfectly. A doctor didn't ask about my caffeine consumption when I complained about lightheadedness.

Dan and I approach the dangerous frame of waves required for entrance to the back halls of the county courthouse for my divorce hearing. The security officers know him, that's not so surprising, but when they wave him around the security area, I have never been so surprised. I face the plastic containers for my keys, my shoes, and the questions about my pockets, watch, belt, and jewelry. The question of the underwire bra has never come up for me, but I have heard tales.

Dan waits patiently and smiles at me even as he chats up the potbellied guy with the pistol at his waist and Mace container clipped to his belt.

We walk toward the elevator. "Dan, why did they let you go through security like that?"

"I have a concealed weapon and a permit. They all know me."

"You would have set off the alarm?"

"Oh, yes, I would have."

The elevator doors open and close behind us.

"Show me."

"What?"

"Show me your gun. Do you ever use it? Where do you carry it?" Since I was on the rifle team in high school, I believe I am qualified to ask.

"On days like today, I carry a Luger in a shoulder holster."

It's just the two of us in the elevator, so he pulls open his jacket. I'm surprised at what a big gun it is. His chest is broad, although it's usually hidden behind his coat, as is the gun. I imagine resting my head against his chest. I sigh audibly, and he smiles.

"When we were at mediation, did you have a gun?" I ask.

"I always carry a gun." He makes sure the door stays open for me as we exit the elevator.

"There's got to be a story behind that, or do all lawyers carry guns?"

"I was once in a courtroom when a crazed, soon-to-be ex-husband pulled a gun. It was before the scanning devices came in. He was angry at his wife, but he was doubly angry at me. I didn't like the look in his eyes or the steel barrel in my face—inches from the brain I'm so very fond of. A quick-acting deputy threw himself against the guy while hitting the hand holding the gun. The noise of the gunshot—I thought I was dead—still reverberates in my head. Clearly, he missed me. All these years later, he's still in prison. I understand he was high on cocaine."

The picture that comes to mind scares me. I wasn't there, yet I experience fear for his life. What if the deputy hadn't been quick? What if the deputy hadn't hit the gun away?

I shudder. "So, every time you come in here, you're on high alert?"

"Something like that," he says.

We move into the waiting room, where another lawyerlike man and a timid young woman sit in a far corner.

"I don't think Steve has it in him," I continue our conversation. "But he did go on the offensive about the squirrels in our yard. One time when I came back from a photo expedition with a sophisticated friend from San Francisco, I was embarrassed to see cop cars lining our street. Steve was handing his BB gun over to an officer. Turns out a shot had ricocheted off the sidewalk and through a neighbor's window."

It's an amusing story, but Dan frowns. "Steve sounds potentially dangerous to me. He doesn't mind acting like a burglar, even if it was only a cake. I remember the squirrel story. He told it to me the first time I met him. He was not exactly threatening but somehow giving me notice he doesn't mind handling a loaded weapon. Also, I noted he likes target practice on living beings, that is, squirrels."

"I've never thought of it like that," I say.

"I try to stay one step ahead of trouble," he offers. His alertness is comforting.

"I'm curious. What will happen today?" I ask.

"The judge will look over the agreement for about ninety seconds, ask each party if they are satisfied and whether there is any possibility of reconciliation. Then everyone signs and you two go your separate ways."

The courtroom doors open. "Merk versus Merk," a guy with a sonorous voice and a gun at his waist proclaims.

Steve and Mr. Castro emerge from a small conference room I hadn't noticed. They follow Dan and me into the courtroom. I keep my eyes averted, but I sense Steve's stare, trying to intimidate me with the same old dynamic so I will go passive. Gritting my teeth, I look him in the eye and do not smile. He is a person but not a friend; he is a non-friend. The heavy door closes softly behind us. We take our seats at two separate tables in front of the high stage.

I remember the paragraph in my *Introduction to Psychology* textbook where it describes how authority is enhanced by the raised platform for the judge and the dark wood of the desk.

"All rise!" The man with the bass voice opens the side door for the judge.

The judge is a woman, who nods to Mr. Castro and to Dan. She asks if we are who she thinks we are. Then she asks if there is any chance of reconciliation. Steve rises to his feet. Suddenly, this is not going the way it's supposed to go.

"I would like to speak to that issue."

"Okay," says the judge, and Mr. Castro puts a hand on Steve's arm, but it's too late.

"We married with the full expectation we would be married 'till death do us part.' I don't know why she left the marriage, really—yes, I do."

I sense he is going from pole to pole even during this last little statement. I also sense that he is just getting started.

"I have a list of all the good things about the marriage." He pulls out the little brown notebook where he records his life. "First of all, she is a great cook; second, she manages money beautifully; third, she keeps the house and yard reasonably well; fourth, she was a wonderful mother to our four children."

The quick nod of his head indicates he believes he has proven his point. He returns the notebook to his inside breast pocket.

"Mr. Merk, you have not mentioned you love her or miss her or want to protect her and care for her. It seems you want her back so she can take care of things for you. It is clear to me reconciliation is not possible in this instance." She taps her gavel.

Sadness constricts my throat when Steve's head drops.

"Have both parties signed off on the financial agreement?"

All of us focus on the judge again. Both lawyers agree simultaneously and quite quickly. The judge smiles at them.

"This divorce is final." She bangs her gavel this time.

Dan gathers up his papers. I sign where requested, then we head for the elevator.

"We'll go down to the basement and get a couple of certified copies, then, if you have time, let's get some lunch," Dan says and moves gently.

Now that it's over, I'm exhausted. The trip to the basement is somber as I review what just happened. The marriage had been fine at first. I remember when he wouldn't include me in his art collecting. The old feeling of not fitting in or being outside the action was so strong I still carry a remnant of it—no, not really. I remember it, but I'm not feeling it now. I feel confident and worthy.

I suppose early on, I had opinions. I edited a book chapter he was working on, but we never discussed it, although I tried to be clear on what I thought an improvement would be. He never asked me to edit any more of his writing. To this day, I still don't know if I was too good or too bad or just not relevant or not understandable. I sigh. I couldn't find a way to be his companion rather than his helpmate, or more accurately, his housekeeper. I now believe he couldn't tolerate my competence.

We both came to understand I would take care of most everything connected with the house. I would also help support the family. He ran his life to make a lot of money. That piece has worked to my advantage at this point. Maybe I didn't value the effort he expended. On the other hand, my life hasn't been financially enriched until now. We always lived like graduate students without any money. Now I appreciate his money-making skills. Now I don't have to be concerned with whether or not I was a good-enough wife. It's over.

Dan is respectfully quiet.

The lady behind the sliding glass window is obviously cheered by seeing him. "Another one finished?" Her voice is bright as she pushes open the glass.

"Yes, we need the usual three copies," he answers.

She is efficient and hands me a folder with the copies. My purse is large enough to hold the folder. Caution had me carry some documents.

"I thought we'd go to the Summit Club to celebrate." Dan gives me the twinkle smile.

"Thanks, I'd love to do that. I have a colleague with a membership. We go there for our Christmas get-together. Do they have a buffet for lunch regularly or just in the holiday season?"

"It's their usual setup. You can order from the menu as well if you like."

I expected to have a feeling of relief or freedom with the finality of the proceeding, but instead, I am a little sad we couldn't find a way to be pleasantly married. I was finished with the verbal abuse. When we'd gone to marital counseling, the therapist had let him rail at me in sessions. I don't allow abuse between partners in therapy. When I have a couple sitting apart from each other on my couch, as they usually do, I call their first rally an example of how their relationship works. Right away, I insist they talk politely to each other. I start teaching communication skills immediately, but I couldn't get it going with Steve. Even after I'd left him, he wasn't respectful.

Main Street is crowded. We walk several blocks to the tallest building in town without talking. As we ride the elevator to the top floor, my spirits rise. The foyer is covered in plush drapes and carpets of dark green, dusty gold, and maroon, with black cut velvet on the chairs. There are chandeliers and white linen in every place possible.

I'm glad I dressed up for today's court appearance. I decided on my slinky black pants to which I added a pale teal jacket. My blouse is black with a small ruffle down the front. I fit in with the young up-and-coming crowd mixed in with the bankers and lawyers who can pay the freight for the Summit Club.

From this height, the view of the city stretches down to the river through floor-to-ceiling windows. The view excites me, and I wonder if I will ever get to walk the path along the river with Dan.

The walk alongside the big river is spiritual for me. The river has moods often matching my own. Frequently, a great blue heron sits on a rock in the middle of the river, and sometimes, there are wood ducks near the shore. The sights and sounds of the water over the grand rocks always soothes me. The river is at the fall line in Columbia, so there are big rocks the water flows around and over unless the river floods. When the river is high, the rocks disappear. The river is never the same, and the light there is always wonderful.

We follow the maître d' past the buffet and salad tables to sit at a table overlooking the city. After a moment's admiration of the view, Dan rises, and I walk beside him to where we get our plates.

"I see they have a nice variety today. I do like a lot of different foods," he says.

I have to stop myself from fainting. He dances, he loves to eat, he's perfect for me.

"That's great, because I love, *love*, to cook." I give a little hop.

I realize immediately my statement is way ahead of where the game is. I blush even though I haven't blushed in, what, twenty or thirty years? Except the time in his conference room when he implied Steve and I had gotten together some because we did have four children.

Dan knows I have broken an invisible barrier. He laughs out loud, and every eye in the hushed dining room is on us. I am painfully aware I don't know what to do. Act haughty? Amused? Sad? Remorseful?

My breath hiccups and I start to laugh. Dan looks into my eyes, and soon, we are both out of control, wheezing and making a lot of noise. I heave a deep breath and straighten myself. I pull on the back of my jacket to fix my disarray.

Dan smiles a big twinkle smile. "Let's get some food."

He still takes short breaths to manage. I know if I look at him, we'll both start in again. I grab a salad plate and start around the table. As I spoon some tuna salad and cucumber slices onto my plate, I sense the entire room relax, and the chatter starts up again.

We compose ourselves at the table with the lovely view. "I'm sorry, I couldn't help it. Tension dissipates when you laugh, and I've been tense for hours," I whisper to Dan.

"Don't be sorry. I know most of the people in here.

They'll be pleased to see me laugh since I've been quiet for several years now."

"Since Lydia died?" I ask.

"That shared hysteria was the first time I've felt light in my heart since then. When we danced, it was a mix, although I do relax when I dance. Lydia was a good dancer, but not as good as you. We enjoyed dancing, but she was more determined and serious than you are."

"Strangely, now that you mention it, I realize I have not had a good laugh since my daughter was diagnosed. Well, my friends and I did go hysterical over the cake theft."

We return to circle the buffet table for entrees, and Dan recommends the trout, which looks moist and delicious. When we return to our seats, the waiter is quick with drinks and bread. I suppose the people who rule the city don't have the patience to wait for their bread.

"Maybe we're both healing. As you say, laughter is good for the body, but so is food. How do you like the trout?" he asks.

"It's just fine. I think it could use a little less oil and a bit more of the lemon flavoring." I smile to show I'm fine with it as it is.

"When I think about it, you're right. Are you ready to go to the dessert table?" he asks.

This is a moment of truth for me. I have a policy not to eat desserts in restaurants as they tend to be disgusting.

"Dan, I have a confession to make. I don't eat any dessert I haven't made myself."

"You don't mind if I get a little pecan pie, do you?" He pretends to be a supplicant, hands together, head bowed.

"Don't be silly, go get all you want." I am pleased I don't add: *After you've had mine, you'll know what they serve here is yucky-sweet. Besides, they don't use fresh pecans toasted to perfection.*

Dan brings a big piece of pie to the table. I smile at him as he takes the loaded fork to his cheerful face.

"What a treat to see someone enjoying their food. Now I have a question. Who do you usually eat with, and what do you usually eat? You mentioned blueberries, and Caroline said you enjoyed my shrimp salad at the Christmas party. I know you like fresh home-baked cookies, and you liked my gourmet sandwich, but who's keeping track?" I roll my eyes.

Dan puts down his fork and engages in another hearty laugh. I smile broadly but keep my chuckle inside.

"Well, to start from the beginning, Lydia had a few nice specialties, frozen waffles with blueberries and Cool Whip, frozen entrees, perfectly heated. Mostly we dined out or ordered in food. I do truly appreciate anything home-cooked. Since her death, I have continued with her pattern. As much as I can justify it, I invite friends to join me. I don't mind eating by myself, but I surely prefer amusing company." He gives me another twinkle smile.

My heart melts to think of this fine man eating by himself.

"Look over there. It's Pam." I watch her come toward us.

"Her boyfriend left her, and she has been acting strangely. I'm worried about her. She's become unpredictable."

Pam stands beside our table. I am unexpectedly enraged. Why is she spoiling this wonderful time?

"Dan, I'm so glad to see you happy." She bends and gives him a shoulder hug while looking at me. "I admired Lydia. She was lovely in every way, a graceful physical presence, a sympathetic soul, and always pleasant." The syrup goes out of her voice. "I have wanted to protect you from conniving females."

She turns to me. "Here is one after you." Her voice gets louder. "I have done the best I could protecting you from the likes of her." She continues to raise her voice and points her index finger at me in a way resembling a gun.

I glance at Dan, who sits back with his jaw dropped. I'm scared of her, but she's crossed a line, so I feel entitled to confront her.

"Pam, Dan has been helpful to me, and I have only his best interests at heart." I have a sudden surge of confidence.

She bends toward me and points. "You are a slut and a whore."

"That is ridiculous and just not true. You need to calm down, Pam." My heart races, but as I want her to come to her senses, my voice continues firmly.

She growls like a crouching animal ready to pounce. "Soon you will be out of the picture."

She turns abruptly toward Dan. Her mood and posture shift. "When Angie's gone, I'll be the one taking care of you." Her voice goes low and guttural.

Dan gives himself a shake. He stands and takes her arm, then he puts her arm into the crook of his and escorts her away from the table.

She turns toward me. "See, he wants me, he is going to take me to his house, he is going to make me his princess." She tosses her head, then lays it against his shoulder and looks up at him.

He looks at her. "Yes, we'll go to my house."

They walk toward the elevators. As they go down the hall, he gives a slight nod to someone at a nearby table who makes the hand sign indicating a telephone call. I understand security or the police will shortly be her escort.

My distress catches up with me. I can't help it, and I begin to shake as tears come to my eyes. A nice lady in an easily recognized Ann Taylor suit tastefully accented with good costume jewelry drags a chair next to where I have thrown myself down. She bends to give me a hug.

"You don't usually see performances like that in this setting."

"Thanks for coming over. I don't know what to do now." Focusing on her soft face decreases my panic.

"Look around. Everyone has gone back to their food. They all know Dan will take care of the poor lady. They all heard Dan laugh, so they are all interested in you and sympathetic toward you. Many of them know Pam tries to mother Dan. Sometimes her protection is useful to Dan. Clearly, this time it was way out of line."

"I experience Pam as only sympathetic to men. She is never respectful or even pleasant to me." My jaw is still clinched.

"You're right. I have also experienced her as a person who is only interested in the men in the room, but I'm not a threat to her office domination."

"Are you suggesting I may be?" I manage to smile at her.

"Maybe you are." She smiles back.

I am not feeling sympathetic toward Pam. Rather, I'm still pissed. The nice lady pats my hand. She tells me her name is Joanne and gives me her card, saying to call anytime.

"I'm an old friend of Lydia's. I personally like your style, so I was delighted to see Dan laughing. He has had a tough go of it."

She signals me to get my purse. She talks about the food as she steers me through the tables. People deliberately tend to their meals, not even glancing at us as we head for the door. At the entrance, she smiles again. "I wish you well."

She disappears back into the dining room. I ask the lady at the hall desk how I pay for my meal.

"Sweetheart, the member will take care of it with his monthly statement."

"Oh, when I've been here before, we always split the bill."

"That's fine. Dan expects the meal to be on his tab. The

third elevator over is express to the street level." She points the way out.

As I walk to my car, the what-ifs start. What if security didn't catch them in time? What if he meant what he said to her? What if she had a gun in her purse?

I sit in my car. What if you stop this silly thinking and drive home? You'd never let a client get away with this nonsense. What if he calls and tells me all about it?

What if he doesn't?

CHAPTER FOURTEEN

Calcutta could not be muggier than Columbia in late June. I try to convince myself the moisture is good for my skin. London is famous for the beauty of its denizens based on the level of wetness in the air. But is it 83 degrees at eight o'clock in the morning in London when its denizens go for their morning stroll? No!

Caroline appears not to sweat, but I'm sticky. We walk slowly, the shade from the trees perceptibly cooler than the sun-exposed sidewalk. We are wearing minimal but still decent tank tops and shorts. She has a light sweatshirt tied around her waist to guarantee comfort in the air-conditioned center. To trick my body into coolness, I imagine a glacier and its freezing runoff. I plan to put myself in the desert to stay warm if I get chilled in the center. I believe in mind over matter, and sometimes, it works.

"I do appreciate your help with my crazy life. I feel pretty bad today since the final hearing is over. I'm adrift. We had lunch together, quite compatible, even fun, except for Pam's breakdown. I'm still having trouble feeling sorry for her. She not only shit in her own nest, but she shit in mine."

"Quite a scene. Did she really say those things?"

"It's still vivid. Maybe I was traumatized since I'm having trouble sleeping. The dreadful scene keeps coming to my mind."

"Sounds like you're having flashbacks."

"Worse yet, I haven't heard from Dan since then. I suppose I need some kind of serious distraction to submerge the trauma, but I don't want anything bad to happen just so I can focus on something else."

"You're telling me you need a serious distraction?"

"Yes."

"What you need is a man in your life."

"I only want Dan. I'm positive he's the one for me. There's no other person out there, real or imagined. He's the only man I've met over the last year and a half I want to cook for."

"I thought you wanted sex. On the other hand, he may be too old for that."

"I guess I don't care so much about sex now. I just want to be with him so I can cook him a decent meal. He's been so tolerant of my mishaps."

She grabs my arm and turns me to face her. "Hey? Do you rule the world? Did you order Pam's breakdown?" She hesitates. "The midnight visit to resurrect Lydia is another matter."

"I didn't want to resurrect her. Just see for myself why he can't let loose of her."

We walk on. Waves of heat rise from where the sun hits the pavement.

"I think I was wrong." Caroline shakes her head in disbelief.

"What?" I rear back, my exaggerated horror almost making me trip over a fallen branch.

"If you're sarcastic, I won't continue my confession."

"Must be serious. I do want to know because it seems to concern me." I arrange my facial features to match her mood.

"I think I was wrong in my conclusion your lawyer is too friendly with other people. I think he is, number one, very friendly, and two, enamored of you."

"Whatever makes you think that?"

"I go back to your party. He was pleasant with me, but he didn't try to put the make on me like a lot of guys do. He remained a pleasant level of friendly. The dance evening seals it for me. The data says it best."

"I wish it were true."

"How do you know it isn't?"

"He doesn't call." My eyes fill with tears.

"The scene with Pam could have embarrassed him, although he's had too much experience in the world to be flummoxed by it. He's probably seen worse breakdowns than that."

"The lunch was so pleasant up till then, I can't figure out why he doesn't call."

"Maybe initiating contact is too much of a leap for him, seeing as you've been his client."

"I wish it were true." I can't help my eyes from misting, so I turn away from her. We are almost to the center, where crying would be the wrong thing to do.

"Test it out." She flips out her arm, pretending to order open the automatic door. She shrugs her shoulders.

"You have another enticing cake scene on your mind?" My annoyance finds its way into my voice.

"Not exactly."

"So what, then?"

"I'm beginning to think you need to take the first step. He might be exceedingly grateful."

"You think I should call him and use the sexy voice you

taught me?" I push out my chest but put my head down at the same time. I don't do coy well.

"Hell no!"

"At least you're not suggesting I play Mae West with her classic line, 'Come up and see me sometime,' with the accompanying leer and suggestive body language. What do you have in mind?"

"Let me turn the tables here. What would work for you?"

Relaxation comes over me. I smile, and Caroline smiles at me. "I'd love to cook for him. But if I invite him to my house, that is, as I understand it, a version of *Come see my etchings*. In other words, it's an invitation to a man saying, 'I'm open to whatever you'd like to do here.'"

"So?" She jumps in front of me, hands on her hips.

"Hmm. You have a point. Exactly the message I want to impart." My spirits rise.

Caroline points her finger at me. "Now don't give me any crap about being too busy."

"How did you know I was going there?"

"I could see it in your eyes, scaredy-cat. You spent way too many years catering to your husband to ever imagine going after what you want. I dare you. I *double* dare you to go after what you want."

How can she do that? Double dare me? I stand up tall and square my shoulders. I work to lift my "headlights" like my gym-class instructor says to do.

"Okay, you're on. I can do it. I'll do it as soon as we get back to my place."

Our usual workout passes in an eyeblink. My mind is elsewhere even as my thoughts are vague. We're mostly quiet on the walk home.

As I get the key from under the porch chair's pillow, I sweat in a way unrelated to the walk in the heat. I do not relax when I see Caroline grinning at me.

"Come on in, let's get some sustenance before I take your dare." Instead of restricting entry, as the key often does, it engages instantly. We walk into the air-conditioned house and head for the kitchen.

I peel kiwis and cut strawberries while she puts out a few nuts and dried apricots. We both get our own glass of water because she likes a lot of ice and I don't. I go to get my cell phone. Unfortunately, the fully charged phone is just where I always put it. My resolve fades, but in the next instant, I remember I have taken on a dare.

"Okay, here goes."

"You've memorized his cell number?" Her eyes sparkle.

"Believe me when I tell you I've had this conversation a million times. Unfortunately, in my mind, he always makes an excuse. Keep quiet," I cut her off when she opens her mouth. "I'll only hang on and talk if you promise to be still."

"I promise." She raises a hip to the kitchen stool and settles down.

I picture the phone ringer sounding at one end of an empty hall lined with antique sideboards and Persian rugs. I start when Dan answers.

"Hello, this is Dan McCloud."

"Hi, Dan, this is Angie. I'm calling because I'm in a cooking mood. I'd love you to join me for dinner tomorrow night."

"Angie, what a kind offer! I'd love to do that. Would it be more convenient if I took you out somewhere?"

"Dan, I've been thinking about having you for dinner for a long time. If you're willing to come, I think you'll prefer my cooking."

"Wow, what time?"

"Come at six thirty."

"I'm looking forward to seeing you and enjoying a meal with you. Can't wait. Bye." His voice has a smile in it.

I disconnect the line. I stare at Caroline like my brain isn't connected to my body.

"How did that happen?"

"He accepted, didn't he?"

"He didn't ask me why my voice was quivering, or what poison did I have in mind, or comment on how Lydia made the best crab cakes in the world."

"I told you he is enamored of you."

"I'm so excited I don't know if I can focus on my cooking. I think I'll make a small version of my red velvet cake. I'll do super buttercream frosting for it. You want to help? I need some fresh vanilla beans."

"Look, I'll go to the store one time to get one item. Then I'm done. You're on your own."

"I may or may not be able to do this on my own."

The ring of the phone jars me.

"Mom," Rachel starts when I answer, "I wanted you to know the tumor markers last time were a false positive. The lab used a weak solvent. They called when they realized what they had done."

"Thanks so much for calling, sweetie. I haven't dwelled on it, but when it came to mind, I did get scared." *Liar, liar pants on fire.* I can't help but babble on. "I'm about to go shopping for dinner with Dan. He is coming over tomorrow night. I've got to put my brain to work."

"You have a day to plan dinner for two?" She snorts. "I bet you'll be able to do that. Have a good time."

Rachel hangs up, and I report the latest to Caroline.

She shakes her head. "I can see your mind is moving onto tomorrow. I'm relieved to hear about Rachel's tumor markers."

"I'm so relieved I could cry. What a day this has been, yet it's only ten o'clock."

She comes around the table and gives me a hug. "I think

the meal with Dan will be the perfect antidote to the poison of months of worry."

"If I can just come up with a decent meal." I laugh at myself at what I have said.

Caroline bangs her head with her hand. She puts her nose in the air, looks down it, and stands tall with one arm outstretched as if to deliver a blessing—her queen pose. She turns to leave.

"I know I can make a decent meal," I shout after her as she closes the front door.

Only a moment elapses before I decide it's time to make my list. When I think about the meal, my mind clears of all other thoughts. What would be a good balance? Healthy but tasty, foolproof.

I was going to cook myself a pork loin and use the extras for sandwiches. A small pork loin will go nicely for two. Cold salmon can wait for a picnic. My AC will keep it cool enough for meat. You are quick with the rationalizations, aren't you?

Roast pork, cooked my way, is delicious. I'll get some fresh rosemary from the bush next door. I have plenty of sea salt and fresh peppercorn. I can cover the pork with some maple-cured bacon. A simple salad will be a reasonable contrast. Of course, I'll make fresh bread. Since there is only one decent cheese store in town, I'll have to make a foray to The Gourmet Shop. What else? Artichokes? Too messy. Brussel sprouts? Too iffy. Squash? Too pedestrian. Asparagus? Overused.

I know what will be nice on the side—carrots with a drizzle of sesame oil. So I'll also need freshly toasted sesame seeds for garnish. Dessert will have to be light. Velvet cake won't do. Is the recipe for lemon madeleines my sister gave me still tucked in *The Gourmet Cookbook*? When I look, I find it.

I call Caroline since she has a stake in helping me. "Caroline, it's me. Turns out the vanilla beans are not necessary. What would be helpful is if you would go to the Indian food store near your house and bring me a packet of raw sesame seeds. Most grocery stores don't have them."

"Perfect, the Indian store is on my list of errands this afternoon. I'll drop them by around six. Maybe we can share a glass of wine?"

"Wonderful, see you then." I catch myself humming as I sit down to finish my list. Maybe I can enjoy the whole thing instead of scaring myself with the worry he won't like it. If he prefers pizza with everything except anchovies, he can take me out next time we eat together.

This list is going to require some running around town. I also want to vacuum and dust a bit. I remember to put flowers on my list. A few for the table will be nice, even if he does bring some too.

So much to do! Am I already late for dinner tomorrow? Steady, Angie. You've done this before many times. It's fun. It always works out just fine.

The cheese shop has a grand selection. When I close the door behind me, I'm enveloped in coolness combined with the not-quite-farm smell of good cheese. My favorite these days is creamy blue cheese. Maybe he only likes a super mild cheese. To heck with it! I'll not worry, just serve what I like; I know what tastes good. The black sesame rice crackers are the perfect base and a foreshadowing of the sesame seeds on the carrots later on. Does anybody else in the world focus on this stuff?

"Give me a taste of each of those two. I'm trying to decide what will be best."

The white-aproned Asian woman smiles and complies, using little wooden sticks.

"I'll take a chunk of the Castello. It's divine."

"It's one of my favorites too." She puts it on the cutting

board and indicates an estimate with a big knife. When I nod, she makes the cut. "Anything else I can help you with?"

"No, thanks."

One part of the dinner is now ready since I know what plate and spreading knife I'll use for the cheese. I head to the nearby Trader Joe's. The parking lot has ample room because the lunch crowd hasn't piled in. In the organic section, the carrots and mushrooms are easy to select. I have decided to surround the pork roast with mushrooms, sautéed in butter, of course. Packaged field greens are where I expect, and the perfect red sweet pepper is in the bin. Thin slices of Asian cucumber will complete the color and shape contrasts for the salad.

After referring to my list, I remember I have coffee in the freezer. My French press makes the right amount for two. Does Dan drink coffee regularly in the evening or only when he wants to be especially lively? Oh, oh! Don't go there. You'll look crazy if you stop dead in the crackers and chips aisle and allow yourself to daydream. What would the store announcer say? *Bring the stretcher and restraints! Lady having an orgasm on Aisle six.*

Keep moving, Angie. My rational self takes over and I head for the coffee grinder; I'll get decaf. If he wants full-strength coffee, I'll use what I have. I already have a selection of tea.

The meat glistens behind the glass. I have seen them spray it, with water, I suppose. The store employee points to the fattiest pork loin in the case. My head shake has him doing better. The store brand of bacon is organic and will taste great. The checkout goes easily, but the packages are light for the amount of money. What else could you expect?

When I return to my house, I see it with fresh eyes. It's just fine. The small front yard, neatly trimmed, the straight walkway, the doorway with its twin concrete pots effervescent with multicolored begonias, are all welcoming.

The uncluttered screened porch complements the not-quite-spare interior. After people visit my house, they go home and throw stuff out. I have café curtains on the windows, mostly white. Because of the lack of clutter, the house looks clean even when it isn't. I love light in the house and the open rooms keep me cheerful.

I put away the groceries and sit down to read. As I relax, the book goes to the side, and I let my eyes close.

Caroline makes the obligatory knock on the front door and comes in speaking loudly. "Hello! I'm sooo pleased you sent me to the Indian store. I was there an hour and a half and could barely carry out the loot. The store has been enlarged and upgraded. What a lovely place to spend time and money. The smells! The colors! Why endure the discomfort of flying all cramped up for hours or days in an airplane when you can push open the door and have a lovely Indian woman taking you around and telling you the secrets of cooking this vegetable or that frozen bread? They must have twenty varieties of rice."

"Now you're making me wish I'd found the time to make the journey. Maybe next week we can go together. Sounds like a lot of fun."

We enjoy the evening, as we always do, and I sleep well.

In the morning, after my breakfast of an egg with mushrooms, I'm ready for the day. I'm grateful eggs have been rehabilitated by the health and diet gurus. They're easy to fix and help with rebounding hunger.

My kitchen is a place of order, relaxation, and activity. I never sit down in my kitchen, I never scold myself, and I make definite decisions quickly. When I make a mistake, I throw it out. If something has been in the fridge so long it's discolored or dry, I throw it out. I am fully myself in the kitchen. Only several hours sitting by a mountain stream can produce the same feeling everything in my life will turn out all right.

Dan's not coming until 6:30, so I have all day. The phone interrupts my state of bliss.

"Mom, I saw your car in the driveway when you're usually at the office. Is anything wrong?"

"Nope. Everything is more than all right. Remember, Dan is coming to dinner."

"So, you're not going to the office today?"

"Nope."

"I have a sick child home from school. Could you come over while I go to the grocery store?"

"Nope."

"I guess you want this day for yourself."

"You're a sweetheart to understand."

"I'll see if my backup sitter can come here for an hour."

I smile after I hang up. I'm proud of myself; I am growing up.

Dessert is attacked first because it can keep for many hours once it's cooled and stored. If for some reason it doesn't work, I can go buy some frozen carrot cake. Frozen pumpkin pie with fresh whipped cream is acceptable as an alternative lifeline, but not this time of year. If the carrot cake becomes required, then asparagus would have to be purchased. Carrots used twice in the same meal would be a travesty. Usually, another trip to the store would push me into panic mode, but not today. I shrug my shoulders. I'll take special care with the dessert since I don't like the idea of a store-bought dessert.

I cream the butter and eggs using extra-large eggs and organic Irish butter. I used to use double-yolk eggs, but they're not available anymore. To heck with cooking oil sprays, only butter with a light dusting of flour allows the cooked cake to exit a pan gracefully. The dry ingredients disappear into the churning beaters, followed by the vanilla and lemon flavoring. Just before I put the batter in the madeleine tins, I add a bit of sour cream. I add sour cream to anything I think won't get soupy. Sour cream keeps everything moist. It's more subtle than butter and adds a tiny tang to combat the sugar. It changes the texture a bit, but I've never had a complaint regarding the extra moisture.

Irish soda bread is failproof, needs to be made ahead, and is quite popular. I'm pleased I remembered buttermilk yesterday. The mix of white flour, whole-wheat flour, oats, salt, and soda becomes sticky with the addition of buttermilk. The buttered cookie sheet readily accepts the blob, while patted flour on top of the dough yields to the knife for the traditional crosscut. The bread is as good as done. In half an hour, the smell of bread infuses the kitchen air. Dan would like this warm cozy feeling; anybody would. Later, I'll have him here when I cook. He can work on a brief or something, occasionally coming into the kitchen to smell the peace and cheer of baking bread.

I glance at the clock. It's time to tend to myself. The pork roast is absorbing the flavors of the garlic and rosemary, and the bacon fat keeps it moist. The sautéed mushrooms sit in a bowl next to the roast. The diagonally cut carrots are in the refrigerator ready to serve except for the sprinkling of sesame seeds. The smell of toasted sesame seeds plus the smell of the bread will be worth the price of admission.

The cheese and butter are coming to room temperature on their serving plates. I'll put out the crackers after my shower. I have been to parties in this town where the crackers were put out too early. They became unappetizing, wilted, and tasteless.

My bathroom is small yet totally appropriate for the house. It's tiled in robin's-egg blue. When my older sister visits, she tells me to redo my bathroom. I know she is talking about her indecision about her own bathroom. I rarely pull out the projection trump card, but I think it's appropriate in this instance. Remember, what you say bounces off me and sticks to you. Usually, I go quiet rather than confront my older sister on any issue. I was pleased the last time she visited and I told her I like my bathroom just as it is. She didn't take offense. Maybe this growing up will work for me. Maybe I'm taking to heart what I tell my clients over and over again. Say something nice about yourself in the face of criticism. I've had clients remind me it works with bullies of all ages.

Recognizing the possibility of a special evening, the shower accoutrements require an upgrade. A recently purchased bottle of shampoo and fresh bar of lavender soap replace the old stuff. My upbeat mood carries into the shower, and I sing old camp songs and the first verses of several Christmas carols. The expensive body and face lotion I save for special occasions calls to me from the cabinet.

I used the time while the carrots were cooking to do my toenails and fingernails. Am I efficient or what?

Since it's an evening at home, I ponder what to wear. Not dressy, but not too casual. Not overly provocative or . . . yes, provocative. Caroline was clear about wearing something easily gotten out of. I don't want to scare Dan, but I don't want to look like a prude.

My gray linen pants fit well. They give me a long line, especially when combined with a V-neck. Only a pink or light blue top would be right. He did like me in pink. I'll wear the pink silk tee with the low neck and short sleeves. He'll be a little dressed up, so I'll match it, I hope. My black Coach flats will be comfortable. I'll put on the fancy linen apron and remove it just after I open the door.

I am not nervous, I am not nervous, I am not nervous. Are these forks perfectly aligned? Are the sharp edges of the knives pointed in the right direction? Is seventy-four degrees the perfect temperature for this time of day and year? Are there any foreign objects on the rug I vacuumed two hours ago? Is the porch inviting?

I take a deep breath, smile, and know everything is just fine.

CHAPTER FIFTEEN

"You're here!" I throw open the door so hard it bangs against the wall. I'm glad to see him after imagining he would not come. I would have cried for a month. Was my greeting too enthusiastic? He looks great. How did he know his cream-colored just-off-the-hanger shirt would match the madeleines?

He stands on my screened-in front porch, where I have friendly chairs and a round table covered with a linen cloth. I sometimes have three or four people for lunch here. My arms flutter, welcoming him into my living room. I don't hug him, just indicate I'm thinking about it.

He looks into my eyes. "Angie, you look beautiful tonight." He steps into the house. He initiates the hug I wanted. "I like the openness of this house. I have a present for you."

He gives me the big twinkle smile, putting butterflies where you don't usually want intrusive, distracting sensations if you have something else to do. Luckily, the meal is ready. I don't mind being forced into awareness of my body.

I don't see flowers or a beautifully wrapped jewelry box.

Instead, Dan reaches into his interior jacket pocket, next to his chest. I sigh. What could it be? He pulls a neatly folded letter from his pocket.

"I don't need a present from you."

Even as I say it, I know I want a present from him. I guess he knows I'd like a present. What is it? Is this letter a form of gift card? Where the hell are the flowers? No wine? I guess he knows I will have the correct wine for the meal.

"This, you don't need, but you want it." He leans over, puts his lips to mine. He hesitates a couple of seconds beyond friendly peck. The accompanying hug cancels any thought he might have the wrong gift. When he steps back, he hands me the piece of paper.

I feel light-headed. Is my blood flow not getting to my brain? As I struggle to focus, he puts a hand on my shoulder, steadying me.

The letter is to Dan from another lawyer. After I force my eyes to see the print, I absorb the content. The first paragraph thanks Dan for the wonderful hunting trip of last month and for his help on a particular case. The second paragraph reads:

I have found the Charitable Trust of 1992. The guardian of the trust is Steven Merk. The name of the trust is Charitable Trust for the Education of my Grandchildren. The financial assets of the trust reside with Bank One of South Carolina, and the account balance is $854,262 as of April 1, 2018 I'm pleased I could provide you with this information, and if there is ever any way I can be helpful to you, please call on me.

Your grateful friend,
Rick Wilson

"So, it does exist." My heart lifts. I feel my pulse in my ears. Is this the beginning of a stroke?

"Yes, and it will be easy to redo the settlement of the marital assets. Possibly, you could insist on being the guardian of the trust since he hid the money from you. You can get anything you want from the court now. I suppose you're too nice a person to send him to prison. He could probably be declared incompetent if we think it would be advantageous to you or your grandchildren."

"I'm not angry enough to send him to prison. I'll have to think if there's anything else I want. It will be hard to spend that much money on the education of five grandchildren."

"Not as hard as you think. How much money have you spent on Sarah's tuition or violin lessons for another grandchild?" He raises his eyebrows.

"You mean I could get reimbursed for the money I've put into educational activities?" I'm vastly relieved.

"You can define educational expenses broadly to include other support as well—computers, cars, food, and rent," Dan says with a half laugh.

"The trust will owe me considerable money right off."

"People skate on thinner ice when they charge European vacations to a trust like this, but if the child takes French lessons, who knows?"

"Wow! That will do it. I already have money for tuition, but if any of the grandchildren want a fancy education, I won't have to starve myself. I've always told my children I would support their children for any education they want. But it would have been difficult for me, and now it won't be. This is great. I won't have to worry about outliving my money, like several articles this week have suggested could happen."

I step close, throwing my arms around his neck. The hair on the back of his neck is still damp from his shower. An image of both of us naked in the shower flashes through my mind. He bends down to put his lips on mine again. This time the big kiss melts into something else. When I step back, I know the evening will be all I want it to be.

"This is the best present I could imagine. You are wonderful."

"It's nice to be appreciated. It's also nice to have you in my arms. I would have liked for this to have happened earlier except for Pam's shenanigans. I regret my own unwillingness to follow my heart. I have turned away when I didn't want to." He smiles.

"Ethical considerations did enter in," he continues. "Unfortunately, Pam's breakdown and yelling were embarrassing to me, but several friends called later and were appalled at her behavior. They all seemed to think I handled it in the best possible way. I feel responsible for her, and I didn't pay close enough attention when she acted strangely after her boyfriend left her. You have a friend in Joanne. She called to ask how the two of us were getting along, and when I revealed my reticence, she swore at me. Her clarity brought me to my senses. I was about to call when I got your welcomed invitation."

While he makes this clever speech, we move to sit on the couch. He runs his hands up and down my arms. Then he pulls me firmly to him and kisses me. At first, my lips tingle, then it's like an avalanche of feeling through my body. Unless I come to the surface right now, dinner is going to be considerably delayed. I did put everything on warm because I didn't want to be cooking when he arrived. I didn't know exactly when he would come.

"This is the best night of my entire life," I whisper. I want to show him I can feed him. I want to show him I care for him with my entire soul. He retreats a smidgen.

"I guess you're not finished talking?" I'd be fine with moving past talking.

"No, I want to explain everything. When you were hurt in the graveyard, I was enraged at myself for being so frightened for you. I couldn't admit to myself I already cared for you. I'm still embarrassed I didn't introduce you to Brent."

"He walked so much like you. I knew it was your son."

Dan is on a roll. I can see he wants me to understand. True, he has a lot of explaining to do. I look into those blue eyes.

"Remember at our second meeting, you were sitting where Lydia always sat when she visited me. She sat tall, and you sit tall. That was the first time I somehow confused you and her. I could focus just fine with you on the other side of the table."

"So, it's been a struggle for you not to believe she's still here."

"I'm not having any more trouble along those lines. She's not you, but she's no longer around when I'm with you or when I'm thinking of you." He smiles. "I'm better now, and your image is solid for me, even when I haven't seen you for a while."

"I'm curious. What other times have been difficult?"

"When we danced and you had the chutzpah to continue with a slit to your waist, my reactions fought within me. I felt I should continue to be sad about Lydia, but instead, I was happy. That night I wanted to take you home. By the way, unless we fight tonight, I do want you to come to my house Saturday night. I'm having a get-together. Pam is not invited." He rolls his eyes as he mentions her name.

"What is it with Pam?"

"I didn't want to hire Pam, but Lydia insisted. Pam's mother had died. Pam had taken care of her mother, who was Lydia's close friend, for a number of years. When Lydia's cousin died, she left nothing for Pam. As an employee, Pam has been a 'mixed bag.' Under the guise of protecting me, she sometimes made things more difficult."

"Maybe you can be too nice. How did she undermine you?"

"There are forms for legal documents. She decided, more than once, she knew a better way. I wouldn't sign documents until they were right. I made her do them over, sometimes more than once. She hated it but finally conformed."

"She did other stuff too?"

"Once, when an important client came in, she was rude to him, so I confronted her in front of him, and she was hopping mad. Sometimes, I had to treat her like a child. There was probably a better way." He shook his head.

"Despite your interventions, she developed a crush on you."

"Yes, I guess she did,"

"Did Pam ever try to get between you and Lydia?"

"Lydia felt sorry for Pam. She and Pam's mother had been close growing up. Pam's father was an early deserter. Lydia's heart was too soft. When I talked to her about Pam's failings, she called me a meanie. I always relented and kept her on."

"What happened when the cancer came?"

"Pam was a little unhinged. She tried to get Lydia to reject standard cancer treatment. She wanted Lydia to try some weird drugs. Again, I stepped in, maybe more harshly than necessary. I so wanted Lydia to survive."

The air is stuffy with his sadness. I want to get back to us. I also want to fully understand what has been going on.

"What happened with Pam after Lydia died?"

"Pam became more compliant in some ways, even disgustingly obsequious sometimes. She did a better job of doing what I wanted, especially just after Lydia's death. Since I was trying to keep myself together, I was grateful. That was probably a mistake."

"She probably felt compliance was the way to your heart. It was her way to be like Lydia."

"Right. Lydia will always be in my heart. She's, however, not here, not now. Pam is in a mental-health facility. I am here with you." He hesitates. "This is hard, but I have another embarrassing item to come clean about. Pam overcharged you, and after two days with my accounts, I found another client she cheated as well. Here is a substantial check to return the money to you. Now I'm clean." He smiles and moves toward me.

We are about to go into a major clinch; I can feel it coming. There is a small knock at the door. Whoever it is deserves some nasty torture.

"Who the devil could that be?" Dan turns quickly, and he's still smiling. Does he know who it is?

I'm so tightly wound I leap off the couch. I crack open the door. I can't see the person holding the flowers because the bouquet of irises and Asian lilies conceals them completely. The flower extravaganza requires both of us to work together to get it to the dining room table.

"They're glorious!" I can't help myself—I cry.

Dan waves away the messenger with a twenty-dollar bill, then he holds me close and guides me back to the couch. He sits me on his lap, and I become aware of how good he smells. I fit so perfectly in his embrace, with my head on his neck. When he pats me on my leg, my tears stop and I feel warm all over, even relaxed.

"Here, we are both dressed up. What I want to do is strip us both down and get onto your bed," he murmurs into my ear.

Since my mind has stirred up a similar vision, my head nod is superfluous. "Dinner can wait."

I kiss him with as much gusto and inventiveness as I have ever been able to fantasize. He takes my hand and leads me to the bedroom. I rip the covers from the bed and turn to him.

"Let's do it and see what happens." He reaches over and pulls my shirt over my head. He emits a low whistle.

I'm pleased with my new black lace bra. I blush after I was determined not to. He chuckles as he takes off his jacket and shirt.

"You didn't wear your weapon."

"I didn't want it to get in the way of anything."

"You're right, a gun doesn't spell romance."

He comes close and begins his fingertip exploration of my body. He removes the rest of my clothes. I remove his. He makes cooing sounds of admiration, and I am amazed at the size and hardness of his penis. We stand close together and touch each other and kiss. I am so ready to have him on top of me in bed, I can barely stand up.

His movements are not rushed, but we somehow end up exactly where I want us to be. He is agile for an old man and so gentle I want to tell him he doesn't have to treat me as if I'll break. Then, as if he can read my mind, he uses some strength to rise above me and tease my nipples with his tongue. I think I will die if he doesn't enter me. But if I die, that's okay because I have gotten everything I want in life. *Take and give.* I touch his hardness; he moans. Great!

When he enters me, pleasure and feeling replace all thoughts. The tension builds, and we break at the same time with, I must say, rather violent thrusts. We are both sweating as he moves to lie by my side.

"I've never had anything so nice happen to me in my whole life." Tears come to my eyes. What is it with the tears when I'm happy, happy, happy?

"A bit hyperbolic, and yet, we do fit together in a special way, first our personalities and now our bodies. I have loved your sense of humor and your kindness. Now I love your body."

"I love what you do to me and for me. I can't get enough of your smell." I snuggle close. We relax into silence.

"Shall we shower together before dinner?" With great effort, I push my noodle of a body onto my elbow. I look down at him. He has thick lashes they're lovely..

"I'd completely forgotten there was another pleasure awaiting me."

"I won't say it can even come close to this, but I did make a roast that will blow your socks off." Then I giggle. Not your most sophisticated ending to sex.

"But you don't even have any socks on." I look him up and down approvingly.

"Probably is a good idea to shower now or we'll never get to dinner. You look so good if we stay here like this, I will be tempted to see what happens if we try again."

"You're right! We should eat dinner now if we're ever going to." I trail my hand slowly over his chest, and he grabs my wrist.

"That is torture for me, lovely torture. I've determined I want food. Then we'll have another go at this. I'll get the water running in the shower." He moves his chest against mine so my nipples harden.

"You're a rotten tease."

"No more than you. Come on, let's do the right thing," he says, and we laugh.

"What is this right thing you're talking about?"

"You know. Let's get a grip on ourselves and go eat dinner."

I sigh dramatically. "If you insist."

We head for the shower, where he insists on washing me. He's good with his hands. He reaches between my legs to "wash" me and brings me to orgasm. He grins wickedly, making it clear he likes to give me pleasure.

"Let's see if what goes around comes around." I turn him

around and vigorously scrub his back. When I turn him back to face me, I see he has enjoyed that. The sensations of the slippery soap, the smell, the sight of his chest muscles engulf me. Nothing else exists.

He watches me lather the soap for my attack on his abdomen and penis. "I don't know if I can take this."

"Grit your teeth and hang on to the stabilizing bar. I'll be gentle."

"That's what I'm afraid of."

I concentrate on what I'm doing so I'll go slowly. He gets harder, then he groans. When he begins to thrust, I put his penis in my hand and kiss him. He shudders when he's finished.

He's still soapy, and I rub against his slippery chest. He holds me close for a long minute while the water caresses us, then he turns to shut off the water.

"That was earthshaking. If I have talent in my fingers, you have wonderful strength in your hand. Now I really need food!"

"How can you think of food when I haven't even dried you off yet?" I cock my head and use a voice I consider sexy.

"There's more? I'll never get to eat." He fakes crying.

I toss him a towel. "Okay, dry yourself off. I'll look forward to drying you off another time."

He takes my face in his hand. He moves toward me. He steps on my foot. "Promise me there'll be another time."

"Look, there'll be no more showering, no more dancing, probably not even food if you don't get your weight off my foot."

Before he moves, he looks down. "I didn't feel the bump. I had my mind on other things."

He laughs; I join him. Soon, we are sharing hysterical laughter. This is a peak moment for me.

"My specially prepared meal is going to be anticlimactic."

"We'll have to see, won't we?"

He wants us to eat nude, and although I'm totally amused, I shake my head.

"I can't see that happening. Meals are to be enjoyed for themselves."

I dress us in robes for our private formal dinner and hope we can make it through dessert.

"Besides, despite the pleasures of the shower, I know my body will not be as attractive in the glare of the dining room light." My finger on his lips stops his protest. "Hey, another time, I'll plan candlelight; I'll even consider lingerie. Do you prefer black or red undies?"

He gulps. "Actually, I hadn't considered anything like that." His eyes get big. "But now that I do, black would show your skin nicely. Will I be able to get through the party on Saturday night if I imagine you in your black lace bra?"

I mimic showing people the door. "Yes, Mrs. Pennington, ten minutes is a short party. It's true, Mr. Cleaver, we didn't get a chance to connect. I'm so sorry you didn't get to finish your drink, Marianne."

"You are quite the actress. Between now and then, I'll practice imagining you in an iron maiden so I can concentrate on my clients."

"I, on the other hand, will imagine you in a Speedo bathing suit that is bulging in front."

He feigns wiping sweat from his brow. Then he doubles over. "I am so hungry, please feed me."

I take him by the hand. When we get to the dining room, I pull out his chair, telling him to sit down as I head for the kitchen. When I return with the pinot noir and the cheese plate, he is smiling to himself. He is quick with the cheese knife; I know a hungry man when I see one.

"This cheese is delicious."

"I get it at The Gourmet Shop. It's called Castelle Creamy Blue."

"Do you still have the cover?"

I nod yes.

"Save it for me, so I'll know what to look for."

"Nope, you'll have to come and visit to get it."

"You know how to torture a man. In more ways than one," he mutters under his breath so I can hear it.

Pleasure with myself suffuses me. I do notice he is deft with the corkscrew, and he knows all the rules about serving wine.

"Nice pinot. How do you choose one from another?"

"By the price and the aesthetics of the label."

"So, a high price and a formal label mean a good wine."

"How do you choose?" I'm interested since I'm inept about wine.

"I never have. Lydia took classes and purchased only the best. Your method is as successful as hers from what I can tell."

"Good! Let me get us some more wine and more crackers."

I can't help myself. I hum as I leave for the kitchen to slice the pork. Deciding it's not as hot as it should be, I put a small flame under the sauce. The flame goes to the perfect level, giving me time to dress the salad and plate it. I know, I know, I should serve the salad separately, but I want it all on the table so we can talk.

More humming—I am way too cheerful. I judge the plates look great.

"I wanted to come in and help, but when I heard the humming, I knew you were in 'the zone.'"

"I have been in my cooking zone since this morning. Only one thing has me feeling more cheerful." I lean and give him a kiss meant to be a peck. He's fast, and his hand is behind my head, and I'm locked into a real kiss before I realize what's happening.

He nibbles at my ear and backs away. "If I weren't so hungry, I'd follow up."

"There's your dinner in front of you, MIK," I purr.

"What does that stand for?"

"I'm from a large family. There were two signals when we had company, one was MIK, the other was FHB. MIK stands for 'More In Kitchen.' FHB stands for 'Family Hold Back.'"

He gives me the twinkle grin. "I like it."

As he picks up his fork, he glances at me. "I don't know if I'll be able to focus on my food." He cuts a bite of pork and adds a mushroom chunk.

"I believe you'll focus on the food."

I'm so sure of myself I don't even bother looking for his reaction. I focus on my own plate. I have done well. The flavors blend together. The salad and carrots cut the heaviness of the pork. He is making small guttural sounds of pleasure.

He looks up. "Since it's MIK, I'd love more."

"The best compliment for the cook is 'I'd love more.' Thanks."

This time, he follows me into the kitchen. I start with small second helpings. He signals I should add more.

"Remember, I have made a dessert."

"I starved myself today so I could eat what I wanted tonight. I'll manage dessert."

I serve myself a few more carrots. They are old-timey, melt-in-your-mouth tasty, not al dente. The hint of roasted sesame oil delights me.

He catches my eye. "I love seeing a healthy eater."

We eat our second helpings slowly as we look at each other, interspersing the relaxed silence with sips of wine. I break the silence. "I will tell you, I considered pecan pie for dessert since I wanted to show you what good pecan pie tastes like. The stuff I won't eat in restaurants is quite a contrast, but I decided pecan pie would be too heavy with the pork, so I'm serving madeleines instead."

"So, you're saying I have to come back for more cheese and pecan pie? You'll have to quit work so you can cook for me."

"You're joking, right?"

"Yes, maybe, no. In life, you don't get everything you want. You have to compromise with yourself. Sometimes, you just take what you can get." He mocks crying.

I laugh.

"So, about dessert?" he asks. "I would eat more pork because it tastes so good, but I just can't."

"I'll bring dessert in a minute or two. It's light."

I stack the salad plates. I take them to the kitchen. He rises to bring the bread and butter. He refrigerates the butter, and I hand him a plastic sack for the bread.

"Thanks for being helpful."

"I do spend some time in the kitchen. Being alone for four years has taught me to put things where they belong when you're finished with them."

"You're a dream date. Do you want coffee?"

"Not this late in the evening. I don't do caffeine after four. I wouldn't mind decaf, but nothing is fine too."

I smile. "I'll fix us both decaf."

"This is a pretty dessert." He carries the madeleines to the table. I follow shortly with the decaf and cream and sugar.

"I like the rich color. I like the taste too." I know the decaf and madeleines are perfect together.

"Your cookies do not take a back seat to the rest of the meal. They're delicious."

The cookies, to my taste, are bland, but they're moist enough what with the amount of butter I used, and the sour cream, of course. I will remember to find a recipe with more lemon and vanilla.

"Do you worry about the future?" I ask since I want to get away from the food talk to a more interesting conversation.

"Interesting you bring up that topic." He takes my hand. "I have come to believe that growing old is just what I want to do."

He pulls me to standing, and we go sit on the couch.

"This, I hope and pray, is my future." He gives me the twinkle smile. My heart almost stops.

"I believe it is."

CHAPTER SIXTEEN

Three days have passed since our tryst. The first day floated by without my feet touching the ground; my clients smiled back at me. The second day, I was puzzled at not getting a repeated invitation to Saturday's party. On the third day, I was annoyed at myself for counting on his connecting. On the fourth morning—it's now Thursday before the party—my anger mixes with sadness. My energy has ebbed, so I call Caroline to decline our regular trip to the senior center.

"What's going on?" she asks.

"I'm just not going today," I say, then hang up.

The persistent chimes of my phone make me angry. I know it's Caroline calling, but I don't want to talk to her. I don't want to talk to anybody.

She will just call again if I let it ring. The stupid talk button requires a response, but not necessarily a decent one.

"He didn't call me yesterday, he isn't going to call today, he'll never call!" I shout.

"Something happened that has delayed his call." Her voice drips sympathy.

"Right!" I use my most sarcastic voice. "He could pick up the damn phone."

I have yelled in her ear, but I don't care. Yes, I do care. Caroline is not my problem.

"You're there, I'm coming."

The phone goes quiet, the green turns to red. I know I don't have to let her in, but I don't get up to lock the front door that I unlocked earlier by habit when I went to the bathroom. The screen door slams.

Caroline doesn't knock because she expects my door to be unlocked. I hear her hurrying down the hall to my bedroom. Deliberately, I keep my back to her and growl.

"He said he would be in touch. He invited me to a party at his house on Saturday night, to be a hostess by his side, meet his old friends, have them meet me, and sample my cooking. All that was going to be so much fun." I put up my hands to cover my face. My tears start anew.

Caroline stays quiet.

"Why aren't you telling me he's just too busy or a child had a car accident?"

I look at her so she can see my pain has turned to anger. She takes my arm, encourages me to stand, and we walk to the kitchen. I bang my fist on the counter. I get a tissue to eliminate the possibility of my snot on my chin.

Caroline stays uncharacteristically quiet. Where is her flippant answer making light of what I'm feeling? What's she doing? Showing me a compassionate side?

My internal scoff must show on my face.

"I'm sorry you're having a difficult time," she says.

"You are using my own trite statement against me."

"Your trite statement?"

"That's what I usually say to clients who are super depressed."

"Does it help?"

"Well, it does help a little. So, what am I going to do? How the hell am I going to recover? Please tell me, Ms. Right-All-The-Time?"

After a few seconds of silence, Caroline looks me in the eye. "I guess you'll have to calm down. If you have clients today, you don't want them to see you as you look now."

She gives me a half smile and moves to give me a hug. Her arms encircle my shoulders with a slight squeeze. Hugs are helpful. Since I'm not friends with my clients, I never hug them. I do try to help them get hugs. I once attended a daylong session with therapists where the topic was should you or shouldn't you touch a client. I decided I shouldn't. The therapist's distance is usually best.

"Chinese proverbs, southern sayings, and my mother all warn against getting what you want. The romantic tryst I got was just what I wanted, but it turned out it was a one-night stand. How will I ever get back to my life?"

"When he invited you to his party, he wasn't thinking of a one-night stand."

"What makes you think you know what he was or wasn't thinking? I was there, remember?"

"Just take a deep breath and know you will be okay."

"I'm struggling to come around."

Caroline remains quiet as I close my eyes to try the deep-breathing thing. It clears my mind a bit.

"I'm sure my mind can handle the disappointment. But I'll be embarrassed to show my face in public."

"So, is it possible here is another situation where you are going to rein yourself in and not get what you want because of what other people might think?"

"I'm back where I was a week ago, before I called him. Are you suggesting I go to the party?"

"You're the one raising the issue."

"You're saying I could take his invitation at face value?"

"Maybe you could."

"I've only got two days to calm myself."

"I suggest you don't bother. You have every right to be angry he didn't call when a call would have tided you over nicely. I think he needs to know how angry and hurt you are."

"I'm angry enough to keep myself in a snit for a week. Since the party is only two days off, that won't be a problem."

My spirits lift. Nothing like righteous anger to soothe the soul. Caroline's magic covers me like a down comforter.

"I will want to look my best. The food I take will stand out from the Costco stuff he will probably inflict on his guests."

"He might have the party catered." She cocks her head.

"No problem. My simple shrimp salad always disappears first at any party. I'll show him he can't ignore me. If he isn't cordial, I'll cause a scene. I could throw a plate of the shrimp salad at him, as long as he's using paper plates."

"Let's go shopping this afternoon. You could use a new dress as a special treat."

"Right. How good can I look? I've only got two days."

THE MALL ISN'T FAR from Caroline's house, so I pick her up. She's excited about helping me choose the right outfit, and she's waiting on her front porch.

We go to the mall that is enclosed and cool. The newer, bigger mall on the outskirts of town is patterned after someone's idea of a village. The stores are small, separate houses, so you have to go outside between each one. Most days have some kind of difficult weather. What were they thinking? We don't go there.

One lone tree at the back of the parking lot has a modicum of shade. The big decision is whether to walk farther in the heat or plan to return to a car that has been sitting in the sun with a blistering steering wheel. We opt for close, in between two big black luxury cars.

The mall is three degrees too cold, but coming in from the heat, it feels delightful.

"Let's go to Talbots. A bit on the expensive side, but less severe than Ann Taylor Loft.

"Good choice. At least you can start there."

The mall is not crowded for a Friday afternoon. The humid heat drives any sane person into their home or office.

The Talbots salesclerks are usually not snooty. When we enter through the red door, a person who looks like a twelve-year-old approaches us. "How may I help you?"

"I'm looking for a party dress. Nothing formal, just a little sexy."

"Is it for a summer party? Beach chic? Garden at dusk? Inside?"

"This will be an inside evening party in an old fancy house with a lot of old friends. I want to impress the host."

"Ahhhh. Come this way."

Caroline and I follow her through the neat racks to the rear.

"You have come at a good time. We have reduced our summer outfits, but we haven't advertised the sales yet." She is solicitous. "What length would be good?"

I turn to Caroline, who grins at me. "Our exercise routine has given you very shapely legs. I recommend just above the knee."

I lean over and whisper to my friend, "If I could get away with it, I would go nude to remind him of what a good time we had and could have again if he would just treat me right."

"Are you interested in a pattern, or would you like a solid color to accessorize with jewelry or a scarf?"

"So many decisions. I find shopping exhausting."

"Hang in there. She has a limited selection of short dresses."

"I would like a solid, light-colored dress with nice lines."

"Here are two that fit the criteria you list."

She shows me a simple, sophisticated navy-blue dress trimmed in cream with a pretty neckline in the front and a low-cut back.

"That navy is pretty, but I don't want to disappear into the background. Won't light colors be more attention-getting?"

"Probably, although the cut of the neckline and the way the skirt fits are attention-getting." Caroline pats my butt.

The sales lady indicates with her head that she agrees.

"High heels are nice with this type of dress, but kitten heels would work."

"I'll try it on. What about this one?" I swing a pale-yellow dress back and forth to show how flirty the skirt is. "This is more like a dance dress." I look at Caroline. "Maybe I can get him to reminisce about how wonderfully we danced together."

"Probably best not to get too worked up until you know what happened."

Her words put me back to the reality of my situation. The saleslady does not interfere. Her quiet cheerfulness is successful. With two dresses in hand, I head toward the arched doorway to the dressing room.

The lighting in the room minimizes my figure flaws. I'm pleased with how I look, and I decide to take both.

Caroline follows me to the register. "You can't wear two dresses at the same time."

"They're on sale. I deserve a treat."

Since the material in the dresses would be the equivalent of a heavy linen napkin, the boxes are easy to carry to the car.

"We're close to the big Mercedes. Can you squeeze in?" Caroline asks.

"If I can get into those dresses, I can manage this."

When I open the car door, a package partly under the car becomes visible. The gallon-sized zippered baggie is crammed with snack-sized bags filled with white powder. Someone is going to make a lot of cookies.

"What do you think this is?" I point to draw Caroline's attention. She's puzzled enough to come around the car. Then she draws back, her eyes wide open.

"Don't touch it," she yells at me as I bend down to pick it up.

I jerk up and bang into the black car. With my senses alerted, I see the luxury car has dark, no, opaque windows, really.

"Is it drugs?" I whisper.

We stare down at the plastic sacks so neatly packed. "I don't know, but it wasn't there when we came." She cocks her head and points her finger. "That much cocaine would be worth a lot of money."

"What makes you think it could be drugs?" I ask.

"Don't you watch CSI?"

"It comes on at the same time as Grey's Anatomy, so I never see it."

"Either pick it up or kick it over here so I can get it back," the angry voice next to my ear jolts me.

I opened my mouth to scream. Caroline's hand on my arm restrains me.

"What is going on here?" she speaks to the three inches of open window.

"It's none of your business. Just kick the stuff to where I can get it, and you won't get hurt."

Caroline's face closes down. She is annoyed; I am scared to death. I probably look like a metronome with my attention going back and forth between Caroline and the window.

Then I see movement in the parking lot behind Caroline.

Three police officers with their drawn guns move slowly toward us. They look like the real thing.

"Look!"

When Caroline turns and sees them, she motions with her hand. "Let's get out of here. Don't worry about the bag. Just get in the car. I'll drive."

I kick the focal point of this drama away from the tires but not close to the door of the black car. I throw myself into the passenger seat, slam the door, scrunch down. Caroline scoots into the driver's side. The next thing I know, we are backing up.

"Hurry!" I say. I look back over my shoulder as Caroline glances into the rearview mirror.

"I don't want to run down a narc. The one I can see is motioning for me to go over there to park. Believe me, that is what I am going to do."

"They've moved to hide behind the other black car," I tell her.

"I guess they know there's someone in the black car."

"Was the guy in the Mercedes a bad guy?"

Caroline backs into a nearby parking slot and turns off the engine.

"Can we go home?" I am sweating badly.

"We get to see what happens, and the policeman hasn't released me. It may be a drug bust. I guess we were supposed to pick up the drugs so someone could claim it wasn't theirs."

"At least you knew not to touch it. If our fingerprints were on it or we had it in the car, we'd be in deep water." I shudder.

"I don't think so. The cops may have been waiting for a drug dealer to get it."

Since Caroline has backed into the parking spot, we can see both the car and the heavily armed cops with enough distance, I hope, not to get caught in any crossfire.

As we sit there for a minute, we watch a tall man in a dark

suit stride toward the Mercedes. All hell breaks loose. First, the back door of the Mercedes opens up and a person jumps out and scoops up the packet. The police make themselves visible with their guns at the ready. They shout something I don't understand. Everything is totally still for a long second.

The tall man, who was almost at the car, raises his hands. The man, who was in the back seat, throws the packet toward the nearest policeman, who pushes it aside with his foot. More words are exchanged. Then a lady in high heels and a short dress, not unlike the one I just purchased, emerges from the other side of the back seat. She looks as though she is swearing at everybody.

The three bad guys get into the back of a police van, which has mysteriously appeared. Two of the good guys get into the Mercedes. When they drive off, another police car pulls up and parks in front of Caroline's car. It's clear we are not leaving the parking lot anytime soon.

I'm pleased I don't scream.

Caroline shrugs her shoulders and rolls down her window. The policeman exits his car and walks to the window with a serious face. "We need you to come to the station and tell us what you saw. You may need a lawyer."

I have a sinking feeling as I try to remember what the bad guys were wearing. What else could they want, and why do they think we need a lawyer?

"Caroline, the only lawyer I can think of is Dan. What will he think if I call him from the police station?"

"One, you can call him on your phone, and two, he will think you are smart to call him. He will want to keep us out of trouble as best he can."

My hand shakes only a little as I dial in his number. "Dan, I don't believe we are in any trouble, but the police are following Caroline and me. Shortly, we will be at headquarters, and they said we needed a lawyer. Could you recommend someone we could call who has a criminal practice?"

"Look, I will be there before you arrive. Do not go into a room with them or answer any questions. Just tell them your lawyer, Dan McCloud, is on his way." His voice is definite, and I repeat what he said to Caroline.

"Great!" is her only response.

We drive slowly to the central office of the Columbia police since the officer is following us. I suppose he thinks we could pull an O. J. Simpson and start a police chase down the freeway. Not likely.

He pulls beside us when Caroline can't see where to park and waves us into a restricted area. We follow him into the hall and surrender our purses and bodies to the machines, I suspect, are the culprit for low semen counts. He indicates he wants to take Caroline into a room, but she tells him her lawyer, Dan McCloud, has told her to sit and wait for him.

"Mr. McCloud is her lawyer too," she says and points to me.

The policeman rolls his eyes, tilts his head in the suggestion of a bow, and waves us toward a long wooden bench.

Dan bangs the door on his way in. "Who's in charge here?" he roars. "Why have you impeded these ladies from going where they are free to go?"

He looks first at one officer, then at another, and each looks away in turn.

"We just need witness statements from these ladies," the man at the desk says.

"I'll oversee it," Dan responds. "Give me the forms."

Caroline and I write our statements of what we witnessed on worn clipboards, and Dan reads over them before we hand them to the clerk. The police officers have disappeared.

The tension in my body drains like the water in a luxury

bathtub when the plug is pulled, leaving me exhausted. We sit quietly for a minute.

I turn to Caroline. "Let's go home. This is enough excitement for today."

Dan takes my arm and escorts me from the building and down the stairs to the car. "Dan, you are my hero and my savior. We might have gotten into real trouble if we had tried to talk our way out of there."

He gives me the twinkle smile. "You're so much fun to have around. My life has been too quiet for too long. Rescue trips make my day. I'll see you tomorrow night."

Once again, I am stunned into silence, like when he embraced me in his office. He believes I am going to his party. He is looking forward to seeing me tomorrow night. Caroline steers me to my car. We both wave at Dan, who cheerily waves back as he exits the parking lot.

We're quiet on the ride home. Since my porch has been in the shade for a couple of hours, the air will be pleasant. The colorful cushions on the chairs and gray-green tablecloth on the round table make the porch inviting.

Caroline plops herself in a chair. "Let's have a drink to help us return to the land of the living."

When I return with the glasses, she smiles. "I like sitting here in the late afternoon. That scene was unnerving."

"You didn't look as unnerved as I felt."

"Really, I was angry with them for spoiling the relaxation coming from our successful shopping trip."

I raise my eyebrows. "When you get up in the morning, you don't usually think you have to stay alert so as not to get sucked into someone else's drama." The first sip of bourbon goes right to my head. "When you think of it, our lives are pretty drama-free. Sure, Rachel can be a worry, but it's not like she'll go to prison for drug dealing."

"I have to deal with Tim's mother's poor health sometimes, but mostly life flows along with few ripples."

Caroline's hand movement suggests the flow and the ripples. We are both amused. The bourbon has relaxed us.

"I guess I can flow into Dan's party tomorrow night and either flow into his life or out of it." I match her flow movements.

Caroline puts her glass on the table and rises to her full height. "Hmm. When I think of the last months, there have been some waves."

She moves her body to suggest the Japanese painter's tsunamic wave, requiring her to start her movement at the floor and stand to finish it overhead. We both collapse into laughter as she sits back down. She's right of course; my life has hardly been drama-free recently, particularly if you include this afternoon.

"Would you like another drink?" I ask her.

"I've had enough for now. Let's go to your bedroom to make sure your dresses are properly accessorized."

In the bedroom, I point to the top shelf of my closet. "I won't be wearing a hat, so we can eliminate everything from up there. Nothing in the closet can be useful." I kneel to approach the lineup of shoes.

"Let's go about this another way. Imagine yourself in the yellow dress. The temperature will be balmy. You will be meeting a lot of people. You want to look great, but not as if you are a Victoria's Secret model. You will want to look confident and friendly."

"I want to look like I know how to dress up for a party, but not like I have to show off. My simple, beautifully cut, perfectly fitted dress is a good start. I will want to wear heels since my legs are trim; my black strappy shoes will be fine. I'll carry a small purse."

I mentally go through my jewel box. "My gold chain is the

wrong color although the style is right. I have a single strand of yellow amber, but it's not right either."

Then I remember, under the other strands, the vintage necklace my sister gave me with yellow and white beads. I pull it out. "These yellow beads match perfectly, and the white beads mean I will change my shoes to strappy white and my purse to white too. The look will be a little less formal, verging on cute, except for the fit of the dress. I know I'll stand out in the yellow. Hopefully, I'll look like someone who could be invited to a pool party."

After I change into the outfit I am going to wear, Caroline looks me up and down.

"Wonderful! Cheerful and young-looking without overdoing it. Just make sure your hair is all fluffed up. It always looks perfect until you've slept on it for two nights. I have to get home since Tim is coming to take me out to dinner. I know you'll cook tomorrow, so I'll get a report on Monday. Bye."

After Caroline leaves, I make myself a tomato sandwich with Hellman's mayonnaise, in-season local tomatoes, fresh sourdough bread, and tiny slivers of fresh basil. Time for the countdown list for tomorrow. In the morning, I'll write part of the report I have due next week, then I'll shop, and then I'll snack for lunch. Then I'll cook the shrimp, chop the celery, onion, and dill, then mix the ingredients with the yogurt and mayonnaise, and refrigerate in the pretty blue bowl. Done! Plenty of time to get clean and dressed and drive to Dan's house. Now that I know Dan wants me at his house and I'm not responsible for a meal, tomorrow will be a piece of cake. My mind wanders to several great cake recipes, but I decide to stick with the shrimp salad.

I sleep well. When I awake with good energy, I smile to myself. *What could possibly go wrong?*

CHAPTER SEVENTEEN

The morning flies by. I had two clients scheduled when I usually don't schedule clients on a weekend, but these clients needed to be seen. The first client was a crying widower. I listened carefully, and he felt better, then we made another appointment. The second client surprised me. Shortly after starting the session, she laughed and told me she s leaving her partner. She turned serious as she told me her partner is very angry, threatening to shoot her and her new love. At this point, I realized what could go wrong, did.

"Tell me where everyone is and what the plans are for the weekend," I said to her. When I got the details, it turned out the partner is only threatening when she is drunk. We call the partner and ask her to bring her gun to the office, which she does. I make appointments for Monday with each of the participants individually and in groups. Have I averted disaster? Let's hope so.

"Calm down," I tell myself. "You have a long day ahead of you."

The noon-hour crowd fills Palmetto Seafood, most of them waiting for a fried flounder sandwich. The tall man behind the counter motions me forward. "Hi, I bet I know what you want."

"Indeed, you do. I'll take two pounds."

"You like the peeled and deveined, don't you?" He scoops out the shrimp from around the ice. The shrimp have never been frozen, so they are always sweet and tender. I like to come here; the metal trays with whole fish and ice stretch down the room. The people who work in the back room will fillet a flounder for you while you wait. It's educational since I have to read the cards to identify some of the fish. Personal service with cheer and a great product. You can't beat it.

Fresh dill is the other ingredient for my shrimp salad requiring a special trip. As far as I know, only The Fresh Market carries bunches of fresh dill, whereas other stores have dill pressed into little plastic containers.

At home, I fill my large pot with cold water and set it to boil. Because of the large parties I have, I have a collection of hand-thrown pottery bowls. I pick one with an interior glaze to complement the shrimp salad. Into this large bowl go the diced celery and onion, the cut dill, and the mayonnaise and yogurt. After the shrimp has cooked with Old Bay seasoning and cooled, I add it to the bowl, put a cover on it, and refrigerate. I know it will taste good. Anticipation of compliments, and surely a hug and a kiss, buoy my spirits. I sing old camp songs. There is no message in the songs, but pleasure in the remembrance of camp and singing.

My high spirits carry over into my shower, where I switch to Christmas carols with no attention to the meaning, only the sensation of singing and hearing myself stay in tune and remain on pitch.

In my housecoat, I stare into the refrigerator. I decide some nice cheese on *ak-mak* crackers will hold me until supper. Summer or no, a cup of Earl Grey tea is a nice accompaniment. It's too early for white wine.

After my snack, I call Caroline. "Hi," I tell her when she answers. "I'm too early. What am I going to do now? My food is ready, I'm showered, and it's too early to dress. What are you doing?"

"I'm just about to shower myself. Tim's coming to take me to dinner." Then she pauses with a *Hmmm*. "What is it you're not doing?"

"I'm not going to clean house or work in the garden. I certainly don't want to sweat or get dirt in my nails."

"Why does it feel to me you are not doing something that needs to be done, something you can do in your bathrobe?"

"How do you know when I don't even know?"

"That's why you call me. What is it?"

"I should just hang up on you right now."

"Fine, then you can go do what needs to be done."

I soften. "Thanks for helping me face a phone call I do want to make. I got distracted by my anticipation of dinner at Dan's place. One of this morning's clients has been threatened. I want to check in on several of the actors in this drama to make certain it doesn't slide into tragedy."

"You are such a caring, good therapist. You know you have a terrific reputation in town."

The thanks I give her is not followed by a self-given put-down, externally or internally. I let my shoulders go down and back in the *Stand Tall* message I give myself.

"See you Monday," I finish the conversation.

"Have a great evening."

"I plan to, bye."

We hang up, and I make my next call. My client answers, recognizes my "hi," and starts right in. "After our discussion this morning, the three of us have had a long talk. We recognized the problems come when we have been drinking, and then we don't do anything, just sit around talking. Since we all want to remain friends, we decided to go bowling tonight."

"That's great. What will you do after bowling? I wouldn't want your ex-partner to get lonely after a fun night."

"She has a sister who has long been after her to come visit. She is going to stay at her sister's house until we get everything settled."

"I'm glad she'll have the support of a family member during this difficult time."

"We're all pleased to feel safer." Her voice has a smile in it. "We'll see you next week. Thanks for calling."

My relief turns into cheerfulness. There is still time to make a list, my favorite time filler. The memo pad comes from Habitat for Humanity. One donation decades ago brings requests twice yearly for money and includes a nicely sized memo pad. The birthday gift list would require too much concentration; clothes and food lists are currently unnecessary. Here's a list suited for now: a list of the places I want to go with Dan.

1. Shagging on the Myrtle Beach Pavilion after a fisherman's fried plate. 2. Just the two of us in his lodge, sometime in the winter. 3. Kayaking on the Black River with lunch in our dry bags. 4. Walking along the River Canal in cold weather, then vegetable lasagna at my house. 5. Visiting the Congaree Swamp on a May evening when the fireflies are out.

Enough local trips, but the foreign travel will have to wait since I have used up my time.

Pink blush and pink lipstick go onto my face and into my small white purse. I check myself in the mirror, pick up the bag with the shrimp salad, pause for a moment to review. Then I put my keys in my hand and head out the door.

CHAPTER EIGHTEEN

Dan's house is lit like a freeway gas station in the middle of nowhere so there is no missing it. Lights shine in every window. As I slow to scope out a parking place, a young man in a bow tie and white shirt runs down the driveway. I stop as he dashes in front of the car and lower my window as he indicates.

"Mr. McCloud is awaiting your arrival. I'm Jim, the valet parking attendant. If you'll just give me your keys, I'll see you to the door."

He seems so sure of himself, no discussion is needed. After he opens the door for me, he offers his arm. His strong young arm is reassuring. I take on the role of a pampered lady, even though in my other hand I have my tiny purse and plastic grocery bag with the shrimp salad.

The door opens as we approach.

"This is Jeeves," Jim says.

"It can't be so." I exaggerate my startled response.

"Not really. His name is Joe, but we call him Jeeves to his face. He takes it just fine because he's a friend of mine." Jim turns to run back to the car.

I stand and look up at the tall man dressed in a black suit. "Is it Jeeves or Joe?" My nerves are somewhat calmer, so I'm able to smile.

"Jeeves is fine. I'm often the butler for English plays at the Township Theater, so it's easy to remember to stay in character. Dan hires us actors when he has a big party. His regular butler is too old to manage this kind of affair. We're all friends."

The level of jokes and non-jokes makes me lightheaded. Maybe it's the change I'm experiencing from mild anxiety to amusement.

"Mr. McCloud is excited for you to arrive." As he talks, he takes the heavy grocery bag from my hand. "I'll take this to the kitchen. Mr. McCloud raves about your cooking prowess."

We move down the hall, which is close to how I envisioned it. Instead of classic red Persian carpets, they are beige silk, and instead of brass sconces, they are pewter. The look is ethereal.

"That is one hell of a good-looking dress," Jeeves notes absently when he takes my jacket.

"Thanks," I murmur.

"You are spectacular. Lydia would have approved."

I grimace and, again, mutter my thanks.

"Announcing the arrival of Dr. Angie Merk." Jeeves displays his theater voice as we pause at the top of the two steps that lead to the living room.

Two actions almost do me in. First, the crowd is instantly quiet, focusing exclusively on me, and second, Dan breaks from the group he is with, bounds up the stairs, and embraces me.

A tear rolls down my cheek. My tension releases like the final pull of a squirt gun. I relax and enjoy the strength of his arms since it reminds me of the other night.

When we separate, Dan gives me the biggest twinkle smile I've ever seen, holds up his hand for quiet, and announces: "I want you all to know Angie since she is now part of my life."

Now I'm annoyed. He thinks he can get around me by showing me off to these people when I haven't even agreed to what he's implying. Then I think, *In a certain way you did agree to a future with him.*

I decide to go with the spirit of the thing for now. In that same second, the crowd in the living room goes wild, cheering and clapping. One would think it was the entrance of the next President of the United States. I blush.

"You look stunning." Dan offers his arm, a gesture I could get used to, especially with the heels I have on. He places his hand over mine in a truly intimate gesture. We step down the stairs. As the excitement of the surprise wears off, people turn back to their friends. We approach a small group, and Dan begins the introductions. I try, unsuccessfully, to associate names with some outstanding aspect of the person, a mnemonic device I've never conquered. I realize I'm likely to remember many of the names because they are people who have their names in the newspaper.

A glass of champagne finds its way into my hand as a balding man says he's delighted to meet me and seems to mean it. *This man is the chief justice of the SC Supreme Court* pops into my head.

As we circle the room, I get other jolts of recognition to the point where I wonder who someone is if I don't recognize their name.

Dan doesn't let go of my hand as he leads me around. I relax and enjoy myself. I have concluded these are regular folks when Dan's hand tenses on mine. The man he introduces is a republican senator.

"So, you're the Angie I've heard so much about." The words are okay, but his intonation drips sarcasm.

I teach relationship strategies, so rather than go on the defensive, I respond, "I presume only good things float around this town regarding me." I give him a big smile.

"I understand you're a psychologist." He draws out the label, implying there is something wrong with it.

I persist with the strategy. "I do enjoy my work." I make my smile more open and warmer.

"Well, yes, I suppose you do." The bully turns away.

Dan's hand relaxes against mine, and he laughs.

"Are you laughing at me?" After my moment of triumph, I am having second thoughts.

"The man is a boor with women."

I can tell Dan is pleased.

"That was the most subtle put-down I've ever witnessed. When he wakes up tomorrow morning, he still won't be sure." He laughs again.

"A bully is not a laughing matter."

"We'll talk after everyone goes." He looks me in the eyes as if I am a lifeline for him. "You are not Lydia, are you? I don't know all about you, but I definitely know you are not Lydia. I can't predict what you are going to do. I am enchanted with you." He pulls me into his arms, but this time, I resist.

"My high heel will spear your toe if you don't release me," I whisper in his ear.

He draws back. "You're right. When I'm with you, neither one of us want her to be in the picture."

A short but very good-looking man appears by Dan's side. "What have I missed out on?"

"By being late, you have missed out on an announcement about what this party celebrates—it's to introduce my dear friend Dr. Angie Merk."

Dan puts his arm around my waist and draws me close. The man looks surprised, then he takes Dan's free hand, looks into Dan's eyes, and smiles broadly. "Wonderful."

"Angie, this is Justin Neeley."

Justin moves his eyes to mine and smiles warmly. "I'm so pleased to have your acquaintance at last."

Dan laughs. "I've gotten the two of you introduced as quickly as possible." Dan turns to me. "Justin is a good man, Whenever I've got a problem, I go to him. He's annoyed I didn't share my good fortune with him earlier, even though he knows I've been busy."

"So, you and Justin are best of friends." I put my face toward Justin's and smile into his eyes. "I couldn't be more pleased to meet you."

Justin turns to Dan. "Wow, she has beautiful eyes."

We all laugh with delight. Dan guides me through the house to a beautifully appointed Florida room. He sits beside me on a cushion so deep and fluffy, I float.

"I have been distracted the last several days. The grandbaby spiked a fever. When we took her to the hospital, I watched her grow still. The fears were like when I took Lydia to the hospital the last time. I struggled to return to the pleasure I have in my life now. When I returned to myself, I knew again we were perfect together. The other problem I have struggled with over the last months is sometimes mixing you and Lydia in my mind and believing you are going to act like she did."

"What did she do?"

"She was willful and demanding, and when I wasn't perfect, she would leave for days, usually staying with her sister. It was hard to remain committed to her. Her other husbands couldn't stand it. She improved over time, but her insecurities remained. You are not like her at all. Come here and snuggle."

"Not on your life. Not until I get a satisfactory explanation for several things. The baby's crisis and your panic are, by the way, satisfactory explanations for your disappearance. You're lucky you rescued Caroline and me at the police station. Earlier I had imagined I would come here to confront you."

"Let's get to the other explanations later, but I want you to know there are several things I'm impressed with." He points a finger at me. "You decided to confront me at my own party. I believed you would come since I had not gotten a turndown, but to imagine you confronting me—could you have done it?"

"Yes."

He whistles a sigh. "You are really not Lydia."

"I had practiced my scene. I was going to get everyone's attention and then shout, 'Mr. McCloud is a hoax. He says things and doesn't mean them. He's a lousy man.' I probably would have collapsed on the floor, anything to add to the drama and get my point across."

Dan's amused by the drama I've described and mimed for him. "Lydia had her ways too. When I didn't behave properly by her lights, she would retreat. Then, after three or four days, I would get her a piece of serious jewelry, find her, and beg forgiveness, sometimes for hours."

"That's only a part of why I would have confronted you."

"I know, and I do apologize for the pain I've caused you." His face becomes serious. "Maybe I can find a way to make it up to you. When I was confused, I did buy you a piece of serious jewelry. I know it won't take away the pain immediately."

I raise one eyebrow. "Try me."

The twinkle smile stays. "We'll go to the bedroom after everyone's gone so I can give it to you." Heat radiates from his body.

"So now I have to get everyone to leave?"

He laughs, then turns to a man who has come in. "Here is someone who is never on time. I've wanted you two to meet, especially. Angie, this is John Trane. We enlisted together because we have been soul mates since elementary school."

"I'm pleased to meet you." It usually takes me a couple of meetings before I can remember a name, but this name I'll remember.

My handshake is firm and met with enthusiasm. His smile warms me to my toes; it is a smile of total acceptance.

"I was in the Summit Club when Pam had her breakdown. You were amazingly self-possessed to handle it the way you did."

"Thanks. Her hostility frightened me."

"Enough talk of the past. John, I want you to be nice to Angie. She has been persuaded to be part of my life."

John laughs. "When have I not been nice to a friend of yours?"

"You obviously didn't like the model I took to the gala."

This time, they laugh together.

"I didn't like her either," Dan continues.

I suppose that was the gala with the dancing. I can be generous given the circumstances and forgive him for not taking me.

A stunning woman, not much different in age from me, joins us. I realize she is the woman who came to sit by me after Pam's breakdown. The sleek dark green dress enhances her height, her hazel eyes, her dark brown hair. "Hi, I'm John's wife, Joanne."

I take her offered hand in both of mine. My throat tightens, and tears come to my eyes.

"I couldn't be more grateful. I had no way to thank you afterward."

"Maybe I could impose on you to come to dinner at my

house next Wednesday. You can bring Dan. The velvet cake he regrets he missed could come too."

"I accept." If I have anything that night, it can be rescheduled or missed.

Joanne moves off with a nod, indicating I should follow her. I would jump off a cliff if she wanted, but her path only leads to the dining room. Heavy silver candelabra with pale candles light the camellia-encrusted buffet table. Martha Stewart could not have done better.

I glance over the offerings, where I note my shrimp salad fits in nicely. It has been dolled up with parsley sprigs and lemon twists adorning the top. I can tell what Dan has purchased and what the women have brought. Dan and John have wandered off, and I am alone in the crowd with this graceful woman.

"Joanne, what time did this party start? I didn't know exactly, so I came when I was ready. What kinds of people are here, what is the cast of characters?" Wine gives me a light-hearted openness. "Is there a purpose for this party?"

"Dan has a reunion of friends once a year. These are all the people he may not see regularly, but who are important to him. It means a lot that you are here." She beckons with her arm for me to follow. "Let's start the food line. You go first since you are clearly the guest of honor. Jeeves told me to find you and start eating."

I take a plate and begin around the table. The table is full but not crowded. I note the sideboard with desserts, some tiered. The beef tenderloin has mostly pink slices, some almost raw, and others browned through. Being hungry, a variety looks good to me, as does the horseradish sauce. Three salads—quinoa with walnuts, my shrimp salad, then watercress and arugula—are attractively lined up. Samples of vegetables and a carefully considered item from the bread basket complete my plate. Joanne and I head to the tables set for eight in the den, which is a friendly room, less formal than the others. No one is yet at the tables.

When I look at the walls, I can't help but comment. "How did Lydia let these prints go to old blue? This room could use a few up-to-date nature photos."

"I understand you are a successful photographer." Joanne's modus operandi is graciousness.

"I do sell prints at the Friday market by the art museum."

"You don't remember, I'm sure, but two or three years ago, I bought a print for my daughter. She had it framed, and it graces her living room fireplace."

"I appreciate your letting me know. When the prints are purchased, I sometimes wonder where they go."

Dan joins us, overhearing the last of our conversation. "Angie is going to redecorate my office with some of her cityscapes."

Ever more surprises. How can I be annoyed? I'm delighted. Dan wanders off again.

Joanne's acceptance blankets me with good feelings. It's clear I fit in, and in fact, I belong here as much as anybody.

"Dan talks of nothing but you. I thought he was making a mistake when he told me he'd take the jewelry to you on Tuesday."

"He had an attack of 'you're Lydia.' I'm not one for fancy jewelry. My one gold chain goes everywhere." I finger the chain to show it's there.

"You are a far cry from Lydia. I believe, in fact, you and Dan are beautifully matched."

I turn away so she can't see my tears. I am so grateful.

"Should we tell John and Dan to start to help themselves to food?" She asks.

Is she deferring to me?

"Go ahead, you do it." Joanne motions with her hand.

"Okay." I stride into the role of honored guest/hostess.

Once I tell Dan Joanne's glass needs filling and he could consider going to the table, he gives me the twinkle smile. The smile tells me he knows what I'm doing, and he approves.

This is a place where I can be comfortable.

Soon everyone is seated around the three tables for eight. Jeeves and Jim freshen wineglasses. Banter and laughter bounce off the walls. I sit between John and Dan as they reminisce.

"It's nice to have a new audience for these stories," John says, radiating pleasure.

John's eyes are light brown with darker depths; I smile into them. Sometimes the stories are funny, but the situations are horrific.

Dan cocks his head. I believe he can see I'm surprised to hear these tales of mayhem.

"I know these stories are awful from an outsider's point of view. It's one of the ways we manage the memories. Another way is distraction." He pauses. "Let's go taste the desserts. Joanne made the éclairs. She says she doesn't like to bother with them, but the pressure of the crowd is too great to resist. I'm always ready for another one. By the way, the shrimp salad is great. I hope you are prepared to make it regularly."

"It's fun to make as long as Dixie Fish continues to have the fresh and already peeled crustaceans."

As we flirt, he stands, pulls my chair out, and takes my arm to direct me to the desserts. The desserts are small, so the three tastes fit onto the small gold-rimmed plates. I had been too busy talking to Joanne to notice the pattern of the matching dinner plates. *Expensive stuff* comes to my mind. Then I realize it's fine with me.

The small eclairs are filled with a custard so light I cannot remember having anything like it before. The dark chocolate frosting hits the sweet note perfectly.

After-dinner liquors are dispensed, and soon after, Jeeves and Jim deliver coats and purses. Dan and I stand together at the front door, saying goodbye to everyone. I find myself totally relaxed without any plans. The guests are all gone when Jeeves brings me my purse. Dan takes it and puts it on the side table.

"She's not leaving now," he says.

Jeeves makes a slight bow, mostly to hide his smile, and turns on his heel. "I'll be on my way."

Dan and I return to the sofa in the living room. He takes my hands in his. "I have been dreaming of this: you being the perfect hostess, everyone having a great time, then our being alone on the sofa." He looks worried. "Do tell me you'll be with me the rest of my life."

"Let's see what the jewelry looks like."

He throws back his head and laughs. Then he pulls me by the hand down the hallway. With a flourish, he throws open the door to what is clearly the master suite. The jewelry box sits on the dresser. More flourish as he opens the box, presents it to me.

I carefully peek inside. "What is this? Is it real?"

He nods, amused. The diamond-and-ruby-encrusted circle sparkles with reflected light.

"I can't take a gift like this. Where would I wear a gold necklace with gems like this?"

"Oh, there will be times. If you'll come with me, we'll go to congressional dinners during the inauguration."

"Hm. What kind of dress and shoes go with a gold-and-gemstone necklace?"

"You always dress perfectly for any occasion. You always fit in perfectly."

My heart lifts. How did he know to say just that? Now I

feel like a queen. "What about cotillions and galas?" I wonder in my new role as queen.

"Yes, it's expected cotillion guests wear real jewelry."

"Do they dance at the cotillion? If they do, I can probably manage to forget I'm a thief magnet."

"We will have a wonderful time. You will fit in perfectly."

I sit quietly for a minute to take in his repeated reassurance.

Dan returns the box to the dresser. "Now let's see if I fit in."

I turn coy. "Salacious talk will get you..." I hesitate. "Just where you want to go."

We undress each other, slowly, with many kisses. The intimacy is transcendent. We are a good match of taking and giving.

After we lie naked with each other for a while, I get up, saunter over to put on the necklace, turn to him.

"I can't believe my eyes. That's the prettiest thing I've ever seen. Please tell me in all seriousness you won't go away."

I try to put away my flippant self. "What you see is what you get." I hesitate. "To be truthful, my dreams coordinate nicely with yours. I love you and want to be with you."

He comes to me. "Now I'm satisfied."

the end

ALSO BY BETTY MANDELL

Keep reading for an exert from the upcoming novel, *The Secret Lily*.

The Secret Lily is one of three romances to be published in 2021 and 2022.

The Secret Lily, set in San Francisco in 1938.

The Sprit Orchid, set in England and Guatemala in 1850.

The French Rose, set in England and South Carolina in 1793.

Each novel in this series features the titular flower playing a pivotal role, a strong-willed heroine, danger, and romance.

Turn the page...

THE SECRET LILY SAMPLE

San Francisco, 1938

*C*laire extended one shapely leg from the back seat of the Bentley limousine into the cool air. The slit in her skirt was high. She paused a moment, then, sensing no audience, placed her rhinestone-studded shoe on the running board and stepped to the sidewalk in front of the San Francisco Opera House. When her hand touched Raymond's proffered arm, she felt and appreciated the fine wool of his driver's uniform. His arm was strong and supportive, as always.

"We're lucky to have a break in the rain." His deep voice, soft in her ear, made her smile. "I'll be here by ten, but if you take longer, don't worry, they'll let me sit here in the car until you come, Miss Savonne."

After two steps, she turned back to him. She valued his support of her. "I won't stay long. Just long enough to show Perfumes by Pierre supports the arts. I want my presence to make clear to certain board members we have an unassailable position in San Francisco society."

"You are your father's heir. They all know he is recovering. He'll be back at the helm of the company within months."

"They know I'm his daughter, but they don't easily give me the same respect. There aren't many female company directors. Some people think a woman can't run a company. At least one board member would take over the company if he could."

"We both know you can run the company and fend off a hostile takeover without having to shoot anyone." Raymond brought his heels together and saluted her.

Raymond's reference to her father's accidental wounding brought chills up her spine. Mr. Savonne's recovery from the gunshot in the forest has been slow but steady. Any reference to the incident brought back the fear for his life the call from the hospital and the dash across the city with her mother to the waiting room engendered. She shook her head to throw off the thoughts and fears and returned herself to Raymond's comments.

"Your support is unwavering and generous." She smiled as one friend to another. "I believe, and my father backs me, my plan to introduce a new scent will fend off any takeover vultures. Besides, we've had several good quarters, so complaints fall on deaf ears."

Raymond stood tall. "You have stabilized the troops through a difficult time. It has taken long hours. You deserve time off. Please have a good time tonight." His slight bow ended the conversation, and Claire moved away from her protector into the uncertain, and possibly, hostile gathering of San Francisco society, the annual fundraising masquerade ball.

The opera house valet, in his medieval costume, offered his arm as she walked toward the classically columned building.

Her polite smile accompanied her "thank you."

He nodded and returned the smile.

The long black car slid away into the fog. Her mid-heeled

shoes clicked against the marble as she strode up the stairs of the newly renovated building with the valet. Removing her arm from his, Claire paused before the massive door and pulled the bent petals of her costume into place. The foot-long triangles of white silk rose into position to frame the mass of her curly black hair. She pulled her mask into place from the top of her head and puffed her curls with her fingers. The sides of the mask echoed the white silk spikes in miniature, additional drama for her sheath of pale pink satin. The sheath moved gracefully over her tall, slim frame. The paisley pattern of crystal beads along the hem gave the skirt heft. The same beads sprinkled in swirls over the fabric transformed the dress from simple to elegant. She pulled open the massive door and continued toward the entrance hall.

A woman, dressed in black, approached her with the guest list. "Miss Savonne, Mr. Racine Johnson was inquiring about you." The attendant took her fur cape.

"Thank you. I guess I have to get that over with." Claire moved into the chandeliered foyer as the attendant smiled knowingly

"What a wonderful costume. You must be Iolanthe, the fairy queen," the attendant called after her.

Claire turned and smiled. "Thanks for confirming my identity."

Claire took a moment to soak in the scene before her. Despite her resolve, she felt excitement snaking into her. Since the foyer was several steps above the vast entrance hall, she could open her senses to the moving kaleidoscope of color, the high-pitched laughter, and the heady mix of perfume. She recognized, within the mix of smells, Perfumes by Pierre's very own high-end Clandestine, and smiled to herself. Somebody paid a lot of money to have that scent float from the crowded room. Clandestine was a subtle combination of rose, gardenia, and lavender, heightened with citrus, and at $320 for three ounces, pricey indeed.

Clandestine is nice, but the new scent is going to be grander. Claire's mind flashed with potential images for the advertising campaign. The lily itself, profiled or close-up, on cards, full-page ads in Vogue. Maybe called The Secret . . . or My Secret . . .

Claire became aware of Racine Johnson when he touched her shoulder. A once-handsome man, Racine retained the open face and tall posture of confidence no longer congruent with his portly body and ruddy cheeks. His tux was up to date and perfectly fitted, clearly new for this occasion.

He stood in front of her. "If you dressed like that for board meetings, we'd get even less done than we do now."

"If I thought I could make you more patient, I might try it." She frowned as she looked at him.

"Come now, Claire." He smiled his crooked smile. "When Luis went on and on about the need to hire Irishmen rather than Chinese as warehouse and dock workers, I thought I would get up on the table and scream 'just be quiet!' to the heavens, but I didn't do it. I can be patient." He smiled broadly.

Claire laughed. She had the image of his overweight body encased in his formal suit, scrambling onto the boardroom table.

Racine's mouth pursed with chagrin. "Okay, so I wouldn't get up on the table."

"Luis follows the popular feeling, but I find the Chinese hardworking, loyal, and honest. How he can have such prejudices when he imports Chinese carved jade and Chinese ancient artifacts for a living, I don't know." Claire frowned, then quickly returned her features to neutral.

Even as she followed Racine's blast at a fellow board member, she understood she was engaging in an inappropriate conversation between an executive director and a board member. *Distance is better*, she said to herself.

Maybe Racine felt her resistance as well. He pulled away from speaking of Luis, although he maintained his serious demeanor. "Enough of that, let's go back to how beautiful you are tonight and whether this is the night I get lucky." He smiled and cocked his head.

Claire looked away from him to gain distance in the crowded room and saw George Nexus, another board member, only a few feet away, staring at her.

Not returning any comment to Racine's inappropriate and purposefully disrespectful insinuation, Claire raised her voice slightly and projected it away from Racine. "George, come over here and be recognized."

The gray-haired man in a toga and black mask positioned himself in front of Claire. "How did you recognize me?"

"You are two inches taller than everyone, and the toga calls to mind you have a Greek last name. When I think Greek, I think of George Nexus rather than any known opera personage," Claire teased.

George gave her his hand and a smile. "Since Racine has obviously not asked you to dance, I get the pleasure."

"See you later," Claire said as they turned from Racine.

George took her arm and led her toward the other end of the great hall where a few people were moving to the music.

"Thanks, George. I appreciate the rescue, but let's get a glass of wine rather than try to dance in this crowd." Claire took a deep breath. She knew Racine and George were mostly on her side, despite Racine's clumsy attempts to seduce her. They all knew if she and the company succeeded, board members profited by association. That wasn't to say George and Racine wouldn't grill her on management decisions. Luis Sarento, the third active board member, was a different matter altogether. His views came from hostility, even when he didn't understand the issues at hand. His interjections at board meetings consisted of throwing some complaint or obstruction into the proceedings. His uninformed objections contrasted with Racine and George's comments, who wanted the company to do well.

Claire was roused from her thoughts by spotting Luis himself across the room. Luis raised a hand to recognize her from twenty feet away but made no move to come closer.

"Luis is satisfied with being seen by us. He and his minions will shortly disappear, and that's fine with me," George said. "Tonight, it looks like you'll get a reprieve from his nastiness." He captured two flutes of champagne from a passing tray in the hands of a skimpily dressed eighteen-year-old.

Claire nodded. "I'm grateful for his disdain of the gala. He's in a habit of purchasing businesses. If our sales were to decrease over several quarters, Perfumes by Pierre might be vulnerable to a strong takeover move. He doesn't like the idea of a woman director. I've seen him be rude to his wife."

"Let's not depress ourselves over an unlikely scenario. Here, take a sip of champagne."

Claire let her shoulders drop. "This bubbly goes right to my brain. I love it. Once a year I have one sip too many, then I remember I have forgotten it gives me a headache." She clicked her glass to his.

He responded with a big smile. "This is a worthwhile celebration. It's nice Perfumes by Pierre had enough profit to be a serious sponsor of this gala. It's good press to be known for something other than scandal in this town."

"We've been able to keep nasty politics at bay, although last year I was frightened when Luis's father-in-law was caught up in the suspicion of bribery for a position on the Port Authority. Luis was not indicted, but it felt close." She shook her head.

"We both know this town thrives on prostitution and gambling interests. We also strongly suspect those interests are supported by our very own crooked mayor."

As they inched toward the food table, Claire watched George's wife, Nicole, a robust sloe-eyed Greek woman with gray in her black hair, approach. The ribbon woven into the braid encircling her head matched the ribbon defining her breasts in her togalike costume. Claire noted the Greek sandals completed the picture.

"There you are." Her eyes were friendly behind the blue velvet of her mask. "I should have known the two of you would have teamed up. Probably deciding whether or not to continue The Spirit Orchid line I like so much but isn't, I hear, doing well on the East Coast."

"I'll try to save it for you, my love." George took his wife's waist and brought her close. "I do like it on you." He bent down to smell below her ear.

"We can always warehouse all the remaining stock for you in one of my shipping warehouses." Claire laughed at the image of an immense space full of small bottles of The Spirit Orchid for Nicole.

"Let me leave you two and go find food." Claire turned and wound her way to the bounty of lace-covered tables. She paused, admiring the ice sculpture of a faun and overwhelmed by the mounds of meat and cake before her.

"I recommend the quail, although the sauce is rich, it's tasty."

Claire turned her head to see who owned the pleasantly resonant voice.

"Here's a plate and napkin." The man placed them in her hand.

He was dressed as a pirate, one eye covered by a black patch. The oddness of having only one blue eye assessing her amused her. He was stepping over the line of formal manners by not seeking a third-party introduction, but the sips of champagne had dulled her sense of decorum, and she responded with a smile.

"Thank you. I guess pirates are known to be bold. I'm having trouble deciding, so your advice is timely." She helped herself to several pieces of quail. His pirate hat was also amusing, incongruously poised atop well-shaped bones under recently barbered skin and neatly cut brown hair. Tall and unreasonably handsome, he wore his silly costume as if it were a tux. He had approached her boldly, but as a supplicant, he bowed slightly at his slim waist. His boots were too big, but he didn't seem to care.

"Do you have a cake recommendation as well?" Claire raised one eyebrow.

He smiled broadly, clearly pleased. "The only cake worth putting a fork to is the Lady Baltimore cake. I tasted several of the others."

He helped her to a portion and continued to hold the dessert plate. "I know a place where there are unoccupied chairs. Come this way." He beckoned with his hand and his head.

I don't need to follow some handsome criminal to a dark, secluded corner, but . . . why not? At least my mind's not on the damn Lily campaign. Claire found herself smiling at the pirate as he held her plates so she could arrange her costume for sitting.

They sat, knees almost touching, plates balanced. His attention dissolved the discomfort of the metal chair with the linen cover draped over the rigid back.

"This quail is good. I don't usually think to eat wild game. Do you hunt?"

The pirate threw back his head, and his deep laugh circled her and drew her in.

"Oh! I guess you're a city dweller, like me," she said, starting to relax.

"The city I usually inhabit is Manhattan. An uncle by marriage, not really related, took me deer hunting once when I was twelve. When he shot a deer, I thought the world had come to an end. Of course, it had come to an end, for the deer. Have you ever pursued a wild animal?" He leaned toward her.

"I caught a trout in a pond made for tourists. I made them put it back in the pond when I saw it was still alive."

Again, the deep laugh. "I guess your wrinkled nose means you didn't like the bait or the thought of the trout in pain."

"You're right there."

In the silence filling the space between them in the midst of the noisy hall, he took her hands in his. His hands were strong yet held hers gently. Claire found herself unexpectedly willing to keep her hands in his, surprised at how she was disappointed when he let them go.

"Come, let's dance. I love a waltz." He rose and put their plates and glasses on a nearby table. His extended hand matched the strength of hers in his as she helped pull herself up. She smiled at him.

I can just dance and let my mind dissolve. I don't have to be in charge, I will just follow his movements. This man is strong, and he doesn't mind being in charge of the dance. He is holding me at a respectful distance, but when we circle and he pulls me closer, I feel calm.

Claire looked up at him, realizing the music had stopped and she had not stepped away as would be the natural thing. A shiver went through her body and lodged in her tummy. She knew she would embarrass herself if she didn't move. He took her hand to lead her back to the chairs.

She removed her hand from his. She was grateful she had the strength to sit down gracefully.

He drew close and whispered, "What shall I call you?"

"I am Iolanthe." Claire put a stern *I am a queen* look on her face.

"You are Iolanthe indeed, but the burst of white gives the impression of a rare lily to me."

She started. *What can he know?*

"Did I step on your toe, or is the lily image too outlandish for you?" He had noticed her shift.

"My toes are fine, and I do love lilies, perhaps best of all the flowers. What devilish pirate are you channeling?"

"I'm Mr. Penzance. If I were half the pirate I've tried to look like, I'd throw you over my shoulder, go to my ship, and then we would sail out over the horizon together." He laughed again. When he suddenly turned somber, Claire could tell he was trying to take in the details of her blue eyes and dark curly hair.

"How can I find you again after tonight?" He captured her hands. "I want your hair in my hands."

Claire felt her attraction to him in her core. She knew color had come to her face. Luckily the mask hid her.

"You are indeed bold. A part of me wouldn't mind at all sailing away from my life." Surprised by what had come from her mouth, Claire shook her head. "I didn't mean that. I'm not interested in dallying. I must go."

Claire pushed her chair back as she rose. She could not believe she was trembling. Her responsiveness to him made her angry. *I can't afford to be feeling this way right now. I have to get out of here before I make a fool of myself.*

"Don't follow me. I will have you arrested. You have been too bold. I have no time for the likes of you." Her legs wanted to run away. She drew herself up, then slithered between the groups of talkers as she headed for the entrance.

Claire moved in tune with her racing thoughts. *It's almost after ten so Raymond will be waiting. How can I be so thoughtless when he always has such patience? I hope he's been able to nap.*

She outpaced the valet, who was smoking behind a marble

column. Grateful she had chosen the less-high heels, she scurried down the steps. Raymond was indeed waiting. He held the passenger door open for her as she indicated on her approach that she would sit beside him.

The Bentley moved smoothly, and Claire spoke up. "Please drive over the new bridge. I'm too excited to consider going home. The house will be so quiet. I'm going to sit here in front with you. No one will know. No one is around to frown at my breach of etiquette."

"Yes, Miss Claire, I know you do get involved when there are lots of people, so I took a nap earlier." The Bentley reached cruising speed along the embarcadero. "So, what happened at the reception?"

"I've always been able to tell you everything."

Raymond sat quietly and smiled. Claire knew he was remembering their many good times together. At the far end of the bridge, he turned the car for the return trip.

Claire interrupted his thoughts. "Look, it's beautiful with the lights on the bridge and the lights of the city. The mist got blown away."

"Miss Claire, sometimes over the years, you've told me things I really would rather not know. I can sense something happened tonight, and you are reluctant to tell me, so please don't."

Claire laughed. "You're the sly one, but this time it won't work. I'll just not tell you."

Silence reigned for only a moment.

"The evening started with an indecent proposal from Racine. Then, the usual rescue by George and his lovely wife. Then I saw Luis. He acknowledged me but didn't speak. It was all the usual stuff. The food was good . . ." She lapsed into silence.

"I've warned you before about Luis. He has a bad family. But that is all the same as ever. What else?"

"I met a man, or rather, he came to meet me, dressed as a pirate. He's from Manhattan. He helped me select food. Even though I thought I wasn't hungry, the food was delicious. We danced and . . . well . . . I've never felt so relaxed and really at home before, never. By the way, he smelled good, the slightest touch of Rough Rider. It was perfect with his own smell."

"Very nice. Then what?"

"Why, of course, I ran away after threatening him. I told him I'd call the police if he followed me." A low rumble of a laugh filled her throat. "How could I do that?" She shook her head.

"You, Miss Claire, are very sensible and protective of yourself, as well you should be."

"What else do you know about this man?"

"He told me he liked the Lady Baltimore cake and the quail. He had a good sense of humor. He said he was from Manhattan, but he didn't say he was raised there."

"What did he say was his business?"

"He didn't say. We didn't get that far. He did say I looked like a lily to him. I wonder if he knows about the secret lily and was somehow baiting me, or if it was simply idle talk?" A chill ran through her. *He couldn't know. No one knows. That's not true, Jessica knows. Raymond himself knows.*

I'm tired. We can go home now. I know I'll sleep. Thanks, Raymond, for hearing me out."

"I also like to drive in the big city late at night. The new bridge is a pleasure. There's calm on the surface of the city at night, and as long as we don't head to the Barbary Coast, we can believe we are safe and the city is at peace."

Claire released some of her tension and leaned her head against the window. Unbidden images of the roguish man floated through her mind. Her response to him scared her. Her responsibilities were too large to play the part of the fairy falling in love with a mortal.

ANGIE & DAN'S FAVORITE RECIPES

Simple Salmon
Ingredients:

- 2 – 4 pound salmon side – ask the employee at the fish counter in your grocery store to skin a salmon side.
- Yellow onion
- Hellman's mayonnaise
- Plain yogurt
- Fresh dill

Instructions:

1. Place the salmon side in the center of a large piece of heavy tinfoil and partially cover with very thinly sliced onion.
2. Enclose the salmon in the tinfoil, making sure the envelope is tight; place on a baking sheet.
3. Cook at 350° for 45 minutes or more, depending on the size of your salmon.

4. Accompany with seafood sauce and serve with a lemon garnish.

Seafood Sauce

- Mix ½ mayonnaise, ½ yogurt, and a palmful of fresh-cut dill in a bowl.

Dan's Favorite Shrimp Salad

Ingredients:

- Peeled and deveined <u>fresh</u> shrimp
- Celery
- Yellow Onion
- Plain Yogurt
- Hellman's mayonnaise
- Fresh dill

Instructions:

1. Boil the shrimp until it is pink.
2. Mince a ½ cup of celery per pound of shrimp; make seafood sauce.
3. Cool the shrimp, add minced celery, and mix in seafood sauce.
4. Garnish with parsley.

Soda Bread – Large Loaf

Ingredients:

- 2 cups white flour
- 2 cups whole-wheat flour
- 1 cup old-fashioned oats
- 1 ½ teaspoons salt

- 1 ½ teaspoons baking soda
- 1 qt buttermilk

Instructions:

1. Mix dry ingredients thoroughly, adding buttermilk as needed to make a soft, sticky dough.
2. Form a 3-inch-deep patty on a heavily buttered cookie tin; score a plus sign to the top of the dough.
3. Bake at 350° for an hour, removing when it's brown along the edges and firm in the middle.

*This bread does not last well. It's best eaten when fresh!

ACKNOWLEDGMENTS

After years of attending book club meetings and writers group meetings, even some writers workshops, the list of those who've aided my journey would fill an encyclopedia. Those who attend the group meetings at the Lexington County library in South Carolina are sophisticated writers. There, the requirement of reading several pages of another's recent work lends to active learning. The writers group at the Richland County Library in Columbia, South Carolina was led by a woman who managed to publish, through the library, a set of the group's short stories. Encouraging, indeed.

Many friends and family members are supportive. When I'm asked what I'm up to and my answer is "I'm working on my novels," they neither laugh nor say, "Still?" Instead, they nod and propose to meet for lunch. There is never a hint of humor. I love them all.

Special people in my writing life are included in my group of friends and family. Becke Turner and Nancy Kreml have been generous with their writing and professional talents. Amelia Mandell, my wonderful, smart granddaughter and computer expert, provided invaluable help. She even co-designed the cover. I couldn't have done this without her. Jennifer Falvey furnished the first edits for this book and moved it along nicely. Jennifer Weingrad completed the final edit. The Covid year of 2020 was hard, but it provided ample time for rewrites.

ABOUT THE AUTHOR

Dr. Betty Mandell retired from her work as a clinical psychologist to publish the novels she wrote alongside her career in Columbia, South Carolina, where she is surrounded by family, friends, and good food. Raised in Denver, Colorado, she established her passion for the outdoors hiking the high peaks in the summer and skiing in the winter. Betty's nature photographs grace many walls in Columbia. Betty graduated college in 1957, and by 1969, she had completed her doctorate in psychology while raising four children.

Dr. Mandell has had several short stories published in a local publication. She also published several articles on managing stress and authored Mind Matters, a monthly column for the *State*. The newspaper column ran with a circulation of 175,000 from 1988-1989. Betty has frequented writers groups, attended a romance-writers workshop, and enjoyed book clubs.

This is a work of fiction. All of the characters, organizations, places and events portrayed in this novel are either products of the author's imagination or are used fictitiously and any resemblance to actual persons, living or dead, or business, is entirely coincidental.

Copyright © 2021 Betty Mandell

All rights reserved.

Library of Congress Cataloging in Publication Data.

Author: Mandell, Betty

Title: The Adventures of Angie Merk: A Romance

Edits by Jennifer Falvey and JJ Kirkmon

ISBN: 978-1-7368678-0-8

Cover art by Erin Iannone

Author photo by Isa Mandell

First Edition

No part of this book may be reproduced in any form or by any electronic or mechanical means including information storage and retrieval systems without written permission by the author. The only exception is by reviewers who may quote short excerpts in a review.

Made in the USA
Columbia, SC
23 October 2024